THE CONJOINED

A Novel

Jen Sookfong Lee

ECW

Published by ECW Press
665 Gerrard Street East
Toronto, Ontario, Canada M4M 1Y2
416-694-3348 / info@ecwpress.com

Editor for the press: Crissy Calhoun
Cover design: Michel Vrana
Cover photo: caracterdesign/iStock
Author photo: Sherri Koop Photography

This is a work of fiction. Names, characters,
places, and incidents either are the product of the
author's imagination or are used fictitiously, and
any resemblance to actual persons, living or dead,
business establishments, events, or locales is entirely
coincidental.

Library and Archives Canada
Cataloguing in Publication

Lee, Jen Sookfong, author
The conjoined / Jen Sookfong Lee.

Issued in print and electronic formats.
ISBN 978-1-77041-284-2 (paperback)
also issued as: 978-1-77090-906-9 (PDF)
978-1-77090-905-2 (ePub)

I. Title.

PS8623.E442C66 2016   C813'.6
C2016-902368-0
C2016-902369-9

The publication of *The Conjoined* has been generously supported by the Canada Council for the Arts,
which last year invested $153 million to bring the arts to Canadians throughout the country, and by
the Government of Canada through the Canada Book Fund. *Nous remercions le Conseil des arts du Canada
de son soutien. L'an dernier, le Conseil a investi 153 millions de dollars pour mettre de l'art dans la vie des Canadiennes
et des Canadiens de tout le pays. Ce livre est financé en partie par le gouvernement du Canada.* We also acknowledge
the support of the Ontario Arts Council (OAC), an agency of the Government of Ontario, which last
year funded 1,737 individual artists and 1,095 organizations in 223 communities across Ontario for a
total of $52.1 million, and the contribution of the Government of Ontario through the Ontario Book
Publishing Tax Credit and the Ontario Media Development Corporation.

ONTARIO ARTS COUNCIL
CONSEIL DES ARTS DE L'ONTARIO
an Ontario government agency
un organisme du gouvernement de l'Ontario

Ontario
Ontario Media Development
Corporation

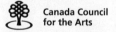

Canada Council
for the Arts

Conseil des Arts
du Canada

Canadä

PRINTED AND BOUND IN CANADA   PRINTING: MARQUIS   5   4   3   2   1

RECYCLED
Paper made from
recycled material
FSC® C103567

for my mother

It didn't take much time at all. So little, in fact, that no one remembered the two days and one night the girls went missing during a windy weekend at the beginning of October. It was a blank spot, penultimate, and so near the end that the end swallowed it up. No one saw it for what it was then, in 1988, and no one saw it for what it was twenty-eight years later.

They were sisters. One was almost done with childhood, while the other was running full speed toward adulthood. They had grown up poor, in Vancouver, near what the rest of us used to call Skid Row, where junkies and old ladies tottered down Powell, weighted with a thick, foggy high or groceries in a rolling wire basket. Still, they had been happy little girls, the kind who dragged produce boxes out of the alleys in Chinatown to build forts in their yard at home, the kind who lay on their stomachs in the living room, waiting for the radio station to play just the right song. Some said they were beautiful, but it was hard to tell. Their real faces, the ones that might have emerged when they were twenty-five or thirty, were still well-hidden by fine, uncombed hair, acne, the traces of babyhood in their cheeks.

We all recognize that kind of perfection. The bony knees. The lines in their palms that crossed skin that was otherwise unmarked and unwrin-kled. It's the perfection that makes us hold our breath, because we know it can never last. Ice cream melts. Sunsets fade. And little girls can't stay happy forever. Storms and men and dark corners behind brick buildings will conspire to wreck them. And so it was.

That weekend in October disappeared from memory in a matter of weeks. And the girls? So did they.

TWO THOUSAND
AND SIXTEEN

ONE

JESSICA STOOD AT THE KITCHEN WINDOW, HER ARMS hanging at her sides, hands in pink rubber gloves. The back-yard was a mess, as it had always been while her mother was alive. On the side, an unchecked patch of rhubarb was begin-ning to push up against a ragged camellia bush. At the back, the old bamboo stakes were still stuck in the ground, dried remnants of pea tendrils and tomato leaves partially tied with twine. Needles from the Douglas fir—taller than any other tree on the block, with a herd of starlings that never stopped complaining—lay like a pilly brown sweater over the lawn.

But the cacophony hinted at other, more ordered things. The minted pea soup her mother would make every spring. The giant peonies bunched in milk bottles on the dining room table. The smell of lavender as it hung upside down from the mud room ceiling, drying. The neighbours might have tidy rows of heather and rhododendrons—hearty and low-maintenance plants that could withstand the stormy North Shore—but it had been Donna who grew her own pumpkins for pie. It had been

3

Donna they turned to for plum jam. And it had been Donna who came to their doors when a husband was dying or a cat had to be found. She didn't need to be invited. She just knew.

Jessica pushed the hair off her forehead, leaving a line of soapy water on her blond eyebrows. Behind her, the cupboard doors were open. Bottles of nut oils and plastic containers filled with flax seeds and kamut lined every shelf in the pantry. For the past month, while her mother was dying in the cancer ward at the hospital, her father had lived on Hamburger Helper, raw carrots and steak burritos from Taco Del Mar. That morning, as Jessica stared at the carefully labelled rows of carob chips and bee pollen, Gerry put his wide hand on her shoulder and said, "I'm not going to miss this shit."

Jessica smiled briefly. "Are you saying you don't want to keep it?"

"What would I do with it? Mix it with some gin and call it a martini?"

"That would be a terrible waste of perfectly good alcohol."

Gerry snorted. "That's my girl."

When she was done, there was almost no trace of her mother in the kitchen. Only her set of handmade clay dishes, glazed blue and brown, and the cross-stitch she had hung above the door that said, *God grant me the patience to accept that which I cannot change.* Jessica packed the recipe binders into a box to take back to her apartment just off Commercial Drive. She doubted she would ever make slow-cooked pulled tofu, but she knew that as soon as she opened the covers the smells of her mother's cooking—muddy and sticky, laced with cumin and soy—would cloud up around her, and she would hear Donna's voice telling her how to gently knead a ball of oat dough so the bread wouldn't turn out stiff and heavy.

"Just fold and pivot, Miss Jess. No need to punch it like it's an ex-boyfriend."

And then she would hear her laugh. That verging-on-manly chuckle that jiggled her belly and shook the grey-blond curls that fell around her shoulders, riotous. Donna might have dropped stray threads and beads from her clothes while she clomped through mulch and mud, but her touch was always light. Just a fingertip, or the brush of her knuckles across her daughter's forehead when she was checking for a fever.

Jessica walked by the big back window and saw her reflection, ghostly against the view of the mountain. She had never looked like her mother. As a teenager, Jessica had grown thin while Donna added to her already substantial body. And her eyes were dark amber like Gerry's, or a cat's. But she had her mother's untameable hair, which Jessica wrangled into submission with a flat iron three times a week. Now, because of all the sweat accumulating on her scalp, she could see the curls forming around her ears, a halo of slowly twisting ringlets. She ran her hand over the top of her head, but this only made it fuzzy, like a baby's. *Time to give up*, she thought. She cared about being pretty most days, but at this very moment, swathed in her mother's hand-sewn apron, she really couldn't give a shit.

Jessica rummaged through the hall closet, looking for a tape gun. She could hear her father in the basement, singing "King of the Road" as he sorted through Donna's canning supplies. Jessica knew they had to empty out the spare bedroom too, the one the foster kids used to sleep in. She could barely remember any of their names and wondered if her mother had kept the photographs she took of them.

"Of course, she did," Jessica muttered. "She kept every last fucking thing."

There had been no kids in the last ten years, but Jessica was sure the twin beds were still set up, and the small dresser was still empty, waiting for the few pieces of clothing the kids brought with them. When Jessica told her fellow social workers at the office what her mother used to do—accepting a new child every few weeks, holding them when they had nightmares, never scolding when they wet the beds—they listened intently and held their hands to their chests.

"She must have been a saint," said Parminder. "All my parents did was prevent me from killing my brother."

"No, not a saint," Jessica had replied. "But close."

One night, when Jessica was six, she had woken up from a nightmare, screaming and pulling at the damp sheets knotted around her legs. Donna came in, fixed the blankets and sat with her, humming a song that was tuneless and wordless but still washed over Jessica like warm water.

She had said, into her mother's belly, "I want you with me always."

Donna laughed and then sighed. "Well, if I were with you all the time, you'd get pretty sick of me."

"No, I wouldn't. For real."

"Sure, you would. When I was a little girl, I always wanted to be somewhere else, somewhere far, far away from home and Granny Beth. But then," Donna paused and tucked a curl behind Jessica's ear, "Granny never wanted me to stick around anyway."

Jessica wasn't sure what her mother had meant when she said that, but as she grew older, she began to see that Granny Beth, unlike other grandmothers she knew, never came to birthday parties or brought her tree ornaments at Christmas. Instead, they drove to Lion's Bay to see her once a year in the summer, in her house on the cliff. Donna had told Jessica every time that she was never to step outside the sliding glass door on to the rain-slicked rocks beyond the living room. The wrought iron fence was solid enough, but when the wind blew from the open sea to the west, everything man-made seemed to shrink, to lose solidity against the sharp-edged air.

Granny Beth gave them tea and Peek Freans and never asked why Gerry didn't come, just as Jessica never asked about her dead grandfather. Once, Jessica said Gerry was working and Granny Beth stared and said, "Is that what he calls it? *Work?*" And Jessica stopped talking. Donna filled the air with stories that withered in the space between them until the hour was up. When they drove away, Donna turned on the car radio as loud as she could. Jessica was glad for the noise.

Her mother was no saint. But her grandmother was even less so. Donna had to fill in the gaps somehow.

"No wonder you're a social worker," Parminder had continued. "You must have felt it was your destiny."

Jessica had nodded, but she hadn't been sure if that's what it was. Now, as she taped shut box after box, she thought there just wasn't anything else she was equipped to do. Of course, she had to try to help kids. Of course, she had wanted her mother to be proud. Of course, it hadn't turned out like she'd expected.

She had quit child protection after nine months. At the time, she had said to her mother, "There has to be a better way than just walking into a house, staying for an hour and taking kids away. The families need support, not upheaval." Donna had agreed, nodding her head and patting Jessica's hand. But then Jessica spent the next six years going from one support agency to another, hoping every time she started a new job that there would be enough funding and time and will. But after a few months, the agency would miss a small detail, or a child wouldn't tell her everything, or she would forget that she was

7

supposed to call and remind a mother about a parenting seminar that evening. And those tiny things would start an inescapable chain that ended up with one more child in foster care and angry parents who couldn't trust a social worker ever again. They talked in meetings about best practices and leaving no child behind, but small changes in messaging or team-building resulted in no change at all for the families reeling from intervention. Children were neglected. Children were abused. Once in a while, the social workers could help. Most of the time, they couldn't. Sometimes, they made it worse. The number of files she couldn't satisfactorily close grew. It didn't matter how many times she moved them, the pile sat—top-heavy and teetering—in her head. She could never shake them. And she was scared of failing, always failing.

Five years before, Jessica had taken a job in the adoption department, planning public outreach so that people would know there were children available for adoption right here and not just in China or Guatemala or Haiti. On paper, it was a noble pursuit, and Jessica almost believed she was making a difference. But every time she put together binders of available children, printing off their most flattering photos and writing descriptions that weren't lies but certainly weren't the truth, she felt like a child pedlar, like she worked in a giant box store selling bright, shiny kids to families who couldn't possibly have any idea how hard it was going to be.

Alexis is a bright and inquisitive seven-year-old, she wrote. *She loves cats and hopes to be a dancer one day. Because of a difficult early childhood, Alexis finds trusting new people a challenge and is learning to appropriately express her feelings. She is best suited to a family where she will be the only or youngest child and where her caregivers have a basic understanding of attachment issues.*

The parents came back to their social workers in tears. The children weren't what they had expected. They didn't know if they could survive this. They needed help. And the social workers gave them books, pointed them to the very same support agencies Jessica used to work for and promised to call in a week. The children stayed or they went back into care. Sometimes they went to mental health units or, worse, the youth detention centre. Nothing was different. Even her cubicle stayed the same. Beige, nubby fake walls. A rubber plant.

And when she went home, Trevor was almost always on the couch, writing in his journal and sniffling. "I couldn't get Gary a room," he'd said last week. "And we found him this morning in a box off Carrall Street with blood all over his face. He said some shitheads from the suburbs kicked him in the head." Jessica had held his hand while he talked. "And you know what? Next week it'll just be some other poor homeless guy with the same story. It's never enough, Jess."

And it wasn't. Trevor could try to find housing for every one of his Downtown Eastside clients, but there was nowhere for them to go. Just condo buildings with recessed lighting. Row houses stuffed full of quaint wooden details and wireless technology. Nothing a welfare or disability cheque could possibly pay for.

Nothing changed. Except there was now silence where her mother's wobbly alto should have been.

Jessica called down the stairs, "Dad, do you need some help?"

"No, I'm fine. I'm just getting ready to deal with the freezers. What kind of meat do you think I'll find in there?"

"I'm afraid to guess."

"Me too."

"Do you want something to drink? I'm going to make some tea."

His voice rose up the stairs. "I could use some water. Thanks."

As Jessica walked back into the kitchen, she could hear the hinges squeaking on the freezer doors and the sounds of her father pawing through the stacks of resealable plastic bags.

She shook a cookie from its bag onto a plate and headed downstairs, glass in her other hand. As she reached the concrete floor, her father staggered out of the storage room, face grey and bloodless.

"Dad? Are you all right? Dad?"

He leaned over the stair railing, hands at his mouth as if he was afraid he might be sick or that words he hadn't planned would spill out all over the steps.

"Dad? Seriously, you're scaring me."

He looked up at her, eyes filmy and wet. "The freezer," he whispered. "There's something—"

Jessica set the plate and glass on the floor and marched into the storage room. "You should have just said so. I'll take care of it. You drink that water." She smiled. "I have an iron stomach."

"Jess, you shouldn't look. Jess, just stay here for a minute so I can tell you. Jess—"

But she didn't stop. She walked around the central worktable, past the utility shelving and up to the two big chest freezers against the back wall. One of them was open, light from the door triangulating up toward the ceiling.

At first, she saw nothing but ice crystals and piles of freezer bags labelled in her mother's slanted handwriting. But as she looked closer, she could see where her father had dug down to the bottom. The freezer was just over waist high, so Jessica leaned in, her hair brushing the ice on the side. "I guess we have to defrost this fucking thing too," she said, sighing.

There was a black garbage bag, dotted with frost, one corner loose. Her father must have pulled it back to see what was inside. Jessica tugged at it some more until the warmth from her hand melted some of the ice weighing it down. She stared. *What kind of weird, wild game is this?*

As soon as the question formed itself in her mind, she knew the answer. It wasn't an animal. It was a small human foot. Five toes. A heel. Frozen.

The scream that filled the basement was hers, but if she had heard it in a movie, she would have sworn it was a raccoon or a dying skunk. "Fuck, fuck, fuck," she said as she backed toward the stairs. And then, because it was the first question that filled her mouth, "Mom, what did you do?"

TWO

FIRST, IT WAS TWO POLICE CARS. THEN A CORONER'S van. Finally, an unmarked car with two plainclothes officers, one a woman in high-waisted navy blue pants hiked over a V-neck sweater. As she propelled herself up the front walk, adjusting the fabric pinching her around the middle, a pale sliver of belly roll escaped and dimpled in the afternoon light. Jessica winced at the injustice this poor woman was doing to her body. And then she thought, *Why do I even give a shit? There's a frozen human in my dead mother's basement.*

Her head ached. As a child, she had always felt on the verge of disaster, as if there were nothing more than a thin line drawn in the dirt that separated her life from another, more dangerous one. In the hours before she fell asleep at night, or during the still moments at school, she imagined her mother getting her hand stuck in the garbage disposal or pictured an earthquake that pulled apart the very foundation of their house and swallowed it piece by piece by piece. On bad nights, when her head ached from the sounds of the late news on the television, she pictured herself being snatched by a man in a ski mask who shoved her into a windowless van, then drove and drove until she could no longer tell if they had been travelling for hours or weeks, or even if she were a little girl anymore. Maybe, instead, she was someone who had grown up without knowing it. Later, as a protection worker, she met small children and witnessed their lives unfolding, one tragedy after another, an inexorable, cruel chess game of events.

But, never, even in her most sleepless moments, had she imagined finding a dead body in her mother's freezer. She wondered if she should be grieving. But for whom? Or what? Instead, she felt a creeping, numbing dread tickling its way through her body, core to limbs. Maybe it was the grief coming. Maybe she was just cold.

The officers stomped through the rooms and hallways saying very little to each other. Jessica and Gerry sat on lawn chairs by the side of the house, out of the way, but still with a clear view to the street. After Jessica had called 911, she found her father opening a beer in the kitchen.

"Dad! Not now. You can't be drinking when the police arrive."

"Why not? If there was ever a time I needed some booze, it's now." But even as he had said it, he started to put the bottle down on the table.

"They're going to have questions. And you have to be able to answer them."

"We don't have to tell them anything. I can be drunk if I want." Gerry brought his fist down on the counter, looking, for a moment, like a shrunken version of his once formidable lawyer self. He had saved old-growth forests, helped activists avoid criminal charges. But now he just stared at his untouched beer.

Jessica sighed. "Dad, this isn't a logging protest. There's a dead body in our house. I think the stakes might be a bit higher. Maybe we should cooperate."

Gerry had nodded. And then shuffled to the sink to fill the kettle for tea.

Outside in the lawn chair, Jessica twisted her hair, watching the police officers opening blinds and moving with surprising slowness through the house. She looked at her hands, white and long, and thought, *They should be shaking.* But they weren't. They were only cold, even as a warm breeze blew in from the southwest. After Donna had died, alone and sleeping, Jessica had stood beside her bed, gazing at her mother's body under the thin sheet, at her mother's face, recognizably hers but empty, like a hollow, three-dimensional rendering. She had cried then, harsh, jagged-edged sobs that came out so quickly they hurt as they spun and ripped through her belly and chest and throat. Maybe now there was nothing left, only this barely tingling detachment and the sense that she should be feeling more, that she would feel more if she only waited.

She started to ask her father if he was worried, but when she looked at him, he was sagging in his chair, staring blankly at the soggy maple leaves from last fall on the lawn. She patted his hand. "You all right?"

"I just want my house back," Gerry said, swirling his mug.

"I don't think you should stay here tonight, Dad. It would be better if you came home with me."

Gerry laughed, a short bear-like rumble. "And sleep where? On your balcony?" Jessica leaned forward, ready to argue, but Gerry put up a hand to stop her. "When your mother died, she asked me not to move. Nothing has changed. This is our house together. Period. No arguments."

The male plainclothes officer stepped out the front door and blinked at the sun. Jessica could see that he used to be an athlete; he stood on the step like he had been placed there by God, as if his body had a divine right to be anywhere it wanted to be, and that this was the way it had always been. For a second, she wondered what it would be like to run her hands over a man like that instead of pale, bony Trevor, who always trembled under her fingers. But then she blushed. This wasn't the time. Really, really wasn't.

The officer turned his head and waved before smoothing down the sides of his curly brown hair. Gerry waved back but couldn't quite hide the half-snarl, half-smile on his face.

"There was a time," he muttered, "when I could have reduced him to jelly under cross-examination." Jessica thought it best to just ignore him.

"Mr. Campbell? I'm Detective Gallo." He strode across the front lawn and pointed at a patch of grass. "Do you mind if I join you?"

Gerry shrugged. "Not at all, *Detective*." Jessica almost laughed.

The detective squatted, one knee on the ground, and looked at Jessica. "Call me Chris. You must be Jessica."

Before she could answer, Chris continued, "I saw your degrees on the wall in the family room. Your mother must have been proud."

What was the point of this small talk? Her mother was dead. Somebody else was dead and lying in the freezer. Someone— anyone—needed to explain everything before Jessica went out of her mind. She had a vision of her brain quivering on the grass at her feet, her skull an empty shell and splintering apart.

But she forced herself to answer. "My mother just wanted me to help others. And to be happy."

"I really should ask you both a few questions, but before I do that, there's something you need to know." Chris looked up at Gerry, his brown eyes squinting against the sunlight.

"Spit it out. I want to get this over with." Jessica could hear the thoughts behind her father's words. *Get the fuck out of my house so I can have a drink.*

Chris hesitated just long enough for Jessica's stomach to flip. "What is it? What's going on?" Her voice sounded weak, like it was cowering in a corner, hunched.

"In the second freezer," he said, and paused. When he started speaking again, his voice was quiet. "There's another body."

Jessica stood up and walked toward the bamboo by the front steps. Her head was pounding. She touched a shiny green leaf. So thin. So easy to shred. When she was a child, it was easy to slide behind the plants in the garden. If she stood still enough, breathed with the wind that blew shadows backward and forward, no one would ever see her and she could watch, undisturbed, anything she wanted.

"What?" Gerry sputtered. "How can there be two bodies?"

"That's what we're wondering too, Mr. Campbell. And we'd really like to know who they are."

Jessica reached out and grabbed a branch of the skinny bamboo. It snapped in her grasp. "I knew it," she said. "I knew it had to be them."

"Who?" Gerry gripped the sides of the lawn chair.

Detective Gallo stood and approached her. He placed a hand on Jessica's arm. "Who are you talking about, Ms. Campbell?"

"The sisters," she said. "Jamie and Casey. The foster kids. The ones who disappeared." Then, before she could finish what she was trying to say, she bent over and threw up, vomit running down her shirt, on the grass and Detective Gallo's shoes. "I'm sorry," she muttered before Gerry caught her in his arms and sat her down on the cool grass.

THREE

IN THE EVENING, JESSICA KNEELED ON THE FLOOR in her living room, her mother's recipe binder on the coffee table in front of her. She stared at the ingredients for Donna's baked falafel balls, reading them mindlessly in the dimming room. Chickpeas. Baking soda. Fennel seeds. She rubbed her eyes with the back of her hand and blinked. There, on the top right hand corner of the page, her mother's oily thumbprint. She bent her head to look closer, examining the looping lines, the spaces between. This was the thumbprint of a woman who cared about fibre and pickles and dying gracefully.

Ten days before she died, she had turned to Jessica and said, "It's going to happen soon, you know." When Jessica started to cry, Donna had patted her hand. "Don't be sad, honey. It's just the end of this journey, that's all. I want you to remember me as a whole person and not just *this*." She waved her newly skinny arms around the mint-green hospital room. "Remember everything. That's the only way to understand my life, or life at all. Every memory, no matter how small, is worth something."

And then she had sighed and closed her eyes. Jessica whispered, "I love you, Mom."

Donna nodded and said, "I was never perfect but you'll want to remember me that way. You have my permission to think about how much I annoyed you too." She laughed quietly and soon fell asleep, breath slow and quiet in the evening sun.

What did that mother, the one Jessica thought she remembered, have to do with the two bodies in the freezers? *Nothing*, she wanted to scream at the walls. Donna loved everyone. She baked and weeded and complained for days if she had to buy cinnamon at a supermarket. "If I could grow it myself, I would," she'd grunt as she slammed the door to the pantry. She constantly told Jessica every last detail of her menstrual cycle. She cried before she had to phone Granny Beth. There was no way, none at all, that she could have kept a secret as big as this for this long. Jessica, as she grew older, realized that her mother had filled every particle of space in every room and that her stories and memories and words were always going to be bigger than anyone else's. Donna wondered aloud why her daughter was so silent, but she never seemed to wait for a response.

The evening before Casey and Jamie arrived, Donna had tucked Jessica into bed and whispered, "I want you to remember one thing: these girls have had a hard life. Their last foster home wasn't safe, not like our house. They deserve kindness and understanding." And she kissed Jessica's forehead and left, before Jessica could ask in response, *Does that mean a little girl with an easy life doesn't deserve anything at all?*

The next morning, they came with almost nothing: just one small backpack between the two of them and even that was only half-full. It was just them, really, and their baggy no-name jeans. Donna's house was full—bulk bin oats; piles of books; unsorted laundry, both dirty and clean—and they slid in, cutting through the air, their girl bodies like slivers.

Jessica was ten, and Jamie and Casey were thirteen and fourteen, the kind of girls who stood at angles, their elbows and knees and shoulders just points on thin, thin bodies. They were beautiful, the two of them, but it was Casey, the older one, who had the eyes that were long and still, whose face was shaped as if it had been drawn with a fine-nibbed pen. Jamie was cute, but Casey made Jessica want to run away and hide under a quilt, ashamed by her huge curly hair, her ungainly height. *If I could*, she thought, *I would peel that face right off her and press it down over mine.*

Two weeks later, Jessica woke up and heard her mother crying in her bed, alone because Gerry was at the office late, as usual. When she crept up to the closed door, she thought she heard Donna moan, "What am I doing wrong?" But the wind was blowing and the branches of the tree in the yard were tapping and scraping on the roof, so she couldn't be sure.

Jessica went back to bed and stayed there, sheets wrapped tight. She didn't want to dream that she was running down a sidewalk, a sweaty, thick man pounding the concrete behind her. In dreams, she could never tell what would happen if the man actually caught her, but when she woke, sharp air in her lungs, she thought of Clifford Olson, of the Paper Bag Rapist, of the girls who disappeared from the streets in New Westminster and Surrey and Skid Row and whose faces she saw on the news. It could happen to anyone. To girls who had grown too tall and ate too much, like her. To girls who were beautiful and would become only more beautiful, like Jamie and Casey.

Three weeks after that, Jessica returned home from school and they were gone.

—

In the living room, the sun had almost disappeared, and Jessica flipped blindly through Donna's old recipe book and said to herself, "It's just a big mistake. An accident." But she couldn't think of an accident that could possibly end like this. And she could hear those words, the ones she had just remembered, bouncing through her head. *What am I doing wrong?* Jessica didn't believe her mother could do anything wrong then. In some ways, she still didn't.

The lock in the front door turned and Trevor walked in wearing his bicycle helmet and carrying a backpack. When he turned on the light, he jumped at the sight of Jessica sitting silently on the floor.

"Jess? What are you doing sitting in the dark?"

Jessica blinked against the light. "I was just looking at my mom's recipes."

"Were you cleaning out her stuff today? Was it hard?" Trevor took off his helmet and sat down on the other side of the coffee table.

"No," she started, but then she began to laugh. "Actually, yes." She stopped laughing and tears spilled onto her cheeks. "We found something."

She watched Trevor's face change as she told him what had happened. In the lamplight, it seemed that he was growing more transparent, becoming a single-layered version of the man she had lived with for three years. When she was done, she slumped forward and rested her forehead on the table in front of her.

"What? I don't understand." Trevor reached out and gripped her arm.

Jessica said nothing and closed her eyes, her lashes brushing the tabletop.

"Jesus Christ. Jess, are you okay? What are you thinking?" He slid his hand down and closed his fingers over her balled-up fist.

"I don't know. I think about my mom and those girls and what my dad is doing right now and then that foot and the rest of the body it belongs to. And then I can't think anymore."

"Are you sure it's them? Could it be anyone else?"

She turned her head so her cheek rested on the smooth wood. It was cool on her burning face. "I suppose they could be anybody, really. Like the nieces of a deranged neighbour who broke into our house to dispose of the evidence. But if I'm being rational, I just know it's those girls. They were the only ones who disappeared. Everyone said they ran away, but now I'm sure that's not true."

"You didn't have to identify the bodies or anything, did you?"

"No, I just told the detective what I remembered. I couldn't even remember their last name. Chan? Chung? Something like that. My dad took the police upstairs to my mom's closet to see if they could find any pictures or old files."

Trevor stood up and rubbed the top of his head, making his wheat-coloured hair stand up in spikes. "But surely she wouldn't have kept anything that reminded her of them."

Jessica lifted her head and sighed. "I don't know, Trev. I don't know how someone thinks after they commit murder."

He stopped moving. "So you think she killed them, then."

"That's not what I said."

"But it came out that way. Subconsciously, you think she did it. Maybe you've got some deeply buried memories that

22

are making you think that. You know, I work sometimes with a psychotherapist at that clinic on Powell who could help you. And then maybe we can figure all of this out." Trevor reached into his back pocket and pulled out his phone, tapping on the screen to look through his contacts.

"Trevor, stop. I don't need one of your flaky therapy friends. God."

"I'm just trying to help, Jess. This is a really challenging situation you're in. Who knows how this will impact you?" He sat down on the floor again and put a hand on her cheek.

Jessica shook him away. "I'm not one of your clients. I don't need you to patronize me like this."

"If you want me to back off, then I'll back off." Trevor put his hands up in a gesture of surrender, but she knew it wasn't that. He was pretending, mocking the very idea of giving in. "But I really think I could help you sort through all of this. I mean, the first thing you have to do is reconcile this mess with the memories you already have of your mother. Donna was a wonderful woman. And even wonderful people do bad things sometimes, right?"

Jessica stared at the vein throbbing in Trevor's neck. What would happen if she just took a sharp pen and pricked it, right there? This wasn't the first time she had thought about hurting Trevor, breaking his thin arms in half or pulling one of his ears until it peeled off. It had started before her mother died. At first, when Donna was diagnosed with ovarian cancer, Jessica and her father were upbeat. "Maddeningly cheery," Donna had said to her oncologist at an early appointment. But then, when surgery, radiation and, finally, chemotherapy tore through her body, Jessica and Gerry stopped joking and simply held Donna's hand while she twisted in her bed, cold sweat beading and running down her face. Jessica couldn't remember how many times she had cleaned up her mother's vomit from that one spot on the carpet just beside her pillow. The stain grew outward—dark, ovoid.

After two treatments, Donna told the doctors she wanted to stop. If chemotherapy was supposed to save her life, then she would rather die. When she explained this to Jessica, it was all very simple. Jessica understood. Donna was proud of her life. She just wanted to rest. She wanted to die knowing that it was a dignified death she had chosen, not a life that she had to scramble and fight to return to.

"I wouldn't be the same when it's over anyway," she said as Jessica rubbed her shoulders. "Even if I survive, I'll have to be careful or take more drugs or stop digging in the garden because I get so tired. Forget it. I'm going to die while I still like myself."

When Jessica went back to their apartment and told Trevor what her mother had decided, he stared at her blankly.

"You mean she's giving up?"

"No. Not giving up. Dying on her own terms."

Trevor shook his head. "Dying on her own terms would mean dying in her sleep at ninety-five, surrounded by incense and candles."

"She can't have that," said Jessica, sighing.

"Sure, she can. She can get through the chemo and get better. She could live forever."

"She has only one choice right now, Trev. Take the chemo or not. And she's chosen not to. We have to respect that."

He pointed out the living room window. "Do you know how many people there are in this city who are dying of AIDS or malnutrition or even hepatitis? These people can't afford shoes, much less choices. Your mother has every opportunity to choose life, and she won't. It's a waste, Jess."

24

Jessica listened to Trevor's words about the world around them and, for the first time, wanted to punch him in the mouth. He could talk about anyone else like this: her boss, the prime minister, their next-door neighbour. But not her mother. Not her mother, who had cried—involuntary, shuddering cries—as Jessica held her over the toilet, her own tears running into Donna's tangled hair. Not her mother, who had screamed, wordlessly, in the middle of the night because there was no human language that could describe her pain. Not her.

"My mother isn't a social problem."

He blinked and his eyes refocused on Jessica's face. He stood there—skinny, his elbows and knees barbed points on what could otherwise be a paper man. "No, of course not," he said quietly. "She has every right to manage her health in any way she wants."

It was an admission that wasn't an apology. He acknowledged her position but refused to admit that his was flawed. This was how he must be at work. Jessica felt her jaw grow tight.

When Donna finally died—sleeping, in a small white hospital room, wearing her favourite necklace of amber beads—Trevor had held Jessica in his arms. He brewed her tea. He greeted people at the memorial service. He drank with Gerry in the garden as nighttime crept through the trees. And yet, she never forgot. His words—those narrow, rigid words—were like hard stones, and she couldn't dig them out. A week passed. Another. When she woke up beside him, she went straight to the bathroom because she knew she couldn't bear it if his voice was the very first noise she heard. She ran the water and flushed the toilet, wondering how she was going to get through another day. Trevor had wiped the snot from Jessica's face with his sleeve the morning of the funeral, whispering, "It's just a shirt. Just a stupid white shirt." For that, she stayed.

Now, as the silence thickened and neither of them moved, Jessica felt heat grow sharply in her stomach, then her chest and up her neck. She swallowed to try to push down the rage, but it didn't work. Her face burned.

"That's enough." She stood up and threw the recipe binder across the room, where it landed with a thud on the scarred hardwood. "I don't want your fucking help, Trevor. Do you understand? It's not like you're so good at it anyway. Didn't you just say last week that your whole job is futile? That you used to think you could change the world, but really all you're doing is moving poor people from one shitty apartment to another? You can't help anyone."

Trevor stared. "Do you even hear what you're saying right now, Jess? I'm just going to chalk it up to grief."

Jessica began to walk into their bedroom. "You're a joke. A failure."

"You know what? Fuck you. I don't care if you are grieving. See you later. I'm going out." He grabbed his bike helmet and slammed the apartment door behind him.

His footsteps marched down the hallway outside, and she began to sob, one hand on the wall. She didn't know what she was crying about—her mother, Trevor or the girls—but it didn't matter. She knew that weeping was its own vortex. It spun and pulled until identifiable feelings were no more than fragments, like half-words that only hinted at meaning. She let her arms and legs curl until she was huddled, small, on the floor of the hallway. Her shoulders heaved and she thought—a brief, crystalline thought in the middle of this mess—her bones might burst through the skin, protruding like sharp, fetal bird wings. When she opened her eyes again, she remembered the apartment was empty. The night would be heavy and quiet soon and she wouldn't even have Trevor's angular arms for comfort.

She stood up, wiping her dripping nose on the hem of her T-shirt, and stared at the walls they had never painted, at the tiny hallway that led to one bedroom and one bathroom—all rented, all poorly constructed. A year ago, Jessica wondered if they were ever going to get married and briefly convinced herself that she wanted to. But then, as she was practising how she would say this to Trevor over dinner, she looked up and saw his narrow, smiling face. He was so happy, sitting at their cheap, second-hand table, eating the braised tempeh and mushrooms Donna had made and frozen in two-person portions. He had never asked her for more, and she saw, in a flash, that he never would. He told her every day that she was beautiful, that he could look into her amber eyes or lie beside her, his feet resting on her long, pale legs, for hours. He didn't want anything else, just this. She felt relief and only once wondered if she would push for something different if she was with a different man. A broader one. One who took an interest in her underwear instead of never seeming to see it. One who radiated warmth in the night.

Until Donna was dying, that is. Then the idea of leaving Trevor came to her in little bursts, prompted by big things and little things in equal numbers. His unwavering politics. The boy-like sounds he made when he came. His perfect, smooth hands that she wanted to break.

She returned to the living room. Remnants of her mother's life lay piled everywhere. She had been through every item. There was nothing that could help explain what had happened today. Sighing, she opened a loose cardboard flap and stuck her hand inside a box, stirring around its contents until she felt something hard and substantial. She pulled out a half-size Mason jar, its contents green and glistening. The handwritten label said *Jalapeno Jelly, 2014*. Her mother had grown and kept everything. She preserved. She remembered every harvest, every aphid infestation, every attack of grey mould. There was a clue somewhere. Jessica just had to know where to find it.

— ⬤ —

The next day, Jessica sat in a rarely used conference room at work, her hands folded on the laminate table. Detective Gallo sipped coffee from a paper cup across from her. Behind him were rows of stacked boxes leaning crookedly against three grey filing cabinets. They had been there for as long as Jessica had, and when she asked Parminder what was in them, Parm had shrugged.

"Who knows? Julie keeps saying she's going to archive them somewhere, but I've never seen her go near them."

Jessica stared at a stringy cobweb hanging from an air vent in the ceiling. Its free end floated and twisted, rested and then shivered. The mess might have embarrassed her on another day, but not now. Might as well be in a gloomy room to talk about heinous things. Jessica had a pen. So did Chris.

"I hope the coffee's okay. The receptionist makes it every morning. I think. I hope." Jessica told herself to stop talking.

He smiled. "It'll do. My taste buds aren't what they used to be anyway. I keep a bottle of hot sauce in my pocket at all times."

Jessica laughed but really wanted to snap her pen in half. She looked at Chris' face, almost perfectly symmetrical but for a small kink on the bridge of his nose. Brown eyes, brown hair. *He looks warm*, she thought. *Like he never wears socks*. Maybe he smelled like cocoa.

He cleared his throat. "Thanks for meeting with me. I know this is a very difficult time for you and your father right now."

28

"I can't say I feel like dancing in my underwear, that's for sure." Why did she keep saying these things? She needed to shut up. Answer questions and that's all. No more editorializing. Stop.

"I should make a note of that." Chris pretended to write in his notebook. *"Interviewee doesn't feel like dancing in underwear. There. That'll make the chief happy."*

Jessica laughed until she had to wipe her eyes with the back of her hand. Her body—so tight and so curled up into itself—hung on to the laughter for longer than Chris' joke was worth. When she caught her breath, she sat up straight. "All right then, Detective. Ask me your goddamned questions. I might actually be ready."

He flipped to a page in his notebook. "Obviously, it's too soon to definitely say that the bodies are the Cheng sisters, but we're working on that assumption. If it weren't for you, it would have taken us much longer to figure that out."

Jessica nodded and Chris continued. "What I want to find out from you are details on their stay with your family."

"I don't know how accurate my memory is."

"Doesn't matter. We'll take as much as we can get. Do you remember the approximate date they arrived at your house?"

"It was the year I turned ten, so 1988. I remember that it was the fall. School had already started, so I want to say it was the middle of September."

"Did anyone ever tell you why they were in foster care?"

"No. My mother never went into details about any of the kids."

Chris angled his head. "Kids can overhear a lot. As I'm sure you know."

Jessica stared at the notepad in front of her. She had always had the feeling that there was something very muddy and insidious in the girls' past. Something that was beyond her ten-year-old self to even imagine. But what?

"They were certainly troubled. I know they were treated badly by some other foster children at their previous placement, but I don't know what happened to them before that. They were the only ones my mother had difficulty handling. And that's saying a lot."

For a minute, she said nothing. She thought about one afternoon, twenty-eight years before, when Donna was in the kitchen, stirring a pot of bison stew. Jessica sat at the counter, reading her mother's old copy of *The Secret Garden*. Casey and Jamie had gone to visit their mother and the house was quiet but for the bubbling coming from the stove. Donna checked the oven. Whole wheat biscuits. She sighed.

"It's going to be windy and rainy tonight. Look at the clouds to the west."

Jessica nodded but kept on reading.

"Granny Beth used to say that she could always feel the rain coming. She'd get a headache and have to lie down. And I had to be quiet. I wasn't even allowed to flush the toilet."

Jessica looked up and saw Donna leaning against the lip of the sink, her hands twisting the tie of her apron. She blinked hard, twice, and Jessica wondered if she was trying not to cry or if the memories of her small, silent self were threatening to seep through her head and spill though her eyes.

"Is that why we never see her? Because she needs quiet all the time?"

Donna smiled. "No, sweetie. After your grandfather died when I was a baby, Granny Beth and I were always alone, just me and her. And after a while, we got on each other's nerves. So when I turned eighteen, I left."

"But why don't we see her now?"

Donna pulled on the ends of her hair and looked at the ceiling. "I guess after I moved out, we got used to not seeing each other. Besides," she said, moving back toward the stove, wooden spoon in her right hand, "she was never very easy to deal with. She was the kind of mother who scared kids. Including me."

Jessica thought she knew what this meant. After all, the kids who stayed with them were scared of something, and she thought that, a lot of the time, it must be their mothers. Mothers who were mean or cheap or always drunk. Granny Beth was mean. Jessica had never seen her hug anyone or smile as if happiness were filling up her whole body. No, she smiled like she had eaten a piece of mouldy bread at a tea party but didn't want to be rude and spit it out.

"Is that why we help foster kids? Because you want to help kids with scary mothers?" All she could see were the broad stripes across the back of her mother's sweater, crossed by apron ties that sagged over her shoulders.

"I always wanted to be the kind of mother that Granny Beth wasn't. The kind of mother who didn't complain or humiliate or pick at old mistakes. I wanted children to love being with me." Donna paused and turned around, spoon dripping dark brown liquid on the floor in front of her. "So, yes, I guess that is why we help foster kids. It's all I ever wanted."

In the conference room, Chris stared at Jessica, his face slightly green from the fluorescent light above. "That's what she said?" he asked. "That being a foster mother was her calling?"

"Yes. I think when the girls were living with us she came to doubt herself a little, which is what happens when a foster family is dealing with children who are particularly challenging."

"What do you mean? How were they challenging?"

Jessica squirmed in her chair and tapped her pen on the table. "They assaulted her a few times. They had a habit of skipping school and staying out too late. They called her names and stole money. That kind of thing."

Chris wrote something down in his notebook. "That's terrible. That must have been really hard for her."

"It was shocking to me then, I suppose. Of course, now I know that lots of kids act out violently all the time. Not so unusual in the grand scheme of things." Jessica shrugged, but her hands were icy and they shook, like bird wings.

"But it would have been upsetting for your mother, right? None of the other foster kids had ever treated her in the same way."

Jessica turned to look out the window, remembering the morning after the girls arrived. She had woken up at dawn, like she did every morning. Her eyes opened as soon as the crows began cawing in the tree behind the house, their brays panicked and irregular, foretelling something evil or catastrophic or just plain bad. Jessica sat up quickly and then lay back down. Her mother had a rule: she had to stay in bed until seven, no matter how long she had been awake or how badly she wanted to put on her socks and shoes and run outside. So she fidgeted under the quilt and stared at the sunlight seeping thicker and brighter through the thin curtains. She could swear there were beetles crawling through her insides, feelers digging at the walls of her body while tiny voices cheeped, *Out there, we must go out there.* The clock's second hand was moving— it had to be—but as she stared at it, it seemed stuck, wedged at six fifty-two, in that time that was clearly morning but also too close to dawn. She closed her eyes and counted to four hundred and eighty. When she opened them again, the hands had moved and she whispered, "Finally," before reaching for last night's socks on the rug beside her bed.

She ran downstairs and pushed open the patio door. The air slid over her cheeks and chin and filled her up, and she felt like she was instantly three inches taller, bigger and tougher than any foster kid who used to live with them. She looked back and listened. Two pairs of cheap canvas running shoes on the mat in the hall. An extra-large ball of bread dough rising on the counter. In the night, she had heard her mother walking through the house, the stops and starts that meant she had been listening at Jessica's door and then Casey and Jamie's. There had been no crying, which Jessica didn't quite understand. The kids always cried the first night. Casey and Jamie, though, stayed in their room and made no sounds at all. Maybe it was because they were older. Maybe it was because they were together. Jessica shrugged and turned away from the brown-tiled floor and dark, cool kitchen and back to the yard and sky and warmth. This moment in the sun—away from the shadows that proliferated in the corners of the house—was what she had been waiting for.

She looked up, the memory receding. Chris sat quietly, still waiting for her to reply. "We were mostly a short-term home and the kids only stayed a few nights," she said. "After I moved out, my mother fostered one boy for about a year, but he was just a toddler." Jessica doodled a lopsided heart on her notepad. "My mother wasn't used to violence. I don't think anyone had ever hit her in her entire life." As soon as she said this, she wasn't sure it was true. Her mother had never really told her what Granny Beth had done to her or described the shape of her cruelty. Granny hadn't even come to the funeral; she'd sent a basket of flowers with a card instead.

"How did your father react to all of this?"

Jessica flinched. "He was never home. I'm pretty sure he barely remembers them at all. He was working a lot. Almost all the time, really."

"He's a lawyer, isn't he?" Chris frowned.

"Not the kind you deal with, I'm sure," she said quickly. "He was an environmental lawyer. One of the first in Vancouver. Back then, he was trying to save Burns Bog. Or maybe it was Camosun Bog. Some kind of bog."

"He had no contact with the girls at all?"

"Well, he must have had some, like at dinner and maybe a bit on the weekends, but I don't think I ever saw them together. At least, not without my mother."

"But is it possible he could have spent more time with them than you remember?"

Jessica shifted her weight from one thigh to the other. "What are you trying to say? That my father had something to do with all this?"

Chris tapped his cheek with his finger before answering. "I'm not trying to say anything. I'm just trying to figure out who the girls saw and talked to before they died."

"My father barely talked to *me*, Detective, never mind the foster kids."

"Chris."

"What?" Jessica knew she sounded like she was barking, but she didn't care. She knew, like anyone who worked in social services, that when women and children were hurt, the first suspects were always the men—the fathers, the boyfriends, the uncles. But still. Not her father. Not him.

"You can call me Chris." His face remained expressionless.

"Can I ask you a question?" she said.

"Of course."

"Do you think my mother killed those girls?"

"I don't know that anyone killed them. There hasn't been a post-mortem yet."

Jessica snorted. "I suppose they could have hit their heads and just fallen into the freezer all on their own."

Chris laughed. "Okay. It certainly *appears* that their deaths are suspicious. I'll give you that."

"Do you think my mother did it?"

He sighed and looked into his empty coffee cup. "All I think is that their lives ended suddenly and far too soon. Whenever we investigate any suspicious death, we work from the inside out and, so far, the inside is really only what you've told me."

"You've just said a whole lot of words that mean absolutely nothing."

Chris placed his hands palms up on the table. "Then I guess that means I have a whole lot of nothing right now."

"You don't have a gut reaction?"

"My gut says a lot of things. It's saying it wants a grilled cheese sandwich right now. Just because I have hunches, that doesn't mean they're accurate."

Jessica stood up and walked around the table to open the door. "I was hoping to find out something from *you*. I want answers too, you know."

Chris looked up. "I guess that means this interview is over."

"I have a job. I should get back to it." She waited as he repacked his briefcase and walked to the door she was holding open.

"I'll probably need to talk to you again, Ms. Campbell."

"Jessica," she said as he moved past her.

"Right."

She watched as he walked down the hall toward the elevator. His feet stepped lightly, rubber soles just grazing the flat blue carpet. If he thought she was pretty, or wanted to touch her, she couldn't tell. She had never spent that much time alone talking with a man as self-possessed as Chris Gallo. Trevor quaked from nerves. She doubted Chris had ever felt a nervous tingle in his entire life. A man who could hold her hand like a promise to never let go.

When she was a child, she would gaze at Gerry; he was tall and unafraid. Every Saturday morning she would crawl into his lap as he read the newspaper in the den and trace the big black letters in the headlines with her fingers. Donna remained in the kitchen, whisking a bowl of buckwheat pancake batter, singing along to "Walk Like an Egyptian" or "Livin' on a Prayer" on the radio. The rest of the week, Jessica sat at the kitchen table alone, watching her mother steer one or more of the foster kids through teeth-brushing, face-washing and breakfast while she ate her oat bran cereal, quiet and well-behaved. Sometimes she heard her father drive off just as she was waking up. Sometimes he made it home in time to eat Donna's slow-cooked, stew-y dinners. Mostly, he didn't.

She picked up her notebook and, her hand on the light switch, scanned the conference room for anything she might have left behind. She gazed at the file boxes and cabinets for a moment. Her mind flickered. The children she tried to adopt out were all in foster care. She could access their files at any time. There were years of files here. Probably lots more somewhere else too. All she had to do was ask.

"Parminder?" she whispered into the phone. "Can you meet me in the conference room?"

FOUR

THE NEXT MORNING, JESSICA WOKE UP, HANDS balled in fists under the sheets, sweaty against her thighs. She sat, Trevor beside her, his blank, sleeping face turned to the window. He was free of lines, those marks around mouths and eyes that betray age or worry or joy. Unformed. Soft.

She knew she had been dreaming about Chris Gallo. It was the type of dream that leaves a shadowy, broken trail: his face in profile against a car window, sunshine hot on her arms, the smell of coffee brewing in a room she had never seen. She didn't know what they had been doing or what he had said, but she knew he had been there, that she had been with him and that, if she could have chosen, she would have stayed asleep just to see what would happen next.

In her underwear, she walked to the living room and lay down, curled on her side on the couch, shivering in the morning chill. She could have gotten a blanket from the closet in the hall, could have found a hoodie in the laundry basket under the dining table, but she wanted this: the bite of cold air on her arms and legs that pricked at her skin like splinters. It was grimly painful. It was the opposite of wanting to fuck someone.

She wanted to fuck Chris Gallo. It was a simple thought, one that was elemental in its directness, and one that was easy enough to construct but hard to think. Because once she started thinking, she knew she would never stop. She wanted to fuck him. She wanted to know the weight of him, the lines of the muscles on his thighs and ass, the temperature of his breath on her neck in a room half-dark, but only half, so she could watch him watching her.

The things I could do to him, she thought.

But then, she knew the fucking could never be in isolation. She wanted him because she wasn't sure she wanted Trevor anymore. She wanted him because she wanted to feel human again, and not this fog of grief and death and the unknown. She wanted him because it was a simple thing to want, even though the impetus and repercussions could never be simple. She wanted him because maybe this was the way she could no longer be scared to leave this apartment and this life and that man in the other room, and it would be a reason, an irrefutable one with hard borders and density and a cruelty that was sharp and fast. This was how it could all end.

If she touched him. If he touched her back. It was just a dream, after all.

In the next room, Trevor snored, that loud snort that meant he would be waking up soon. Like every morning, he would reach for her, his hand groping through the sheets for her hip. Years ago, she had smiled drowsily at the touch. Now, she was relieved she was in the other room and the air was cold enough that she didn't even want to cry.

—

It took three hours for Parminder to get an answer from the administration office in Victoria. The location of closed files older than fifteen years was difficult to pinpoint. Record-keeping was a challenge, especially now that no one budgeted for paper storage. Parminder frowned at the receiver and crossed her eyes at Jessica, who was standing at the entrance to her cubicle, snapping her fingers.

When Parminder hung up after muttering a thin thank you, Jessica pulled on the ends of her hair.

"Well," she asked, "where are they?"

"Her most accurate guess is that they're in the office in Burnaby, in one of the basement storage rooms."

"Her most *accurate* guess? What does that mean?"

Parminder sighed. "It means that the Ministry hasn't implemented a province-wide record-keeping protocol yet. They're still in the development stage."

Jessica groaned and hung her head.

"She's pretty sure all the Lower Mainland files are in Burnaby. They have the most space there and she thinks she remembers one of the ministerial assistants ordering that they be centralized and archived by region. But she's not sure."

"Jesus. I hate the government."

Parminder laughed and then tried to choke it back. "Quiet. You never know when they're listening." She pointed at an air vent in the ceiling. "There could be hidden cameras every-where."

When Jessica phoned the Burnaby office, she got an auto-mated message informing callers that all personnel were attending a team-building exercise and would return the next day. The following morning, she called again and was put on hold, transferred and transferred again before getting through to the communications officer who had been there the longest.

"Yeah, I think one of the storage rooms is now an archive."
He paused. "Yes, definitely that one in the basement that used
to be for bikes. Wait a minute. Let me ask Gill, the office manager. She has the keys to everything."

She was put on hold again. No music this time, just crackling silence.

The next afternoon, Jessica and Parminder stood in a windowless room lined with industrial metal shelving. The office
manager had led them into the back then left, dropping her
ring of keys for the locked cabinets on a small, round table.
As the door closed behind her, she called out, "I came in here
yesterday to take a look and I'm pretty sure everything is orga-
nized by year of first contact with child protection, and then
by last name. But I can't say what's in the files themselves—
they may cross-reference other files that are somewhere else
or don't exist anymore. Good luck!" The door closed with a
soft sucking sound.

"Welcome to the pre-digital world," Parminder muttered,
then laughed.

"I think I see a box marked 1963. Is that even possible?"
Jessica wandered to a dimly lit corner and gingerly lifted a
flattened lid.

"Anything is possible. God, I feel like Doctor Who."

Jessica stood and turned to look at the rest of the room.
The shelves radiated outward—long and dusty, marked by
rusting bolts and strands of shredded paper. There were years
here. Handwritten notes on other people's lives, just like the
ones she used to scribble as she sat in her car between cases.
Lines about what they ate. How they punished their children.
The damage they might have done. Boxes sagged and cabinet
drawers gaped. The entire structure was collapsing under the
weight of paper that wasn't just paper. These were words that

changed families, that separated children from their parents and passed those children to strangers, as if the strangers were better. Maybe they were. Sometimes they weren't.

"I wonder how many of these kids went on to prison. And how many of them turned out just fine," she said as she walked toward a row of cabinets that looked slightly newer than the rest.

Parminder laughed sharply. "I ask myself questions like that all the time. And then I get so depressed I want to quit my job and do something with no impact on people at all. For about a week, I thought I wanted to be a notary. I don't even know what notaries do, which was the whole point."

"Am I doing the right thing? This isn't ethical, is it?" Jessica paused, one hand already half-hidden in a folder.

"Of course it's not ethical. But it's what you need to do. Those girls are dead. Your mother is dead. Their social worker is probably dead too. There's no one alive whose life will change because you're looking for their files. You need the truth. Think about that."

Jessica nodded and tried to smile. Parminder tucked a black curl behind her ear. "Me, on the other hand, I'm just here because this is exciting. So I guess I'm being totally unethical, like a tobacco company or Vladimir Putin. Hooray for me!" She punched the air above her head with a tightly closed fist and laughed.

· It took Jessica and Parminder an hour to figure out where the files from 1988 were kept. In the grey filing cabinet they opened, the folders were no longer in alphabetical order, if they ever had been in the first place. After Parminder cut her finger on an old spiral-bound notebook, Jessica finally found two thick folders, one labelled *Cheng, Casey,* and the other, *Cheng, Jamie (see Cheng, Casey).*

Jessica opened the first cover. A faded photograph of a thin Chinese girl was stapled on the underside. Her pointed chin was angled slightly upward. *The facial equivalent of a fuck-you*, Jessica thought. *The face of a girl who had to walk down city streets, protecting herself.* Her bangs were crookedly cut and acne dotted her forehead. But she was pretty. She might have been skinny and angry, but she stood there like a dust-coloured bird, waiting for someone to notice the complication of beautiful bones and muscles underneath. The line of her cheek. The full, wide mouth. The suggestion of the woman she might have become.

"Oh," whispered Parminder as she looked over Jessica's shoulder. "That's quite a face."

Jessica shivered. She felt small and afraid, as if Casey's eyes were seeing her as she was in 1988. Grubby, uncombed, clumsy.

There were many days when she woke up then—stuffed animals thrown to the floor, hair sticky with the drool that had collected on her pillow overnight—that she could hear the rhythmic thudding of her mother's mixing bowl against the kitchen counter or her father running through the house, gathering up the detritus that he needed to go to work. These were the good sounds, the ones that meant they were the only ones home. No other children would peer at her from behind their plates, eyes big or small but all with the same emptiness that indicated a bland acceptance. They were here. There was no point having any feelings about it.

But there were other days too: days when her mother never seemed to see her, when she was the only kid who was allowed to walk home from school alone. After Casey and Jamie began living with them, Jessica noticed that everyone else's parents picked their kids up or made them walk in groups, eyes darting from shrub to van to mailbox. On the news, sullen, ugly men went to jail for taking children and women, and yet it seemed that people kept disappearing, from places that Jessica had never heard of, which meant that they must be ordinary neighbourhoods like hers. Sometimes, she wanted to ask her mother if she was afraid, but then she stopped herself. Donna always picked up Casey and Jamie. It was them she was scared for. What was the point in asking questions if the answers were already so obvious?

One afternoon, Jessica stopped at the convenience store. She opened the front door, knocking the bell. The man behind the counter looked up from his newspaper and smiled.

"Hello. School over already?"

Jessica stopped and shook off her hood. "Hi, Mr. Kim."

"What chocolate bar are we getting today?"

"Shh. What if my mother hears you?"

Mr. Kim laughed. "Your mother is a smart lady, but I don't think she can hear you all the way in here."

She walked to the candy aisle and gazed at the Skors, Oh Henrys and Coffee Crisps. Every Friday, when her elementary school let out early, she came in to buy one chocolate bar, then ate it on the way home, careful to wipe her face with the tissue she kept in her coat pocket for just this instance. Her mother always had date rolls or molasses oat cookies waiting for her—sticky and sweet, but they filled Jessica's mouth with tiny strands of fibre and nuts and filled her stomach in a distressingly healthy way. She wanted sugar that melted in her mouth and zipped through her veins until she felt dizzy.

Twix. Because you got two bars in one.

Jessica brought the package up to the counter and felt in her backpack's side pocket for her two-dollar bill. It wasn't there. Quickly, she shrugged off the pack and set it on the floor, where she opened up the main pocket and pulled out

43

her lunch bag, binder and social studies textbook. Still not there. She checked her coat and jeans. Nothing.

"Sorry, Mr. Kim, but I think I lost my money." She thought she might cry from shame.

"Don't worry. You can just come back later. I've got lots of Twix here."

Jessica stuffed all her things into her backpack and ran out, down the street and around the corner. Quickly, she opened the back door and went up the stairs to her room. She pulled out her desk drawer and lifted out an old cookie tin. She shook it. Silence. She popped the lid off. Empty.

She sat on her bed and tried to remember the last time she had counted her money. It had been Sunday, after Donna had taken her shopping. Forty-seven dollars and thirty-one cents. And it was all gone.

"Jessica, is that you?" Her mother's footsteps were coming down the hall. "Jess? Why are you just sitting there in your coat?"

Jessica tilted the tin so her mother could see. "It's gone, Mom. All of it."

Donna stood with her hands on her hips, filling the doorway with her wide-legged pants. "What do you mean? Did you lose it?"

"No, I didn't lose it! Someone must have taken it. *They* must have taken it." Jessica threw the tin on the floor and watched it bounce and roll.

"Are you saying Casey and Jamie took your money?"

"Who else? You?"

Donna looked up at the ceiling for a minute before sitting down on the bed and taking Jessica's hand. "Listen, we don't know if they took it or not. But even if they did, what would we do about it?"

"You're my mother. You make them give it back."

"It's not that simple. Our family dynamic is very delicate right now. If we start accusing them of stealing, then they might run away or hurt themselves. I can replace your money, Jess. But I think we should just leave it between us. What do you say?" She patted the top of Jessica's head, her touch soft but still forceful, and Jessica knew she didn't have a choice. Jamie and Casey were the ones who had never had much money, who were living here because their parents hurt them or didn't care or couldn't cope. Jessica knew this and so she was quiet and sat down at her desk, back to her mother.

Later that evening, when Jamie and Casey passed by her closed bedroom door, she imagined their bodies sliding through the air. She could swear she heard a dry rasping, like snakes uncoiling in desert sand.

Quickly, Jessica shook her head, closed the cover of the file and stuffed both folders into her bag. She hurried over to the open cabinets and began to shut them, slamming the drawers, metal on metal.

"I know this is obvious, but I don't think we're supposed to take files out of this room." Parminder winked as she watched Jessica fumble with the manager's keys.

"Come on, Parm. Let's get out of here before I start feeling guilty."

They left the room exactly as they found it. Jessica knew it was only a matter of days before the police came looking for the files, so she would have to read quickly and return them as soon as possible. Her bag hung off her shoulder, heavy and strangely red-hot, as if she were carrying a box of freshly cooked French fries. She walked with Parminder down the hall to the elevator, imagining the folders nestled against her wallet and phone, spines bending when the lining pushed against them. Photocopies were soulless. She had to touch the photographs, the indentations of pen on paper. She had to be alone to read every word. No Trevor, no Gerry, no Detective Gallo. This was between her and Donna.

"What would your mother say?" Parminder asked as she stared at the elevator lights.

Jessica looked down at her black flats. "I don't know," she said. But she did know. The mother she remembered would never have used her credentials inappropriately. *How can we hold those in power to account if we don't live ethically too?* Jessica looked over her shoulder, half-expecting to see Donna standing behind her, arms crossed over her chest. *That's right, I'm talking to you, Miss Jess.*

"Thank god. The elevator's finally here." Parminder's voice seemed far away.

Jessica blinked. The doors slid open and she began to walk in, but then she stopped, mid-step. There was time. She could return the files right now and it wouldn't make any difference. She could call Chris Gallo. She could do the right thing, as she always had.

But then she placed her palm on her bag. Her fingers twitched. "Fuck the guilt," she said. "We're leaving."

Jessica ran on the damp streets, her hair trailing behind her in a long, messy ponytail. It had started to mist, and she could feel the drops being pulled into her lungs every time she took a breath. The pounding of her feet on the pavement sounded loud and hard and simple. Her breath was just breath. There was no need to think.

She came to an intersection and stopped. Casey's photograph flashed in her mind. The files were waiting for her at home, piled on the coffee table, a pad of paper and a pencil placed on top. Panting in the cold, wet air, Jessica tried to calculate how long it would take her to read each piece of paper and examine each photograph. And she wondered if she would be able to detect a sliver of her mother. Maybe her words, spoken to the social worker, on a page of notes. Maybe a lock of her hair, blurry and overexposed, captured in the corner of a picture. It already felt like so long since Donna had touched her shoulder or held her hand. Maybe, just maybe, her mother had touched one of those sheets of paper and left a faint print, a finger outlined in the oils from her skin.

During the nights that Donna had spent in another child's room, her sturdy arms holding him as he panted from fear, Jessica lay in her bed and wished her mother would come in for just one minute, just to untangle Jessica's hair or kiss her cheek. Now, she wanted her again.

The walk sign blinked on. Jessica wiped her nose on her sleeve and started running. She was two kilometres away from home. If she went fast, she could be reading in fifteen minutes. She raised her chin and darted forward, hands in fists.

▬◄

The evening air seeped through Jessica's quilt, icing the knees of her jeans and creeping up her arms. She sat on her narrow balcony on a folding chair, wedged between Trevor's bike and a stack of plastic bins filled with camping gear and the remains of the container garden she had tried to grow two years earlier. She had placed a flashlight on the floor beside a mug of tea. It would be dark soon and she didn't want to go inside, where Trevor was stirring a pot of vegetarian chili and singing to a Tom Waits record. She couldn't smell spices and beans and listen to his wavering, pubescent singing while reading Casey's and Jamie's files.

She imagined him flipping through the papers, his fingers long and white. He would shake his head and say things like, *The system never works for immigrant families* or *Remember how girls disappeared then and no one gave a shit* or *They never had a chance*. It would be like one of their potluck dinner parties. Someone would tell a story about an addict or a prostitute or a child, and everyone else would try to outdo each other with how much empathy they felt, or how much they wished they could really, truly understand. Trevor would try to filter Casey and Jamie through his brain and reorder their story until it made sense to him and his mental system of privilege and risks and best practices. Jessica frowned. This one belonged to her.

At first, she just stared at the closed folders, running her hands over the paper and blinking against the dim, grey sunset. Everything might be here. Or nothing.

After ten minutes, Jessica slowly opened Casey's file and began reading. The social worker's notes were short and she offered no detail, but sometimes a line pushed itself forward and Jessica felt the pulse of that day, smelled the food that was cooking in the background, saw the light changing from dawn to day to evening.

They trust only each other.

Mrs. Cheng cried in my office after an exhausting interview.

Jamie's anger masks her fear.

They both love and hate their father.

Donna is doing her best.

Jessica blinked and remembered her mother sitting at her desk, writing a letter to Granny Beth. Donna wrote letters all the time, to dozens of people, but Jessica always knew when she was writing to Granny. She turned on Bach, as if the bombast and swells could somehow drive her letter forward, give it a shape that was less concave, less ephemeral. And she murmured to herself as she wrote, words that Jessica never tried to listen to but would hear nonetheless.

"I don't want to bring up the past."

"How is your knee?"

"It was an accident."

"I did my best."

Now, Jessica shivered at the memory. Donna had been apologizing for something, over and over again. And Granny Beth had refused to listen. She shook her head and pulled the blanket tighter over her knees before turning over one more page in the folder. A transcript. A copy of the police officer's first interview with Mrs. Cheng, only two hours after the girls were admitted to the hospital. As the daylight dimmed, Jessica read faster and faster, and the story grew. The questions, the photographs of the girls' room at their family home, the medical reports—everything churned and stuck, reassembled and took shape until Jessica felt like she was following Casey and Jamie everywhere they went, carefully placing her own foot in their footprints, still warm and soft.

For a moment, she was afraid. It had been three days since her father had found those bodies, and she couldn't remember sleeping or stopping or sitting on the toilet just to stare at the white wall of her bathroom. She felt as if she were standing at the top of a high, high hill, and the only way to get down was to hurtle herself toward the steepest side as fast as she could, feet stumbling and rolling and tripping as she went. She breathed deeply and looked out over the alley.

It was dark now. Trevor would soon come to the patio door and ask her to come inside. But she wasn't finished and there was an extra set of flashlight batteries tucked in her pocket. She kept reading.

Before they went missing, the older girl was hurt, and the younger saw it all and was punished. They were taken from their parents and went into foster care, first to a home where the boys were mean and hard and whispered things in their ears as they walked past them in the hall. Then, they were moved to a second home, one with a mother who never left them alone, who cooked meals that made them shit immediately afterward, who wanted to love them and really, really tried. For a couple of weeks, they stared at her, having learned how to be hard from the boys who had touched them. But they weren't hard by nature and this foster mother wasn't so bad, even if she always said the wrong thing. Had they stayed, they might have eventually loved her back.

They were restless. At night, they lay in unfamiliar beds and listened to the wind and rain, could feel the cold, clean air when they pressed their palms to the windows. It would be something, they thought, to run outside, down the hill, across the bridge, and back to their old neighbourhood, their old house, their old, lumpy beds. This foster home was clean and bright and quiet, pressed up against trees the girls didn't know the names of. If they had been younger, they would have picked up snails in the backyard, jumped into piles of leaves that were wet with rain and nothing else. But they weren't younger. They were just old enough to make a plan.

**NINETEEN
EIGHTY-FOUR**
to
**NINETEEN
EIGHTY-EIGHT**

FIVE

WHEN BILL AND GINNY CHENG MOVED TO UNION
Street, they took pictures on the front lawn. Bill and Ginny in
the back, Casey and Jamie in front, their little girl shoulders
narrow under their parents' hands. The grass was patchy and
the porch needed to be painted, but it didn't matter. They had
a yard and a basement for storage. And they didn't have to
share a bathroom with anyone, not like in the attic apartment
they had just left with its steep staircase and gaping windows.

The girls were in school at Lord Strathcona, grades four
and five, and Bill had been working as a longshoreman for
six months, saving up for a car and now the extra rent on
this little blue house. Ginny was working nights at the Patricia
Hotel—cleaning, filing, answering phones. Of course, if the
family had had the choice, they would have chosen a newer
house in one of the quieter East Vancouver neighbourhoods.
Maybe by Hastings Park. Or even near Main Street, south
of the cemetery. But this is what they could afford. Besides,
it was close to work. The girls didn't have to change schools.

MacLean Park was only two blocks away. Ginny reasoned that the park was pretty safe, in the daytime anyway.

During the week, Bill left the house by six and Ginny got the girls all to herself before school. She crept into their room in the mornings and watched them sleep. Casey slept by the window, her arm flung over the top of her head, mouth open. Jamie's bed was up against the wall by the closet. She curled up, knees tucked into her stomach. Their breathing was always in tandem, even when one had a cold or the other was snoring. In and out, like they didn't know any other way.

Ginny blew on their ears. They woke up, stretching slowly, smiling when they heard their mother say, "Breakfast is almost ready." They ate and ate, but stayed skinny. Ginny wondered if all her girls could grow were bones and long, thick night-black hair. Sometimes Ginny would make rice congee or steam the pork dumplings she kept in the freezer. Mostly though, Casey and Jamie weren't interested in the kind of breakfast Ginny's own mother used to make for her in their old Chinatown rooming house. Instead, they ate toast with jam, or sugary cereal. Ginny shivered as she watched them slurp up the pink-tinged milk. She could never understand why anyone would eat cold food first thing in the morning.

The girls sang as they got ready for school. Songs they learned in class or the pop songs they heard on the radio.

"It's 'Karma Chameleon,' James! Come on, sing with me."

After she dropped them off and returned home, she replayed their off-key warbling in her head to fill the empty rooms as she tidied and ironed her clothes for work. When she lay down to sleep, she could smell their musty child-sweat from the tops of their heads. She wished she could dip her sheets in that smell and wrap herself up, warm and drowsy.

When Bill came home, she rushed through dinner and homework, bathed the girls as quickly as possible and then left, taking small, quick steps to the hotel in the dark night. She never took the new blue Chrysler because it seemed like such a waste to drive when she could walk in eight minutes. But she never stopped peering into the bushes beside the sidewalk, or speeding up when she passed a windowless van. Things happened to women in Chinatown. The police had been asking questions at the hotel, asking if Ginny had noticed when the hooker who usually stood on the corner outside had just stopped showing up.

"Why?" she asked. "Did something happen to her?"

The police officer winced. "I can't really say. We've found her purse and shoes. But not her."

She never heard anything about it on the news, but she knew that girl was dead. She had come to expect it. Everyone who had to work or live down here thought the same way.

When Ginny was younger and getting ready for school or work, her mother used to say in Cantonese, "Watch out. You can't always trust other people. They're not all like us." Back then, she used to shrug and continue out the door, purposely not looking at her mother's body in the window, wavering and thin behind the cheap, sheer curtains.

But as she grew older, her mother's words grew heavier inside her head. When she and Bill got married, she heard *careful, careful, careful* as she walked down the street. What would he do if she disappeared or got hurt? When she began working at the Patricia, she watched the girls who stood on the corners in their wedge sandals and short denim skirts and wondered if they had the voices of their mothers echoing in their ears. Ginny silently begged them to walk away from the slow-driving cars, to put on a long coat and just go. Anyplace but here, where Chinatown and the Downtown Eastside bled into each other and where nobody ever wanted to stay. Ginny kept her eyes open and walked quickly. To stay safe, she needed to look like a woman who had something to live for.

When Casey and Jamie grew big enough to leave the house by themselves, fear prickled through Ginny's skin every time she had to go to work and leave them. Where would they go? Who might knock on the door? Had she remembered to tell them to stay away from the Carnegie Centre, where human misery had snowballed so that vomit and shit and dirty sexual favours in exchange for drugs seemed normal? There were so many hidden doorways and spaces between buildings where men could lurk, the kind of men who looked for young girls without their mothers.

Bill told her to carry a knife. He had even given her a folding one that his best friend Wayne had bought from the pawnshop, but she just tossed it into the junk drawer in the kitchen and never thought of it again. It was a cold, hard, palm-length piece of fear, a solidification of what she already felt. She didn't need that. She needed to be smart. As she had always been, ever since her father had died and she and her mother had moved to their small room with the sink but no toilet. Her mother had stuffed Chinese sausages at the Dollar Meat Store while Ginny had left school in grade ten and learned to clean hotels. Now, she practically ran the Patricia at night. She learned to protect what she had. Her job. The girls. She called home from work as often as she could. She never stopped thinking about them, reasoning that if she kept them alive in her head, the universe would know they were wanted and loved and therefore nothing bad would ever happen to them. She told them to be careful. She told them other people weren't like her.

Ginny's mother had also said, "Don't give your husband everything. He's just another person. He will make mistakes. And then where will you be?"

So Ginny took ten dollars out of her paycheque every week and deposited it in a bank account in her name. She felt guilty, but then she reasoned that she might never use that money anyway. Nevertheless, a digging feeling scraped at her insides.

She loved Bill. He had charmed her mother even though he had come to Canada as a teenager. "He'll never get anywhere with that accent, you know," her mother had said. "People hear me and they think I'm stupid. And I'm not a man who will have to support a family one day." Ginny was mad that her mother would say such a thing out loud, but then, she also knew she was right. Bill had once been a teenager who dreamed of becoming an electrician, but school and reading became harder and harder until he dropped out at the beginning of his grade eleven year. Even then, he thought he could get a good union job in construction or at CN Rail. He worked and worked, leaving positions because there was nowhere to go, sometimes getting fired for mouthing off in his staccato, angry-sounding accent, never quite making it into the union because he could never stay in one job long enough, and bouncing from one shitty apartment to the next. It was only now, at the age of thirty-seven, that he seemed to be getting anywhere, even as Wayne and his other friends still struggled to find work. A year ago, he drank beer until he fell asleep every night. Ginny would come home in the mornings and have to hide the empty cans before the girls woke up.

"I want to forget," he had said. "Every week, I line up at construction sites begging for work. I'm better than that." Then he had punched the wall and his fist went all the way through the aging plaster, lath splintering around his tensed arm. "If I could," he had whispered to her, "I would hit myself like that."

But now, it was better. He had proved himself with the house and the car. Ginny told her mother that he was going to keep at it. That there was nothing but progress and good things from now on. She looked in the bathroom mirror every morning and reminded herself that each day would be better than the one that came before. They would work hard, and they would be rewarded. There was no room for error.

SIX

ONE FOGGY AFTERNOON THREE YEARS LATER, BILL came home from work early, his boots and coveralls clean. Ginny had just given the girls crackers and cheese for their after-school snack and they were now lying on the rug in the living room watching *Degrassi Junior High*. Bill sat down heavily on a kitchen chair. Ginny wondered if she should allow the girls to watch the show. One of the characters was pregnant. It was too real. Too scary. Or not scary enough.

"I got fired," Bill muttered, tugging at the laces of his boots.

Ginny stared. "What? Why?"

"I got into a fight with the new foreman this morning."

"Oh no. *Bill.*"

"He acts like he knows everything, that fucking kid. I don't know how he got that job, so I asked him, and he got all mad and said he was one hundred percent qualified. Then I said I might just call the union and ask if he's legit. He laughed. *Laughed* at me, Ginny. And then he said, 'As soon as they hear your stupid-ass accent on the phone, they won't believe a word you say. If they can understand you in the first place.' So I punched him in the mouth."

Ginny bent her head and looked at her hands folded in her lap. "Jesus," she whispered.

"The police came and took me to the station. The union lawyer got me out on bail. He said the foreman might get disciplined, but I'm the one who got charged. I could go to jail. I'm done, Ginny. Done."

Bill looked small. A lock of glossy black hair fell over his forehead, but Ginny didn't move to smooth it back. *Damn him*, she thought. *After all the work I've done.*

But still she smiled. "You can find another job. You have a good reputation."

He laughed, then shrugged off his coat. "Maybe. Not anymore. I don't know. Remember how hard it was for me to find this job?"

So she stopped asking. He looked for work for a while, sometimes taking temporary jobs at construction sites with Wayne, other times signing up for free information sessions at community colleges where he would sit through some seminar on welding or electrician certification. But as soon as he sat down with the application forms, he gave up.

"I don't have any transcripts. Where the hell am I supposed to get those?"

Ginny sighed. "You have to phone your old high school and ask."

"What? You mean the high school I didn't graduate from?"

"You could get your high school equivalency first," Ginny said quietly.

"Sure. I'll get on that as soon as you do." And that was the end of that.

When Ginny came home from work, Bill was asleep on the couch, empty beer cans lined up on the rug beside him. It all looked so familiar that Ginny felt a sharp twist in her stomach, as if this was the way she always knew they would end up. Her mother barked over the phone, "Has that redneck found a job yet?" And Ginny couldn't lie because it already hurt too much. Even when he was granted a conditional discharge with no criminal record, Bill still said nothing as he ate lunch. Ginny tried to talk about the weather or who was on Phil Donahue but then gave up.

After a few months, there was no money left, only the bank account that Bill knew nothing about. Ginny stared at her transaction booklet and felt her face bloom red and angry. She was not going to pay for his drinking with *her* money. She had saved it. It was hers.

She watched him fail over and over again. In the mornings, when she got up and looked at his sleeping face in the half-light, she could see how the failure was dragging down his jaw, the endpoint of his nose. He was drooping with defeat, and she hated it. No one was going to hire a man with a face like that. A man who stared blankly ahead like a friendless, homeless dog afraid of its next beating. Ginny couldn't kiss him or touch him, couldn't even look at him without forming fists with her hands.

It wouldn't be long before they had to leave this house and move into another apartment with walls that let the winds blow through as if they were huddled in a tent made of muslin. This house was where her girls were going to grow up. They had agreed, but now she knew: he was never going to match her contributions.

The next morning, still in her navy blue work pants and white shirt, Ginny kicked Bill's hand as it dangled over the edge of the sofa. His eyelids fluttered and he ran his palm over his cheek, spreading out the drool, shiny in the pre-dawn light.

"Just five more minutes," he mumbled, burying his head further into the cushions.

"No. Wake up."

Bill's eyes were wide open now. "What's wrong? What time is it?"

"It's almost six."

"I'm going back to sleep."

Ginny bent down, cupped her hand under his chin and stared into his eyes. "You're going to get up and have a shower. When you're done, you're going to pack up all your clothes and get out of here. I don't care where you go, just leave before the girls wake up."

"What are you talking about?"

"I'm sick of this, Bill. I can't support all four of us. You have to go."

Bill sat up, knocking over beer cans as he swung his feet on to the floor. "Like hell I am. If you want to get rid of me, then you go."

"How will you pay the rent without me? How will you cook for the girls? How will you do anything?" Ginny crossed her arms in front of her.

"Listen to you. So high and mighty just because you have a job. I had a job once too, you know."

"Exactly. You had one. You don't anymore."

Bill's rage wilted. He lowered his head and spoke into his chest. "I can find a job, Ginny. Soon. Just give me a chance."

"I don't give out chances. This is my life too. And you're not going to wreck it."

Ginny turned around and opened the hall closet. She pulled out an old duffel bag and threw it into the living room. "You can have this. I never liked it anyway."

When the girls woke up, Ginny told them that their father wasn't going to be living with them anymore. Casey blinked and said, "Are you getting divorced?"

"I don't know. But he's moved out."

Later that afternoon, she found a folded piece of paper in the kitchen. On the front, in Bill's handwriting: "For Casey and Jamie." Ginny held it for a long time, pressing down on the folds as she sat at the table, running her finger over the letters in blue ballpoint ink. She could smell the promises inside, the written evidence of Bill's inability to do as he wanted. She knew that he was promising visits and gifts and love, always love. Maybe he could do it. Maybe he could live apart from them and still be the father they needed. Her lips twitched as she remembered how he had stared into her eyes on their wedding day, as if her face was the only thing he ever needed to look at to make it in this world. Love had never been their problem. She loved him still. But it hadn't done any good. She tore up the paper without reading it and threw it in the trash.

━

Ginny found a second job waitressing at a diner during the breakfast rush. After her shift at the hotel, she went straight to the restaurant five blocks west on Hastings. There, she worked until ten thirty and then walked home, her shoes like hooves, hitting the sidewalk loud and heavy. She slept until the girls came home and sat with them while they ate their snacks.

Casey was in high school now and said very little, even though Ginny asked about her day every afternoon. Instead, Casey stared out the window and chewed her cheese or carrot sticks or cookie silently. Jamie never shut up.

"Today, Miss Humphrey brought in a real live chameleon. And we're all going to take turns bringing him home on the weekends. We get to feed him dried brine shrimp. Cool, right?" Jamie looked hopefully at her older sister. Casey shrugged.

"The grade seven dance is tomorrow, Case. Will you help me pick something to wear?"

The silence felt suspended above their heads, stormy. Ginny looked at Casey's expressionless face and then back at Jamie's disappointed one.

"I can help you, Jamie. I can alter one of my dresses for you if you want." Ginny smiled.

"Oh. Sure. Thanks, Mom."

But Ginny knew this wasn't the same. Her clothes weren't right. They never would be.

Out of the silence, Ginny heard Casey's voice. "Why did he leave?" Casey tilted her chin up and stared at her mother. "Is it because of something you said?"

Ginny started to speak, but her words tangled in her mouth. The answer was in her throat. Why couldn't she just say it?

"It's because you were nagging him, isn't it?"

"Casey, it's not that simple."

"Maybe it is, Mom. Maybe you're the one who makes everything complicated. Maybe if you had just stopped bugging him, Dad would be sitting here right now."

Casey's face was starting to contort and she was trying her hardest not to cry. Ginny reached out and put her hand on her daughter's wrist. "Even if he was here, what would he be doing? Would he be talking to you? Or would he be lying on the couch, drunk again?"

Casey shook off her mother's fingers. "You have no idea what we talked about when you weren't home."

"Why don't you tell me, then? I want to hear what you have to say too."

"You wouldn't understand." Casey stood up, leaving her plate on the table.

"Try me."

The phone rang. Ginny looked at the clock and saw that it was close to five. It was probably her boss at the hotel, calling to tell her that she needed to come in early, or that she needed to pick up some more Windex on her way to work. She stood up and reached for the receiver hanging on the wall.

Casey grabbed the phone and hung it back up so violently that the bell inside rang loudly and briefly, like a yelp. Ginny stared.

"What are you doing? That was probably my boss."

"Don't you see? It's all about work for you. Work at the hotel or the diner or work at home. You *like* work. You like working and eating and sleeping and then starting all over again. You're a psycho." Casey wrapped her arms around herself. "If that's what life is, then I don't want to live it."

Ginny extended a hand to draw her daughter into a hug, but Casey just spun in her spot, shoulders hunched, out of reach.

"Your life doesn't have to be like mine," Ginny said. "You can finish school, get training, do whatever you want."

"Come on, Mom," Casey muttered. "We all know that's not how it works. How would we pay for university? How would I even get into university? I'm almost flunking already." She looked up at her mother's face and blinked hard. "I don't

65

want a cleaning job or a restaurant job. I want nice jeans and hoop earrings. I want to be happy."

Ginny wanted to tell her that she did understand, that she felt these same things when she was younger. But it wasn't true. She knew, deep down in her belly, that she had only gone from job to job, from the apartment she could afford to the house she could barely keep, never thinking about the possibilities that existed outside of Chinatown, outside of cleaning and replacing toilet paper rolls in small, bare bathrooms. She bought her mother's groceries every week and swept out her dark, L-shaped room in the boarding house around the corner. She balanced her chequebook. She rotated household chores—Monday for floors, Tuesday for laundry, Wednesday for dust and tidying . . . When she slept in the middle of day, she didn't dream. She just sank into a darkness that simultaneously pulled and pushed her down. She had never wanted anything else than this. She had never found the time.

In that moment, she knew this was Bill's problem. He wanted stuff. A nicer home, a flashy car, a job he could brag about, a wife who was happy. But there was no way for him to get any of those things.

"You can be happy, honey. We can figure something out. You're so young. You have so much time." But even Ginny could hear the falseness in her voice. There wasn't time. Casey could leave school and be working within the year. Wringing out grey mops in grey water. Ginny shivered.

"Sure, Mom. Whatever you say." Casey's body seemed to crumple under her baggy sweatshirt. "I'm going to my room. I've got homework." And she left, her thin socks dragging on the floor.

Jamie stood up too. "I guess I should go."

But Ginny caught her by the arm and pulled her into a hug, Jamie's face squashing against her chest. She said to herself, "I hope they never know how hard it is to be a grown-up."

Jamie squirmed and pushed back from Ginny's body. "Did you say something, Mom?"

If she thought it would help, Ginny would have told Jamie everything she was thinking. *Do more than I did. Think and learn. Leave Chinatown. Run if you have to.* But these were abstractions, words that would mean little to a twelve-year-old girl who went at her tasks one at a time. There was no way for Ginny to tell her all of this in a way that she would understand, remember and use when she grew older. She would have to wait for the right time, for the exact moment that her advice might mean the difference between a bad choice and a better one.

Ginny smoothed down the top of Jamie's head. "Never mind. Get going on your homework. Dinner is at six. And then I have to go to work."

SEVEN

AT FIRST, GINNY DIDN'T KNOW WHERE BILL WENT, although she assumed he must have gone to stay with his old high school friend Wayne, who still lived with his parents on the other side of Chinatown. Bill didn't phone. He didn't send any letters. This relieved her. His total absence was like a tonic, a complete cleansing of his existence. In the morning, when she returned home from her shift at the hotel, the house was quiet and clean, everything as she had left it. She could almost believe that she had never been married at all, and that the girls had been conceived by her alone.

That didn't stop her, of course, from changing the locks. In the afternoons, Ginny's mother came from her apartment to stay at the house, usually watching television and dozing in the old armchair in the living room. When Ginny was getting ready to leave after dinner, her mother was often asleep and Ginny had to shake her by both shoulders before she would wake up. Her eyelids trembled, and Ginny wondered if this was how her mother was going to die—shaky, thin-skinned, just barely aware of the people around her. If someone broke the glass in the back door and slipped inside, he might not even notice the sleeping old woman wrapped in a knitted vest and fraying quilt.

In the early evenings, when she saw Casey, Jamie and her mother sitting at the kitchen table together, she exhaled and closed her eyes, content.

One morning two months later, she walked home in the blue winter light, the hood of her parka blowing fake fur against her cheek. She opened the gate into the front yard and looked at the living room window. The curtains were slightly open. When she had left, she had closed them tight, like she did every evening. Ginny's stomach turned. She ran up the walk. Her hands shook as she unlocked the door.

Inside, her mother was asleep in the armchair. Ginny rushed to Casey and Jamie's bedroom. Empty, with just the usual mess of clothes and shoes, the way they always left things before school. She stepped out into the hall and sat on the floor, head on her knees. Her lungs heaved, pushing against her ribs. After a few minutes, she raised her head and put her hands on the floor beside her to steady herself as she stood up. The fingers on her left hand felt something sticky. She squinted but couldn't see anything in the unlit hall. She bent down and sniffed. A drop of drying beer. As if someone had walked from the kitchen to the living room sipping from a full, dribbling can.

Ginny shook her mother. "Ma! Wake up. Ma!"

"Ginny. What time is it?" she asked.

"Was he here? Was Bill here?"

Her mother rubbed her eyes with her knobbly hands. "No, of course not."

"Are you sure? Are you sure he didn't come while you were sleeping last night?"

"I might be old, but I'm not stupid. I fell asleep while the girls were watching a show. You know, the one with all the horses. *Dallas?* I made them breakfast and they walked to school. And then I thought I would take a little nap before I went home. Nothing else happened."

But Ginny had turned around and run into the kitchen. Her eyes examined the stove, the fridge, the table. Everything seemed fine. She opened the back door and stepped out on the porch. There it was, lingering and faint, but there nonetheless. Cigarette smoke. She looked down at the crooked wooden steps. A skinny trail of ashes.

She didn't know when he had come or left. But she knew the girls had let him in. *Everything I do is for them*, she thought. *And still they want him.* When they came home, she could ask them, but she knew Casey would lie and Jamie would too, or at least not say anything so as not to betray anyone. She had no phone number for him, had no idea where he was staying. How could she tell him what she wanted to shout in his face?

You have contributed nothing. You don't deserve them. If you hurt them, I will kill you.

Four hours later, as Casey and Jamie walked into the kitchen after school, Ginny turned away from the stove and said, "If you ever talk to your father, remember that he makes a lot of promises that he never keeps. He loves you and he means well. But he's not reliable."

Jamie was struggling with the toggles on her coat and didn't seem to be listening. But Casey stared at her mother, her face pale under the fluorescent bulb mounted on the kitchen ceiling. She opened her mouth to say something, but then shut it quickly, pursing her lips together as if she were afraid a stray word might just fall out. Ginny placed two plates on the table. Grilled cheese.

"Eat. There's not a lot of time before we have to get started on your homework."

Ginny's mother walked slowly into the kitchen through the back door. She sat down, her bones almost creaking out loud, and smiled. "Nothing to worry about. Everyone's safe." And she patted Casey's arm with her brown, spotted hand.

—

It happened once, maybe twice a week. Ginny came home in the mornings and could see the outline of Bill's body on their bed, an imprecise, man-sized dent on the quilt. If she bent down and sniffed the pillows, she could smell his hair gel— citrusy, tinged with scalp. Sometimes, she closed her eyes and imagined him holding her like he used to, when he had a job and she didn't worry about what he was drinking or where he was going next. He had smooth arms, almost free of hair, and he would wrap them around her waist and kiss the back of her neck. At those times, he made her feel perfect.

Casey and Jamie never said a word. Ginny's mother slept through everything.

When the crocuses began to push up in the back garden, Ginny saw that Bill was getting sloppy. She found a tin can with half a dozen cigarette butts right by the back door. A muddy bootprint on the mat on the front porch. She saw a dry spot on the street where a car had been parked all through the windy, rainy night. And the girls, especially Casey, were slower and drowsier after school, as if he had kept them up. Maybe he was telling them stories as he sat outside, smoking. Maybe they just wanted to look at his face and couldn't sleep as long as he was there. Ginny wasn't sure, but she cleaned up the crumbs on the kitchen table that smelled like pizza and rinsed out the cloth twice, in water so hot she had to wear rubber gloves.

But the girls seemed happier. Casey began chatting again after school while Jamie showed off gymnastics moves she had learned that morning.

"What if I got a part-time job, Mom? So I could get some new clothes?"

"Sure, Casey, if that's what you want. But you have to make sure it doesn't affect your schoolwork."

"Mom! We should get a guinea pig!" Jamie said, sitting on the floor with her legs split.

Eventually, Ginny began to expect Bill's ghost around the house. Liked it, even. It was easy to love him when he was making the girls happy and when she wasn't watching him drink beer after beer while he watched reruns of *M*A*S*H* late into the night. His smell was like a touch. Just enough.

EIGHT

IT WAS SUMMER. GINNY'S MOTHER DIDN'T NEED TO GET the girls ready for school anymore, so she no longer slept at the house. Ginny came home from work in the late mornings and made lunch for Casey and Jamie before going to bed. The bedroom grew cool when she opened the window, and a breeze that was mercifully fresh and not scented with the durians and barbecued pork of Chinatown swept past the curtains and over her face. Everything was quiet and Ginny slept, uninterrupted, until five, when she heard the girls calling for her from the hall.

On her days off, they spent all afternoon together. Sometimes they went shopping for groceries. Other times, they walked through the city, going to Stanley Park to see the Rose Garden and Lumberman's Arch and the animals in the zoo. Casey loved going downtown to stare at the diamonds in the windows at Birk's or the dresses on display at The Bay.

"When I get married, I want a dress like this," Casey said, pointing at a full-skirted ball gown with rosettes on the hem.

Jamie wrinkled her nose. "That's so girly. What about something like this?" She put out a hand to touch a straight white column. Ginny caught her dirty fingers just in time.

"That's for old ladies, James. I want something romantic. Because weddings are all about romance, you know."

Ginny laughed, but her heart beat hard against her chest. Casey was a beautiful girl, small and sharp, with eyes that seemed to see everything. Liquid and dark, bottomless. Not everyone would think she was pretty, but those who saw how lovely she could be would chase her until they owned her. Until she could fit in a box of their choosing, like a dried butterfly with its wings pinned open. She ran her hands over the goosebumps on her arms.

Jamie punched her sister in the arm. "You're just talking like that because you're in *love*." Ginny stared and Jamie bent her head, already understanding the mistake she had made. Casey sat on a white chair.

"What are you talking about?" Ginny could barely breathe through the words, but she had to say them.

Casey rubbed her eyes and smiled like she didn't want to. "It's nothing, Mom. Jamie's just shooting off her mouth again." Jamie nodded but looked small, still folded in a corner.

"Is there a boy from school? Has he asked you out?"

"Yeah, a boy from school." Casey looked at her mother and then away again. "He's been calling."

"Do you like him?"

"I think he's nice."

Ginny put a hand on Casey's shoulder. "Maybe he should come by for lunch and I can meet him."

Casey stood up and shrugged off her mother's touch. "Oh, Mom. It's nothing. He's just some boy. We're not getting married or anything."

"But don't you think I should meet the boy you're dating?"

"Yuck. Who says *dating* anymore? Mom, if it gets serious, I'll tell you. Okay?"

And Ginny said nothing, only watched as her two daughters walked toward the bathing suit section, giggling at the string bikinis on display. She didn't want to follow them but knew she had to. After all, how would they ever find their way back home without her? They might fall into that shifting, unnamed place where girls disappeared, the place that sucked away their identities so cleanly that only their mothers remembered the weight of their bodies, the women they once hoped to be. Ginny stepped forward, her feet like stones.

━

There was peace. A heavy contentment that settled over their house like a favourite quilt. Ginny watched the summer mornings bloom and thicken from the hotel's front desk, remembering the sunrises she watched when her daughters were babies and she nursed them in a chair by an uncovered window. She missed those hours, but now, when she returned home from work and saw the girls watching TV or trying to duplicate outfits they had seen in fashion magazines with what they already owned, she thought to herself that perhaps this was just as good. Because their faces still looked up with smiles when she walked in the front door. Because the tops of their heads were warm when she kissed them. Because they were still hers.

She knew Bill was still coming at night, could practically smell the exhaust from his car as she came home some mornings. Whatever promise he had made Casey and Jamie, he was keeping it. So Ginny carried on.

The fall was still warm and sunny when the girls started school again, both now in high school and old enough, Ginny thought, to get themselves to bed and up again. On their way to the bus stop most mornings, they walked past the hotel and Ginny waved to them through the front window, watching as they struggled to balance their overstuffed school bags. After her shift at the diner, she went home and showered, breathing in the traces of Casey's shampoo—ghosts of fruit, an undercurrent of soap.

One afternoon, Ginny sat at the kitchen table with Casey and Jamie, listening as they gossiped.

"She's not a slut, she's just lonely," Casey said.

"What's the difference?"

"Maybe she just needs a friend."

"Whatever. She's gross." Jamie rolled her eyes.

The sunshine slanted through the back window and spilled yellow over the girls' faces. Ginny looked at Jamie—smooth-faced, with a mouth that smiled wide. She could have been a baby in that light.

When Ginny turned to Casey, she sucked in her breath and blinked. Her daughter sat leaning her head on her hand, shadows tracing the lines of her face. Ginny had always known she was beautiful, but as she looked at her now, she saw that it wasn't about the shape of her eyes or the shininess of her hair. At this very moment, on a sunny Saturday in early September, there was something else spilling out through Casey's skin and lips and neck. She was still, moving only as much as she needed to in order to breathe. Ginny could almost see the weight of Casey's body, as if she were an anchor and the rest of the room relied on her gravitational pull for its order and comfort. When Ginny closed her eyes, she felt sure she could feel pulses of warmth, the pump of her daughter's blood. Casey looked calm. Happy. Red-cheeked. Like there was no other person in the world she would rather be.

Later that night, as Ginny was stocking toilet paper in the vacant rooms at the hotel, she combed through her mind, searching for the reason Casey might look so happy. There was the boy she talked about in the summer. There were the continuing visits from their father. But Ginny could think of nothing else.

Maybe Casey was just growing up. Maybe she just didn't want to be a surly teenager anymore. Maybe she had decided she was going to stay in school.

Ginny knew that she wanted this dreamy contentedness to continue. How nice to come home to a family who smiled, who never looked at you with hate, who said *goodbye* when you left for work instead of ignoring you. And she knew that it might not last, that any word or sideways glance or unkind wind might break the thin wall between this and the sulky, sweating world outside.

NINE

GINNY HURRIED THROUGH THE GREY-LIT STREET. Shivering moonlight pushed its way through a gap in the clouds. She had forgotten her apron at home and needed to run back to grab it before her break was over. Every footstep drummed with the one thought in her head: *shit, shit, shit*.

She never forgot anything. Why today?

As she turned the corner onto Union, she squinted and paused for a half-second. That was Bill's car parked in front. She checked her watch. One fifteen. The girls should be long asleep by now. All the way home, she had been hoping this was the one day he wouldn't show up, but there was the battered blue Chrysler, its rear end poking crookedly out into the street. She sucked in her breath and smoothed down the front of her jacket. If she had to see him, she had better look decent.

From the street, she could see the living room curtains were wide open. Bill was standing by the fireplace, the already short sleeves on his T-shirt rolled up even further. His shoulders. When was the last time she had seen his shoulders? She reached into her pocket for her keys but noticed the front door open, unlocked and not even pushed into its frame. Ginny stepped in, hands already curled into fists. "Idiot," she whispered. "Can't even lock the damned door."

She was about to stride across the room and ask him what the hell was happening, when she looked down and saw a man lying on the rug. He was face up and breathing heavily. He held one of her kitchen towels to his nose but the blood had already soaked through. Drips were running down his hand and onto the floor. Ginny dropped to her knees and touched the top of his head.

"Wayne?" she said. "Is that you?"

Wayne, Bill's old friend from the New Canadian class in high school. The only one, he always said, who understood what it was like to come to this country expecting everything before realizing that they were going to achieve nothing at all.

Bill pulled Ginny's arm and yanked her up to a standing position. "Do you know what you've done?" he hissed.

She tried to pull away, but his grip grew tighter as she struggled. "What are you talking about?"

"This filth has been fucking your daughter."

Ginny stared. "No. That's not true."

Bill pointed at Wayne. "Tell her, motherfucker."

Wayne moaned and pulled the towel away from his face. Ginny gasped at his swollen nose and eyes. "I didn't mean for anyone to get hurt. I love her, Ginny."

"I don't understand." Never in her life had Ginny felt this stupid. Her brain twisted and rattled and still she felt like she was running through a swamp, batting slowly at words that floated around her.

Bill shouted in her face. "He says he loves her! *Your* daughter. Your *slutty* daughter. Get it?"

"I'm sorry, Ginny. I love her. I'll marry her."

Bill grabbed Ginny by the shoulders and shook her. "You're never home. What kind of mother are you?"

Ginny pulled her arm back and punched Bill in the throat. He staggered away, and she ran to the girls' bedroom and pushed open the door. Casey lay on her bed and Jamie crouched at its foot. At first, all Ginny could see was a mess of blankets and sheets and Casey's long hair on the pillow beneath her. But when Jamie stood up, Ginny saw her younger daughter's swollen left eye. She looked down. A ball of towels between Casey's legs. They looked and smelled red and wet and fresh.

Casey mumbled, "Mom's home. Mom's home. Mom's home." And put out her hand.

Ginny kneeled on the floor beside the bed. Jamie said, "Dad kicked her in the stomach. I didn't know what to do. Mom, what are we going to do?"

Ginny cupped Casey's cheek in her hand and kissed her forehead. "Was there a baby?"

"Yes. My baby. Our baby. Did Wayne ask you if we could get married?" Casey smiled, then grimaced. "It hurts, Mom. Like a knife over and over again."

Ginny was crying so hard she could no longer see, only feel her daughter's head with her fingers and smell the burnt flesh odour of blood and more blood. Jamie's face was pressed into her back and their bodies heaved together, each inhale of breath shuddering through mouths and throats and lungs. Her daughters wanted her to fix this, to calmly patch and kiss and settle, but she couldn't think where to begin. All she knew was that she had failed, that all the hard work she had spent nights and days immersing herself in had ended up like this.

She rested her forehead on the edge of Casey's bed and sighed so deeply, she could have sworn she had turned inside out.

"I'm going to call an ambulance," she said to Jamie, who nodded with her eyes closed. "You stay here and hold your sister's hand."

She pulled the door closed behind her. Bill had collapsed into the armchair, his jaw hard and his eyes whittled down to slivers. Wayne hadn't moved. Ginny stared at the phone hanging on the wall. There would be questions. From doctors; police officers too. No one would believe that she was a good mother. No one would think she had tried her best. She was on the verge of losing her girls, not to a bearded, smelly man in a rusty pick-up truck, but to a phalanx of people who would look at her and see her mistakes, the gaps of time that she had left her daughters alone, the frank conversations she might have started with them but didn't. She had worried over the wrong threats.

She looked into the living room, at the triangle of light on the floor from the kitchen, down the hall toward her quiet, neat bedroom. This was her house. Somehow, she had let in something crawling and slick with evil. She rubbed her hands together and knew, finally and with no exceptions, that all her hard work and misplaced caution had been no use. Ginny picked up the receiver. She might as well call. Maybe there was a chance that someone would understand.

One Friday after school, the sisters ran away. They took a bus, a SeaBus, and then walked the narrow streets along the waterfront, turning to watch the trains grinding on the tracks. They headed east, to Skid Row, the neighbourhood they knew so well, that their mother would say they had never feared enough. The older girl, the brave one, was looking for a man, one she hadn't spoken to in weeks, but she knew where he drank, where he bought doughnuts, where his parents lived, just around the corner from the smokehouse. His clothes always smelled of ham.

They waited outside, across the street. Wind pushed at them as if it had picked up speed rolling down the mountains and then erupted along this very sidewalk. Rain fell, but not fast enough to send the girls to the ripped awning at the abandoned gas station down the block. So they stood, shivering in the Cowichan sweaters their foster mother had forced them to wear that morning.

They waited until nine thirty. No lights behind the unmoving curtains. The older sighed and said, "Fuck this," and began walking toward the pub he sometimes fell asleep in, his head on the sticky bar, a hand still grasping a pint glass half-full.

They had never walked these streets at night. In the day, people on benches were still and sleeping and the pigeons were grey and pink and purple and cute. In the day, the solids in the puddles of vomit had been picked clean by rats and seagulls, and the store owners stood on their thresholds, hosing down the curbs in wide arcs. In the night, nothing human was a secret, especially if it was ugly or mean or dirty. In the night, no one could see they were still children, or no one cared. The younger slipped her hand into her sister's and whispered, "Let's go back. We can wait at the house for a while longer." But just as the words left her mouth, the girls were grabbed from behind and pulled into a half-alley where garbage coated the ground, slick. They reached for lamp posts or finger holds in crumbling brick walls, but they weren't fast enough or strong enough and they were dragged back and back and back until their bones were limp. They heard hard breathing behind them and closed their eyes.

TWO THOUSAND
AND SIXTEEN

TEN

IT HAD STARTED TO RAIN AGAIN. JESSICA LOOKED UP from the foster care files and blinked at the dark alley beyond the balcony rail. The flashlight illuminated only the papers on her lap, so all she could see were the lights in the apartment building across the lane. The pavement sounded slick as cars sped through the street on her right. She shivered. The blanket had stopped helping an hour ago.

Jessica blew on her fingers and thought of how her mother had reacted when she'd told her she was going to major in social work at university. Donna had been raking the last of the fallen leaves, her scarf wrapped around her neck and up over her chin. Jessica, just home from school, touched her on her woolly sleeve.

"The university admissions people came to talk to us today," she said, hair blowing into her mouth.

Donna nodded and asked, "Learn anything?"

"I talked to the one lady from UBC for a while about what I should do and—," Jessica looked up at the sky, at the blue patches closing over as clouds from the southwest bunched and grew seamless, "—we both thought that I should apply to the Faculty of Social Work."

Donna dropped the rake on the grass and clapped her hands together, a smile so wide and bright that Jessica closed her eyes. Her mother hugged her and whispered in her ear, "It's what I always wanted for you. I'm so proud."

That night, Gerry came home early and the three of them went out for pasta and red wine. Gerry made toasts about his daughter's social conscience and generations of community involvement. Jessica said nothing, but smiled when her parents looked at her. She didn't know what she had started, but maybe it was worth it. Donna ordered three pieces of tiramisu and then rested her head on Gerry's shoulder. Yes, it was worth it.

Jessica looked down at the open folders on her lap, created by another social worker twenty-eight years ago. The files were maddeningly inconsistent. The social worker's notes on the interview with Ginny were full of detail, as if she were giving her every chance to prove she was a fit mother. But in the end, it didn't matter because it was clear that the girls had been abused, and the social worker couldn't let them go home until she had the time to adequately assess their safety there. Besides, Ginny was renting a house she couldn't afford and her absence while working to make the rent wasn't acceptable. Until she could find one well-paying job or an appropriate and cheaper home, the girls would have to live somewhere else.

I've referred her to BC Housing, she wrote, *but the waitlists are long. The girls will have to stay in care for the time being.*

There were two medical reports, which documented Casey and Jamie's overnight stay at St. Paul's hospital. Casey suffered a miscarriage at approximately ten weeks. Signs of physical assault, including bruising on the abdomen, back and thighs. Treated for shock. Vaginal bleeding moderate to light. Otherwise healthy. Jamie had a black eye and broken rib. The social worker noted that Bill was taken into custody, while Wayne received medical attention. Nothing on charges or trials or prison terms. Jessica supposed Detective Gallo already knew that part of the story. Besides, it would only be Bill who would have been charged with anything criminal. In 1988, Casey was fourteen, the age of consent. Her relationship with Wayne, as strange and inappropriate as it was, had at least been legal.

SEP. 10, '88: *C and J discharged. Emergency placement at the Tindalls'.*

SEP. 14, '88: *Girls silent during placement visit. Peggy Tindall seemed distracted by the two boys I placed with her three weeks ago.*

Jessica had been looking for Donna, for traces of her mother in these notes, but there was very little—only one sheet of paper with five handwritten lines.

SEP. 21, '88: *Dropped C and J at home of Donna Campbell. Clear that the older boys at the Tindalls' were mistreating them. Donna's experience is necessary here.*

SEP. 27, '88: *Phone conversation with D. Girls acting out. D admits this is hardest placement so far. Needed some reassurance that she was doing a good job.*

OCT. 1, '88: *Girls ran away to Stanley Park overnight, although this may be a fabrication. Returned to D the next morning and slept 10 hours straight. D feels she needs to watch them 24 hours a day.*

OCT. 17, '88: *D phoned office. Sounded tired. Inquired about mother's housing application. Reports that C and J are unhappy with placement.*

OCT. 21, '88: *Home visit after phone call from D. Girls have run away again. Police are investigating.*

Jessica knew how the social worker was feeling. She had dozens of files, dozens of children to track and find homes for.

If she started caring, or spending more time on one particular family, her whole system would collapse and then she would be unable to keep all those kids in order. She had wanted Casey and Jamie to stay with Donna because she was capable. Donna always said yes. She didn't need handholding. Donna was the foster mother she counted on. If there were problems, the social worker always said she needed to know. But that didn't mean she *wanted* to know. There was only one way to walk with a responsibility so weighted and omnipresent. You needed people you trusted. People who could be independent and make their own decisions. You needed Donna.

And once the girls had disappeared, as so many girls and women did back then, the police took over and the file was pushed to the back of the social worker's drawer.

Jessica could smell Trevor's chili through the glass balcony door. Her belly churned and she sat, crunched into a ball against the cold. Still, she didn't want to go in. Eating with another human seemed blasphemous. She should suffer out in the early spring air because Donna needed help and didn't get it. Because the girls needed an adult who knew more. Because the social worker needed a lighter workload. Because everyone cared, but wrongly, or not enough. In the alley, a cat darted from car to Dumpster to hydro pole, its skinny body twitching with hunger or longing or rage. Jessica couldn't tell and she wanted to cry for her own ignorance.

The door slid open behind her and the cat sprinted into the shadows, gone. "Jess? Hon, come inside and have some dinner. I used chipotles this time." Trevor's voice squeaked in the cold, like the first time she heard him say his own name.

The day they met, it had been sunny and warm, the kind of afternoon where light thickens and pools as it pushes its way through windows and cracks around doors. Jessica lay in

Trevor's bed, toes in a square of sunshine on the sheets. Three hours before, she had been on her way to a blind date. Now, she held his thin, nervy body in her hands and he said, "Tell me what you want."

And she did. She told him how she wanted him to run his fingers gently down her skin, and how long she wanted him to move beside her. When she wanted him to kiss between her thighs, she breathed, "Now," and he knew what she meant. She told him, and he did exactly as she said. He replied with almost nothing, only murmuring into her, "So beautiful."

Afterward, she rested her head on his shoulder and stared at the cheap, round light fixture mounted on the ceiling. She knew that Trevor would always do what she asked. He would whisper in the mornings before she was awake, reshape her bras when he pulled them out of the washer, pack her lunch the evening before in an insulated bag. She felt the hair on his chest against her cheek. It was like down.

There were no secrets. He was skinny and the muscles under his skin moved in full view. When he smiled at her for the first time in that coffee shop, she felt she could read his entire life in his face. His mother was a nurse. His father was a printer. His childhood bicycle was green. And he never lied.

In his bed, warm and damp with twisted feet, she felt certain. This was it. Trevor kissed the top of her head and asked quietly, "How are you feeling?"

"Fine," she said. "Safe." And she felt his chest fall with an exhale, as if he had been holding his breath the entire time, waiting for her to say those precise words.

Out on the balcony, Jessica shook off the memory and stood, arching her back in a stretch before stepping inside. As they sat at their small pine table, she could feel Trevor watching her. He was observing her as if she were a skittish, endangered goat clinging to the side of a mountain. She refused to look up and instead stared at the mess of beans and peppers and tomatoes in her bowl. Maybe if she was quiet, he'd get the hint and be quiet too.

"Did you find anything interesting?"

She lifted her head and looked at his face, so smooth and boyish that the stubble lining his jaw seemed like an accident. He was still cute, still politely attractive in a way that was reassuringly inoffensive. But if she lived with a real man, one who knew how to fix a garbage disposal and carved animals out of wood, she would be sitting down to a meal of steak and good red wine and listening to classic rock. Instead, she had Trevor, soy cheese and Bon Iver.

Jessica shrugged. "Lots about the girls and their mother. But hardly anything about Mom."

Trevor put down his spoon and picked up a piece of cornbread. "Is that what you were looking for? Stuff about your mom?"

"What else?"

Trevor chewed for a minute before answering. "I thought you were trying to figure out how the girls died. I mean, you *knew* your mother. What else do you need?"

Jessica sighed. "But only she knew what happened. She's the missing link. Don't you see?"

"I guess," he said, slightly shaking his head in a way that made Jessica want to push beans into his eyes. "What are you going to do next?"

"Well, I could talk to the police again. Detective Gallo might tell me something if I pass him the files. You know, like a trade."

"You're going into business with the police?"

Jessica frowned. "You make it sound like I'm a snitch or something. God."

"That's not what I meant." Trevor looked up at the ceiling and exhaled before going on. "Why don't I help you? Maybe we can brainstorm another way you can find out what went on."

She stared at the apartment door behind his head. "This is my thing, Trev. She was my mother. If I find out something awful," Jessica paused and rubbed her eyes with her hand, "I need to just deal with it alone, even if I get scared or over-whelmed. Besides, you're used to pushing people and playing the system to get what your clients need. This has to be done my own way, in my own time."

Trevor left his chair and kneeled down on the floor beside her, his hands on her lap. "Jess, I want you to take a break. Take some time to breathe. You're still grieving your mother. Maybe it would be better if you left the investigating to the police. Or let me help you."

She could feel the blood behind her eyes—hot and insis-tent. "Would you stop helping a client just because it was someone you cared about? Do you think I would?"

"That's different, Jess. That's work. This is personal."

"Exactly. All the more reason for me to keep going."

"You're a social worker. You know how hard it is for fami-lies to be impartial."

"So? I'm not those families."

Trevor rested his head on her thigh. Jessica put her hand in his hair, separating the wiry, light brown strands with her fingers. She used to kiss him, holding him by the hair, just like this. After a moment, he looked up. "Those girls were your family. Your mother is your family. You're the ones everyone else is investi-gating." He looked up and patted her hand. "You should worry about yourself and leave the detective work alone."

Jessica slapped him away and stood up. "Stop treating me like one of your clients," she snapped as she grabbed her coat

from the hook in the hall. "You have no idea, Trevor. None."
She pulled on her boots and opened the door. "And for future
reference, I hate vegetarian chili. Eat a hot dog, for fuck's sake."

As the door closed behind her, she started to turn to see
the look on Trevor's face, but then stopped. It was better to
leave blindly.

By the time Jessica pulled up to her parents' house, the rain
had stopped. She looked up at the sky—a swirling grey, clouds
reflecting the city lights across the inlet. Everything on and
around her felt damp. The still-dripping stand of bamboo by
the front walk, her jeans, the wooden stairs leading to the front
door. No rain, but the evidence of it had soaked in everywhere.

She walked in, leaving her shoes on the mat in the hall. Lights
were on in the kitchen and living room, but Gerry wasn't there.
Traces of his meals littered the surfaces. Jessica ran her finger
through a line of crumbs on the counter. A pile of unopened
mail sat on an armchair, half-covered by an afghan.

After the police had left the house, Jessica had asked her
father if he wanted to stay with her or go to a hotel, but Gerry
had simply repeated, "This is still our house. That hasn't
changed." At first, Jessica argued with him, but now, standing
at the foot of the stairs, she understood. There had been
dead bodies here, but here was also where Gerry's smell was,
where his oldest slippers skimmed the carpet as they always
had. There was no comfort in a hotel room, no cocoon of his
softest, favourite things. The basement door could be closed.
His shape in the mattress was only here.

Upstairs, it didn't look any better. Gerry's clothes were in
piles, and some seemed cleaner than others. It smelled musty,

92

as if her father had been showering and pissing for days without opening a window or turning on a fan. The only thing that wasn't covered in Gerry's mess was her mother's desk in the nook at the top of the stairs.

She found her father in the master bedroom, sitting on the floor in front of the big window that looked north up the mountain. He was wearing his old flannel pyjamas, the ones Donna had sewn for him out of fabric that had been left over from all the clothes she had made for the foster kids over the years. The top, baggy and worn around the collar, was printed with white, fuzzy lambs. The pants featured Big Bird. Jessica knocked on the open door.

"I heard you pull up," Gerry said without turning. "Your brakes sound like shit."

"What are you doing?"

"I was trying to clean up a little, but I got distracted with these." Gerry waved his hand at a pile of photo albums on the floor beside him. "They were in your mother's desk. That's all I got done, you see, her desk. Everything else is still a disaster."

Jessica sat down on the carpet and pulled an album into her lap. Her mother's handwriting on the cover said 1996. She flipped through and found the awkward photos of her high school graduation. She wore a crushed velvet baby-doll dress and a black and gold choker that cut into the flesh on her neck. Her date stood in a baggy tuxedo, holding her by the waist as if this pose were the most natural way for teenagers to stand together. *We should be slouching against a wall, looking at each other's shoes*, she thought.

Gerry leaned over. "You look nice there."

"Are you kidding? Look at my hair. I think I used a crimping iron."

"You've always been much prettier than you think, you know."

Jessica leaned her head on his shoulder. "You're just saying that because you're my father."

Gerry chuckled. "Maybe. But it's still true." He put his arm around her. "What are you doing here this late?"

She scratched at the stain on the knee of her jeans. "I don't know. I just didn't want to stay home anymore. Misery loves company, right?"

"If you say so. I suppose it's a cliché for a reason."

For a few minutes, Gerry and Jessica said nothing, only stared at the lights at the top of the mountain, waiting for the rain to return and batter the metal roof. She wasn't thinking or moving or trying to find anything out. She was just there with her father who asked no questions. *Finally*.

Rain landed on the roof in heavy drops. Jessica shook her head and traced her finger on the window, invisibly connecting the water now dotting the glass. Gerry coughed and met her eyes.

"The police were here today."

"What?" Jessica sat up straight. "Why?"

"They want me to go to the station for an interview." Gerry laughed. "I suppose that means I'm a suspect."

"That's ridiculous. Chris should know better."

Gerry stared. "Chris? Oh, Detective Gallo. Since when have you two been so friendly?"

Jessica turned so she was no longer facing her father. She told him all about her own interview with Chris, how he hadn't told her anything, and how she resolved to find out what had happened on her own. And then she told Gerry about the files.

Gerry scratched the top of his head. "What did you do with them? Have you returned them yet?"

"I haven't had a chance, Dad. I just finished reading two hours ago. Actually, they're in the car."

"Jess, you have to return them. The police will be looking."

"I will, I will. I just want to keep them for a little while. There was so much there and so much that wasn't." Quickly, Jessica told her father about Bill and Wayne and Ginny, about how their lives had all collapsed around them.

"Wait—do the police know any of this?"

Jessica paused. "I'm not sure. I mean, they must know about Wayne and Bill because it was a police incident. But I don't know how much they know about the abuse, or Casey's state of mind."

Gerry stood up and began heading to the hall. "I'm going to get those files right now and bring them to the station tomorrow. They have to know about the abuse. There are other suspects they haven't even thought about yet."

"Dad, come back here. It's pouring out."

He turned around, one slipper on his left foot, the other in his hand. "They have to know, Jess. What if Wayne had something to do with it? Or Bill?"

Jessica stood up and held her father's arm. "The bodies were in *our* freezers, Dad. How could someone else kill them and put them there?"

"Well, maybe one of them snuck in when your mother wasn't home and put them there without her knowing. Or maybe she came home after the girls were already dead and just hid the bodies. She might have panicked."

She put her arms around Gerry and sighed. "Do you hear how crazy that sounds? You know and I know that it didn't happen that way."

His body slumped against hers and she could feel him breathing deeply, inhaling and exhaling against the urge to sob. "How could she leave us with this, Jess? Why did she do it? Why didn't she just ask me for help?"

Her father quaked against her, as if his sadness was a hard ball deep in his gut, shaking and shaking to find its way out. He cried silently and she wondered what would happen if he opened his mouth, if he let the beastly sounds escape—hurtling, wild. She wept too. The two of them, arms tangled, the dark expanse of sky on the other side of the window. Crying and crying and crying. When she opened her eyes again, she felt knifed from the inside out.

Gerry's breathing steadied. Jessica wanted to tell him that Donna didn't do it, that they would soon find out it had just been a tragic accident. She wanted to tell him that he had always been a present and committed husband and father, and that Donna had trusted him with even her ugliest secrets. But she knew these things weren't true. And she knew that if she said them out loud, her father wouldn't believe her anyway.

For a moment, she wanted to ask him if he remembered. One night when she was thirteen, she had been staying up late, watching *The Kids in the Hall*, when she heard the car pull up in the driveway. Quickly, she ran upstairs to her bedroom. The front door unlocked. Someone stumbled and there was a crash on the floor.

By the time Jessica stepped off the stairs and into the hall, Donna was on her hands and knees, picking up the pieces of the broken pot and ficus plant that lay in a heap. The skinny table was on its side. Donna's one fancy purse had been dropped in the pile of potting soil.

"What happened?"

Gerry came striding down the hall, a broom in his hand. "Your mother had too much to drink. She tripped and fell, as you can see."

Donna looked up and smiled, but her eyes were unfocused and filmy. "I shouldn't have had that last Tom Collins."

Gerry snorted. "No kidding. But it was a bad party. What else could you do?"

They were talking like Jessica wasn't even there. She thought that she should say something, remind them of her presence, but then she thought that if she stayed, half-hidden by the shadows in the dimly lit hall, they might say something she wouldn't hear otherwise. She willed herself to be still, to breathe as lightly as possible.

"It was bad. So bad. Your friends' wives are just awful human beings," Donna said as she wiped her dirty hands on her skirt.

"They're just unhappy, Donna. I can't even tell you how many of those guys are sleeping with their secretaries. And have been ever since we left law school."

"Then they're overcompensating for a hell of a lot. I think Marge has had three facelifts since the last time I saw her."

Gerry laughed, then shook open a plastic bag. "Put the sharp pieces in here."

"And what about you?"

"What? Hon, stop picking them up by the edges. You'll cut yourself."

Donna stared at a tiny piece of glass in her hand, glittering even in the hallway in the dim light. "Have you slept with any of your secretaries? You can tell me the truth."

"Come on, Donna. If you were sober, you would know the answer to that." Gerry squatted and ran his hands over the floor. "Let's just get this cleaned up and go to bed."

"Gerry. Look at me. Have you ever cheated on me? All those trips to Prince George and the Queen Charlottes. Surely there was someone? A waitress? A young protestor?"

Gerry put his hands on Donna's shoulders. "I've never kept any secrets from you. I may not be the easiest man to live with, but I have never lied to you."

"I'm sorry. Do you remember how my father died?"

"Of course I remember. You told me all of that when we were dating."

Donna stopped and bent her head so that she was looking at the floor. "I work hard to trust people. To trust myself." She placed a hand on his slipper. "It's not easy, considering how everyone in my family dies or is just an asshole."

"You're not an asshole. Your mother, on the other hand . . ."

"Not just her. I never did tell you," Donna said, then fell silent. "There was just never enough kindness to go around, that's all."

Jessica watched as her parents finished cleaning up the mess. As soon as they had both walked into the kitchen, she quietly crept back up the stairs and to her room. She rubbed her feet together under the sheets and promised herself she would always be kind and try to make her mother happy. She had to make up for the sad, small Donna who was afraid of her own mother, who wanted to escape, who wanted to be trusting. And then she had fallen asleep.

But Jessica knew her father wouldn't remember this. These moments had been small to him, even though they had stayed rooted in her brain all these years. And if she told him that story now, he would only feel guilty that he hadn't tried harder and, once again, cry sharp, masculine tears.

"I don't know why she did anything, Dad. But I can try to find out."

And then she led him to the kitchen, where she made him toast with butter and honey. Soon after, he went back upstairs to bed, his grey head bobbing weakly as he climbed the steps.

He paused on a stair and looked back. "Once, I asked your mother if she thought all these other children coming and going might upset you."

Jessica felt a tingle in the back of her neck but smiled and tried to look unconcerned. "Really? What did she say?"

"That you were strong and smart and knew the foster kids needed her help. I remember her saying, 'Even if she feels neglected sometimes, she'll know it's for the greater good.'"

Jessica didn't answer, instead staring at the dripping tap above the sink. She had always felt she had never done enough good. Not then, not now. Donna knew she would survive. Even as she stayed in her bedroom while the other children cried and clung to her mother because they were scared and didn't have anyone else.

Gerry started walking up the stairs again. "Are you staying?" he called.

"I think so. If you don't mind."

"Whatever you like. I assume Trevor knows where you are?"

"Of course," she lied.

"All right. Good night."

"Good night, Dad."

Jessica moved through the house, consolidating piles, dusting the furniture and throwing food wrappers into the garbage. It had been only a week since she was here last and it seemed as if her father had been living alone and dirty for three months. By ten o'clock, she had put the rubber gloves and spray cleaner back in the hall closet and began to walk upstairs. Halfway up, she could hear Gerry snoring, a deep, low vibration that meant the house could tip on its side and he still wouldn't wake up.

She stood in the hall and opened the door to her old bedroom. The twin bed was still there, and an old white bookcase that used to be filled with *Little House* and *Sweet Valley High* books. But everything else was gone. All her cheap Klimt posters, the stuffed animals she kept on the floor under the windowsill.

Even the old plaid wallpaper had been stripped, the walls repainted a noncommittal cream. When she had moved out, she had cleaned the room herself, telling her mother that she should turn it into a home gym, or maybe even a crafting room. Her mother had shrugged and said nothing, and the room remained Jessica's, only empty. She sat on the bed, grateful for her mother's resistance to purge and change.

When Jessica was a child and there were no other children in the house, Donna kneeled on the floor beside her bed every night and read three chapters from their latest book. *Harriet the Spy. The Secret Garden. Are You There God? It's Me, Margaret.* In the lamplight, with rain or snow or wind blowing against the window, Donna's voice was measured and even, the kind of voice that Jessica often imagined Mrs. Ingalls had in the *Little House* books. The kind of voice that sang lullabies without fanfare. The kind of voice that woke children up with words that poured out like warm milk.

Donna wasn't big or loud or obvious then. She was soft and quiet and amused. It was the best way to fall asleep.

When a foster child arrived, Donna no longer had time to read for forty minutes every night, so instead she settled Jessica into bed, passed her the book and kissed her on the forehead. "Only three chapters, no more," she said as she shut the door. Jessica could hear her heavy footsteps in the hall, and the squeak of the hinges as her mother entered the spare room, where another child screamed or sniffled or lay quietly, eyes fixed to the white ceiling.

Jessica knew she was expected to be a good example, to go through her day without much instruction and to be independent, so her mother could pat and hush and love the other children through all the bad things that had happened to them. Sometimes Jessica saw their scars or bruises, or heard them calling for their mothers in the middle of the night, panic sharpening the pitch of their small, high voices. She felt bad for them, of course. When she curled up in a ball in her bed and listened to her mother running to get a glass of water or an extra blanket or a stuffed animal from the basement, she still felt bad.

In her own house, she was small and orderly. She wasn't allowed to feel lonely. She couldn't misbehave. Donna never made an emergency trip to the mall to buy a Lego set for her. Sometimes Jessica would look into the bathroom mirror before she took her shower and thought she could see her face starting to crack and another, sadder face emerging from behind. She looked down, blinked twice and then looked again. The sad face retreated. It had to. She wasn't allowed. Her life had been too easy.

Jessica stretched her legs in the twin bed, her grown-up body filling the space. With her eyes closed, she felt exactly as she had when she was younger, maneuvering her body around the lumps in the mattress, finding the right spot for her feet that wasn't too hot or too cold. She forgot about the bodies that had rested, undiscovered, in the basement for twenty-eight years. She forgot about Trevor. She could hear only the window screen rattling against the glass as it always had. As she fell asleep, she thought she could feel the narrow bed tilting underneath her, but she didn't even open her eyes to see. She just wanted to sleep, even if the earth was getting ready to yawn and swallow her whole.

In her dream, she was ten again, hiding under her mother's desk as Donna vacuumed the carpet in the hall, unaware of Jessica's curled and crouched body behind the office chair. The roar of the vacuum grew louder and louder until the noise seemed to give off sparks that glittered and popped behind

Jessica's eyelids. As her mother got closer, Jessica could see the spinning gears in the motor, turning and turning, sucking up dust and grime and whatever else Donna wanted to disappear. Jessica thought she could feel herself shrinking. The pile on the carpet grew taller. The vacuum was bearing down on her and she screamed, but her mother couldn't hear over the noise. She waved her arms, but she was too small, no bigger than a dime standing on its edge.

"Mom! Mom, can't you see me?" The wind tunnel had started and her voice was pulled out of her chest and away, lost.

Jessica felt the gears on her toes as she tried to crawl away. It was no use. She was going to be sucked in.

When she awoke, the sheets were wound around her ankles and damp with sweat. She sat up and pulled them apart, brushing the hair out of her face as she worked at the twists and knots. When she was free, she stood up and walked to the window. There wasn't much to see, just the lights on the mountain high above the house, and the dimly illuminated underside of low-hanging cloud, half-visible, half-immersed in the black, black sky.

Jessica was reading a *National Geographic* from 1997 on her old twin bed when her phone chimed. It was a text message from Parminder. *It's past eleven, but it's not too late to get drunk.* Half an hour later, Jessica, in pair of white cotton capris and a pale pink button-down shirt (Donna's version of dressy casual), sat in a pub on Main Street, drinking craft beer that inexplicably tasted like apricots and sweaty feet. Parminder sat across from her, sipping a fruity cocktail from a straw with a wrinkle between her eyes.

"I mean, it looks like it would be good, but it tastes like someone muddled an old man's cardigan and then dumped some raspberries on top." She stared at the drinks menu written in chalk above the bar. "There are thirty-eight beers on that board. I hate this city."

"Craft beer and backyard chickens. You can't say Vancouver doesn't have priorities." Jessica laughed but then stopped abruptly when she looked down at her lap. "I look terrible."

"You're very youthful for a lady in her seventies."

"Watch it. I get testy when I haven't had enough glucosamine."

It was easy to sit and pretend nothing was wrong, that her parents' house had been full of slow cookers and old photographs and quilts folded in on themselves, and nothing else. Not the ghosts of frightened children, untethered from their now-adult selves. Not the stories from Jessica's childhood that Gerry could never remember. Not Jamie and Casey, dead and frozen and almost totally forgotten. None of that. There was only Parminder's face, smooth and dreamy in the dim candlelight, the rapid-fire voice of Nicki Minaj punching holes in the air above their heads, and the layers of drunkenness accumulating on their tongues and eyes and brains. They had begun shouting to cut through the blur.

"How does Trevor fuck?" Parminder pointed a finger at Jessica's nose. "He looks like the type who keeps apologizing for shit you can't even feel."

Jessica snorted. "No, he's better in bed than he looks. He's sweet, I guess. Considerate. Asks me what I want." She tilted her head and looked at the lights suspended from the ceiling. "Maybe he asks too much."

Right now, she wanted to know what it would be like to have sex with someone who never spoke, who did things without asking beforehand because he knew and she knew that this was the place to give tacit consent, that the next touch or taste might be unexpected but that it would turn out to be exactly what she wanted, even if she hadn't known it before. Questions and answers would be rendered superfluous. Just bodies—hers and someone who held a ninety degree angle in his shoulders, whose skin barely covered the twist of tendons and muscle underneath.

But then, this imaginary man would be perfect. How could anyone know what she wanted unless he asked? Jessica scanned the bar. There were men everywhere, men who could be all right or pretty bad or serviceable for one night with a woman who was wearing her dead mother's clothes. She felt sad, her heart straining under the beer and short rib sliders Parminder had insisted she eat. She wanted a man to look at her, and her body to split open without anyone uttering a word or forming a coherent thought. She wanted that. Now. Or soon.

Parminder took a sip of her drink and frowned. "He looks like a glass of milk, that Trevor. Like a tasteless glass of skim milk. Which is super-sexy, right?" And she laughed, her head thrown back, her long black hair swinging across her back.

"You're the love of my life, Parm. You know that, don't you?"

"Sweetie, that's just the booze talking. Tomorrow morning you'll have a torturous headache and you'll want to kill me. And I'll be at work, cursing you just as hard."

Jessica slammed her empty pint glass on the table. "Sounds like every married couple I've ever heard of."

"Well then, I love you too. You saucy senior citizen, you."

This was easy. This night, with Parminder and a crowd of drunken people in a bar she half-hated, might end hard, with a parched mouth and hair tangled from dried beer, but this moment? These minutes in a conversation that floated above the surface of her real problems? This was easy. She waved at the server and smiled. *Yes*, she thought. *More.*

ELEVEN

WHEN JESSICA OPENED HER EYES, THE LIGHT IN THE room was thick, and the air warm and damp. She blinked and stared at the curtains—white and thin, backlit. No birds, just a faint hum from the hydroelectric cables running up the mountain behind the house. She rolled over and looked at the clock on the nightstand: 11:26. *Fuck*, she thought. *I'm supposed to be at work today.*

Slowly, she swung her legs over the side of the bed and looked down at her bare thighs. When was the last time she and Trevor had had sex? When was the last time he had hovered above her body, looking and looking because in that moment he believed she was the most beautiful woman in the world? Last month? Three months ago? When Donna was sick, Trevor had never even tried, never trailed his hand on her neck as she lay in bed. And she had been so tired, all she had wanted was a glass of wine and a warm quilt. And silence.

Sometimes, when Jessica would come home from work to her apartment, she wanted to crawl into bed, covers wrapped around her, and just breathe with her hot cheek resting against the pillow. The weight of saving children or, at the very least, keeping them from harm, pushed down on her shoulders until she thought she could no longer walk or stand or even sit upright. And so she unlocked the apartment door and dropped her bag and keys on the floor, ready to stagger into the bedroom.

But if Trevor was home, he took her hand and led her to the sofa, where he patted and smiled, propping her up with cushions. She said, "I can't do it anymore," or "I'm not helping anyone," or "I have to quit, and my mother will be so disappointed."

And he nodded and looked thoughtfully at her drooping face. After a few minutes of silence, he pulled softly on her hair and said, "It's been a hard day. Don't make decisions when you're feeling this frustrated."

At first, Jessica tried to explain. "But maybe there's something different for me to do. I've only ever been a social worker. I've never tried anything else." And it was true. Her life had been certain, pre-mapped, a trajectory that excluded questions. Until now, this was fine.

"Honey, you feel doubt because you're smart, because you care about your kids. There would be something wrong with you if you didn't get down once in a while." Trevor kissed her forehead. "These feelings show just how perfect you are for your job. And for me."

Jessica stared at Trevor's smooth face and steady blue eyes. He knew. He knew how it was all going to work. She didn't need to worry. He winked. "We're going to be fine. Better than fine. We're going to work together to save the world, like Lois Lane and Superman." Trevor punched the air and laughed so hard Jessica had to smile. *This is bigger than me*, she thought.

It's both of us and everyone else who needs us. Maybe she could do some good after all.

It felt like it had been a long time since he had been all she needed, since his touch on her belly had slowed and calmed her breathing so she could sleep or smile or have sex. *Coffee*, she thought as she puttered around her childhood bedroom, looking for clean clothes. *If I don't have some coffee, I just might die*.

In the kitchen, she dumped a spoonful of instant coffee into a mug and stared at the kettle as it heated up, the beat in her head a painful echo of the hip hop that had pounded in last night's bar. *Milk. Milk would make all of this taste less like shit*. As she reached for the handle on the fridge, she saw a piece of paper stuck to the door with a horn-of-plenty magnet. Her name was scrawled across the top in black ink.

Gone to see Det. Gallo. Wish me luck. Love, Dad.

Jessica punched the fridge and cried out, bringing her red knuckles to her mouth. In her T-shirt and underwear and bare feet, she ran out the front door and peered into the backseat of her car. The files were still there, locked up. What did her father think he was going to do without them?

Back in the house, she grabbed her phone from her purse and dialled the direct number Chris had given her. A woman's voice answered. "RCMP North Vancouver."

"I'm sorry. I thought I dialled the direct line for Detective Gallo."

"His line is on forward. You've reached the front desk. Do you want his voice mail?"

"No. Listen, my father is there talking to him. I need to speak to Detective Gallo right now. It's urgent."

"What's your name?"

"Jessica Campbell."

"I'll see if I can reach him."

The music playing into her ear was unidentifiable, just a string of notes that were pleasant but not distinctive enough to be good. Jessica drummed her fingers on the counter and exhaled loudly, blowing the hair off her forehead.

"Jessica?"

"Chris. Is my father there?"

"Did he tell you he was here?"

The kettle began to whistle, a strange, breathy, high-pitched sound that was almost human. "Damn," Jessica whispered as she strode across the kitchen to turn off the stove.

"Did you say something?"

"No, I'm just turning off the kettle and I'm in my under-wear and I'm trying not to sound like a bitch or an idiot but it's not working, so whatever. Is my father there or not, Chris?"

The pause was tangible. She could practically hear him debating what to reveal and how much. She wanted to reach into the phone and tear his face open with her hands, just so she could get to what he knew without waiting for him to be fair or deliberate.

"He's here."

"I want you to know that interviewing him is a waste of time. I was there when those girls were living in our house, not him. He was never home, never tried to parent them. However those girls died, my father had nothing to do with it."

"He's not under arrest, you know."

"Yes, but he's a suspect. Which is ridiculous. I was there when he found the first body. I was there when he called the police. If he had killed them, why would he call the police in at all? Why wouldn't he have just gotten rid of the bodies quietly and be done with it?"

"Like I said, he's not under arrest."

Jessica started to cry, tears leaving hot trails on her cheeks.

"He's not himself right now. My mother just died, Chris. He thinks he can handle everything, but he can't. He's old, and I didn't get that until now, but he's *old*."

It was the first time she had said it, that her father was old. He hadn't been old a year ago or even six months ago. He skied. He hiked. He went to the pub with his friends and drank pints of bitter. But when Donna was dying, he stopped. He hovered in the house, wiping at surfaces that he had never noticed before. In the mornings, he pulled out all of the mostly empty cereal boxes and methodically ate the stale flakes and puffs that had sat there for months, maybe years, because there wasn't enough for one serving, but there was too much to throw away. Jessica had seen him then, one sunny evening, sitting on the front step in his stained and baggy gardening clothes, with his face turned toward the light, eyes closed, like an arthritic cat in the sunshine who needed warmth in his bones to withstand the inevitable cold and dark night.

This is what she was crying for. His death was a certainty, had always been, but it was here, in this kitchen with its yellow tiles and streaky windows, that she knew it was looming. She wasn't ready. There had been so much death, so many dead people stuck inside her head, expecting the truth, or turning away from it. There was no room for her father. None.

She could hear Chris' breathing, even and slow, as if he were trying to calm her.

"Jessica, I appreciate what you're feeling right now. It's natural to be worried about your father, but he's still a strong man."

"No, he can't fix everything. He can't even cook a meal by himself."

"You're not that different, you know. You're calling here, trying to convince me to release your father even though he knows and I know that he can leave anytime. You found those foster care files and kept them from us. Are you sure you can handle everything you're taking on?"

Jessica said nothing for a second. "How do you know about the files? Did my dad tell you?"

"No. I went looking for the files myself yesterday afternoon and the woman at the archives told me you had been there just that morning. It's not often they get people inquiring after twenty-eight-year-old files, so two in one day was quite an event over there."

"I was going to bring them to you."

"Sure, of course." Chris laughed, and it was the first time she heard a trace of annoyance in his voice. "Do you realize how this looks to me? You stole and kept relevant documents from the police. To some, it looks like you might be trying to protect someone. Someone like your father."

"He has nothing to do with this. The files say nothing about him."

"Why should I believe you?"

"Because I'm telling you the truth. I'll bring you these files right now and you can see for yourself. Tell my father to wait."

She ran upstairs, tripping on the carpeted steps. Finally, she was sober and wide awake.

Jessica stood in front of the police station, sweaty hands holding the files to her chest. She looked down at the clothes that she had dug out of her mother's closet. The wind picked up the hem of the ankle-length skirt embroidered with small circular mirrors and twisting, dark green vines. The sweater stopped just short of her knees, pulling as it stretched across her hips and ass.

She knew she looked like death in this colour—an unnameable shade of wheat or beige or manila—but her T-shirt and jeans from the day before were stained and dusty from the hours she'd spent cleaning late into the night. At least her blond hair was brushed and bundled into a decent ponytail.

She didn't know if this razored, shallow breathing was panic, if the dark spots at the corners of her vision meant she was having a stroke, if this was the way her mother had felt when it became clear that Jamie and Casey would never love her. Jessica pushed down on her chest with her right hand and closed her eyes.

After the girls had been with them for a week and a half, they disappeared. Donna called anyone who might have been a friend and was getting nowhere. Jessica listened to the same conversation repeating itself every ten minutes. *Have you seen them? Do you know where they are?* The exchanges were short and no one offered to help. The girls didn't have many friends. Every time Donna put down the receiver, Jessica wanted to clap with glee. Maybe they were gone for good. The back door opened. It was Gerry.

"The girls are gone. I need you to look for them."

Gerry dropped his keys on the table. "Now? I have a client coming in twenty minutes for an affidavit. I can't leave."

Donna whirled around and stared. "Fine. Stay. I'll go. You just have to listen for the phone."

He shook his head. "I can't just get up in the middle of an interview and take personal phone calls. Jessica can answer the phone. Right, sport?" Jessica smiled and looked at her mother.

"You're ridiculous. The social worker might call back. Jessica can't talk to her."

"Donna, how many times did you come home late when you were a teenager?"

"I don't know. Why does it matter?"

Gerry sighed. "Because you always came back. I don't think there's any need to panic."

"Do I have to remind you that things are different now? It's not safe out there for young girls. You watch the news. You know this."

"They've only been gone for a few hours. Give it some time before you come to the conclusion that they've been abducted off the street."

Donna stood with one hand on the receiver. Jessica thought she could see her mother's brain cycling through everything Gerry had just said, trying to find one word that could help her right now, in this moment of spinning, muddled confusion. Donna dropped her head and closed her eyes.

"Fine. Go do whatever you have to do. I'll stay here."

After Gerry had disappeared into the den, Donna sat on a kitchen chair and watched the phone. Jessica watched too and could have sworn she saw it twitch. She didn't want to break the silence, so she sat still, listening and listening.

The next morning, the social worker and the police came. They asked questions, took a few things away with them, but stayed for only one hour. Jessica wondered if sixty minutes was enough time to understand the shape of missing people, if the officers could know so quickly what the girls smelled like or walked like or wanted to eat. Or if they cared.

One of them, an older man with a white moustache, nodded at Jessica and said, "It'll be fine, sweetheart. They'll come back."

And he was right: the next afternoon, Jamie and Casey walked into the house, their clothes covered in grey-brown dust, their hair tangled from the overnight windstorm. When Donna ran toward them, her arms out to pull them both into a hug, they backed up, fast, until they were flat against the wall.

Donna touched Jamie's cheek and Jamie gasped, her eyes shut so tight, the lids were wrinkled and narrow. They had slept in the park, they said, but they were back, so what did it matter? It didn't, really, except that afterward everything in the house shifted, as if the tectonic plates beneath them were grinding and tilting, pushing at the houses and streets and oceans above, preparing for a schism greater than anyone had ever seen.

Jessica stared at the police station. Casey and Jamie had gone missing once before and returned, but when they did, they had said very little about where they had gone or how they had spent their time. She was sure her mother had never asked them. Why not? Quickly, Jessica pushed the past away and yanked at her sweater one more time before opening the door.

Inside, an officer sat behind a wide desk, phone cradled under her ear. Plastic chairs lined the walls of the room, and people sat, staring at their phones or into space. Gerry sat in the corner closest to the front window. His hands were clasped in his lap and his eyes were shut against the fluorescent light.

"Dad?" Jessica placed a hand on his shoulder. "Are you awake?"

Gerry opened his eyes. "Did you bring the files?"

"Right here."

"Good. Detective Gallo really wants to see them. Almost as much as he wanted to see me." Gerry smiled and shook his head. "He most definitely considers me a suspect."

Jessica rolled her eyes. "What did he ask you?"

"You know. Where was I when the girls disappeared. Did I resent them. Did I ask you to find and hide those files. That sort of thing. I told him I barely remember the girls. He doesn't seem to believe me. Or maybe he does and he's just trying to be clever."

"I'll tell him again. Just let me talk to the front desk."

"All right. And then maybe we should get some lunch. What do you think? My treat."

"It's a date."

Gerry closed his eyes again and rested his head on the wall behind. He seemed small and grey and still. Jessica bit her lip and stood up straight. She turned to walk to the desk, but then saw Chris standing behind her, hand extended to take the files.

"We should use an interview room," he said, leading her to a hallway. "We have lots to talk about."

Jessica followed him past offices and water coolers and cubicles, all lined with colourless carpet and paint. Her sweater blended right in. As they passed her reflection in a framed print of the Capilano suspension bridge, she grimly noted that she looked like a floating head.

Chris opened the door to a small room and she said, "These are my mother's clothes."

"What's that?"

Jessica wanted to pull out her own tongue for speaking at all, but there was no going back now. She had to explain. "I spent the night at my parents' house and it was kind of unexpected, and I had nothing to wear. So I had to rummage through my mother's old clothes and this is what I found." She waved a hand at her body and smiled tentatively. "You should have seen the outfits I rejected."

Chris laughed. "I was going to say that I didn't notice, but I actually did. You don't often see an attractive woman dressed like a hippie grandmother."

Jessica looked down at the floor. All she could hear was her own voice in her head yelling, *He thinks I'm pretty. I knew it. I knew it.* She wished she could slap herself in the mouth. *Don't be a dumb-ass.* Out loud, she said, "My father had nothing to do with those girls. Not alive, not dead."

Chris pointed her to a padded office chair and said, "So you keep saying."

"It's the truth. Treating him like a suspect is waste of time."

"Let me ask you something, then. How is it that in the twenty-eight years Casey and Jamie Cheng were missing your father never looked into the bottom of those freezers? Hell, how is it that *you* never looked?"

Jessica placed her hands on the table, tightly closed in fists. "My father was never home. He never cooked. Even when my mother was dying, he could barely make a pot of coffee. Do you not listen? *He was never home.*"

"What about you, then? Didn't your mother ever send you to the basement to get a steak?"

"I hated her food. Everything she cooked was wild game or grains and seeds. It was all I could do to step foot in the kitchen, much less the basement." She looked at his face, willing her own to go blank. "Are we really having this conversation right now? I was ten years old when they disappeared. I had just learned to ride a bike. God."

She could see on Chris' face that he believed her but that it still made no sense to him that those bodies—those small, contorted bodies—could have rested, undisturbed, in the basement of a home where people lived and slept and ate. Jessica understood that the story needed to be linear, that, in Chris' head, one event had to lead logically to the next. But it didn't need to include her father.

She leaned forward, the edge of the table digging into her ribs. "Shouldn't you be trying to find out the real story?"

Chris glanced at the files on the table in front of him. "We're still waiting on the post-mortem. Until then, I'm doing what I can, which includes questioning anyone who knew those two girls. That's all. May I remind you that we don't have a homicide yet and therefore no suspects. Yet."

"Why is the post-mortem taking so long?"

"It hasn't started."

Jessica wanted to howl. "Why not?"

Chris sighed and looked up at the ceiling. "Those bodies were frozen, as I'm sure you remember. It takes time to," he paused and his eyes flicked back down and settled on Jessica's face, "defrost them."

For a minute, Jessica felt sick again. *Of course. Of course.* And yet, who would ever think about the mechanics of bodies buried in deep chest freezers or about the intricacies in removing and preparing them for examination? With her hands clasped on the table in front of her, she whispered, "I'm sorry. I should have realized."

"Don't be sorry. You're not the only one who wants this case to be resolved. Dead girls from the eighties are a big deal around here, especially for my boss." Chris cleared his throat and when he spoke again, his voice was quieter, smoother. "Why were you at your dad's last night?"

She looked up and shrugged. "It's stupid, really. I got into a fight with my boyfriend and I just wanted to be with someone who understands, you know? And my dad has been lonely anyway, so I went."

"Did you show him the files?"

"No, I left them in the car. But I told him what was in them."

"What did you tell him?"

Jessica explained it all to Chris: why the girls were taken into care in the first place, and the names of their parents and Casey's boyfriend. When she was done, she rested her chin in her hands. "It's a terrible story, but not that surprising, in some ways."

"How so?"

"I already knew they were troubled, so it all just makes sense. I can see why my mother wanted to help. Who wouldn't?"

Jessica stared at the wall, sifting through the images in her head of the girls arriving, then unpacking, then walking to the car on their way to school. Every time she thought of them, the girls seemed to be walking away with her mother hurrying after. Her ten-year-old self was rooted to the spot, it felt, as if she knew there was no point in chasing Casey and Jamie and Donna, as if she knew they needed to sort it out among themselves and that she, younger and unknowing, was safer being left behind.

On a Saturday evening, after the girls had returned, Jessica sat behind the Douglas fir, digging a hole with her mother's favourite spade. The remnants of her napkin-wrapped dinner lay on the dirt beside her—tempeh steak, braised beets and barley pilaf. When the hole was the size of a pie plate, Jessica dropped in her food and began filling it again, carefully gathering up stray needles and sticks to strew over the dirt. She peered up toward the back porch, looking for her mother's face in the kitchen window. It was close to sunset and the lights were still off inside. With a lift of her chin, Jessica could see almost everything.

Casey and Jamie had been back for six days. In that time, Jessica had learned to stay away, to never speak to them and, above all else, to never let them see her watching. Her mother, on the other hand, still hadn't figured it out.

Through the window, she saw Casey's and Jamie's heads, and then her mother's, her hair bouncing as she hurried past. Quickly, Jessica pulled her legs in so that her entire body was hidden by the fir's gnarly trunk. The back door opened and the girls ran out, wearing thin jackets. Donna followed, waving her hands.

"You can't just leave, girls! I'm responsible for you. I have to know where you're going."

"Leave us alone," Casey hissed. Jamie giggled before opening the gate to the back steps.

"You don't have to run off just because I wanted to talk. Come back inside. We can watch TV. I can make popcorn."

For a moment, the girls stopped and seemed to be considering Donna's offer. Jamie took her hand off the gate and Casey fiddled with the zipper on her jacket.

"Look, I know about your parents and the abuse. Your social worker has to tell me these things. We don't need to talk right now, but you might want to think about talking to *someone*. Especially you, Casey."

"Oh no," whispered Jessica to the pine cone in her hand.

Casey's back straightened and she took a step forward. Donna smiled and held out her hand. But then, Casey drew her arm back and punched Donna in the mouth.

"We weren't *abused*, you bitch. If it weren't for you or those fucking social workers, we would be perfectly happy. Do you understand? Or do you need me to punch you again?"

Donna shook her head and held her chin in both hands. From where Jessica was sitting, she could see that her mother was bleeding over her teeth.

"That wasn't happiness, Casey," Donna said, wiping blood from her mouth.

Jamie jumped forward and pulled at Donna's hair with both hands, fingers buried deep in the mess of curls. Jessica stood up and took a step toward the house. None of the other kids had ever hurt her mother like this. None.

Donna grabbed Jamie's wrists and propelled her into a deck chair. Casey pushed at the gate and started running down the stairs.

"Come on, James. Let's get the fuck out of here."

The two girls rushed through the yard, past Jessica and the big tree and out through the back fence. Jessica could hear their footsteps in the alley, and the sound of them overturning a metal trash can onto the gravel. "Fucking white people," Casey said. "Let them pick up their own garbage for once."

Donna sat heavily on the wooden lounge chair, her knees splayed over the edges. Jessica wanted to run to her but felt strangely rooted to the ground. Her mother had never looked so helpless, so downtrodden, so *crumpled*. Jessica kneeled back down. She just couldn't watch anymore.

Chris' voice cut through the fog of memory. "These files are a big help in filling in the gaps."

Jessica stared at the table in front of her. Something had happened to those girls that weekend they had run away. She was sure of it. When they had come back, they were filled with a rage she never saw again, not even when she was taking children away from abusive homes. Bill was neglectful and beat them once. But there was something else. There had to be.

Finally, she spoke. "What was Bill charged with?"

Chris twirled his pen between his fingers and looked down at his notes, as if he needed the time to think about what he should reveal and what he shouldn't. Before he could speak, Jessica almost shouted, "Just tell me, for fuck's sake."

"One charge of assault related to Wayne Chow, and another related to Casey Cheng."

"What happened to the charges?"

"If you really want to know, I'm sure you could find out. It's all part of the public record and you seem pretty good at digging up old paperwork." He drank from his coffee cup and then smiled. "Did you find anything about your mother in the files?"

She pulled at the sleeve of her sweater in frustration. He was changing the subject, something she used to do when the parents she was interviewing grew defensive or silent. There was no point in fighting his questions. He would tell what he wanted to and no more. She sighed. "No. The notes basically stop as soon as the girls were left at our house. I looked, but there was nothing there."

"So you still have no insight into your mother's role in their deaths?"

Jessica shook her head. "None. I wish I did."

As soon as the two bodies were found, she had known that Donna had done something to those girls. She had spent the last four days careening from possibility to possibility, searching through notes that said almost nothing. But as she sat there, swallowing the urge to cry, she could think only of the small, bare foot she had seen in the freezer, dusted with ice. The longer it took for her to find out the truth, the more she began to believe that her mother—the singing, stewing, musky woman she knew—had killed two children. And this thought made her want to light her own head on fire, just so she wouldn't have to think anymore.

Sighing, she rubbed her eyes with the tips of her fingers. "If she were here, I would shake her. It's so unfair, leaving those bodies for us to find. What did she think was going to happen? That we wouldn't notice? Or that we'd just leave them alone?" Snot began running down over her mouth and she sniffed, but it didn't make any difference.

Chris handed her a handkerchief. "I'm the only man under ninety who carries one of these."

Jessica blew her nose and stared down at the damp square of cloth. "I don't suppose you want this back now."

"Just take it home and throw it in the wash. You can give it back the next time I see you."

"Next time? Will it be for official business or something else?" As soon as she said it, Jessica felt her body wilt. For a moment, she could see herself—eyes swollen, nose red with wiping, shoulders bent forward from the strain. She shouldn't be flirting. Why was she flirting?

He smiled and picked up the files. "I'm sure I'll run into you somewhere. Who knows? Maybe I'll go for a sandwich and find out you got there first."

Jessica laughed and pushed up the sleeves of her sweater. She felt hot, as if the floor were radiating upward and wrapping itself around her.

He held the door open for her and, as she walked closer to him, she extended her hand. He held her by the wrist, his fingers grazing the veins that pulsed under the thin skin. She took another step forward and he looked down at her, brown eyes narrowed. For a moment, she thought he was going to kiss her. In the middle of this mess, a kiss would make a perfect kind of sense, as if it could be the unmoving centre of a wildly spinning universe. Jessica knew it would be messy, that kissing the man who was investigating suspicious deaths in her mother's house would be a bubbling mass of sadness and complication and the kind of sex that was both freeing and confining. But she didn't care. Not now. If he would just kiss her, maybe everything would fall into place.

In half a minute, she imagined that one kiss leading to long emails, to sentences that were heavy with longing and words that were about sex but weren't, words like *want* and *pull* and *tonight*. She saw, in her head, her own feet walking quickly out of her apartment, carefully paced so Trevor wouldn't hear her running like mad toward another man in a waiting car. Afterward, Chris would leave his smell on her, and she would press her nose up against her own shoulder every twenty minutes for a whole day and breathe in the remnants of his sweat, that scent that was him but also her because it was both of them, locked tight together in his bed or a bed in a hotel or anywhere. And if she left Trevor then, it would be her fault, but it would incontestable, a separation easily understood, easily defined by relationships and their ruination.

But then she heard a photocopier whirring to the left and the slide of a drawer being pushed back into its cabinet. Chris turned his head away and waved a hand toward the hall. "Your dad is waiting," he said before walking quickly to the front room, not even looking behind to see if she was following.

Jessica wondered if she was still drunk, or insane with grief, or both. As she waited for her father to put on his jacket, she thought of Trevor again. Poor Trevor, always trying to help and never quite succeeding. With her, with anyone. She felt sorry for him, and guilty. If she could, she would lie with him right now in their bed and rest her forehead against his. Surely that way he would know that she cared, understood even. He was like a mouse in her hands, quivering and cold. If she went back, she would try to be more careful. She could try.

Gerry stood outside in the sunshine, shading his eyes with his hand. "Where to, Jess?"

"Someplace with meat. And beer." She took her father's arm and led him to her car, her mother's skirt swirling around her ankles.

They drove down Marine Drive and stopped at an old barbecue restaurant hidden behind a trellis and a small parking lot. Gerry pointed to a table in the back that was pushed up against the faux-wooden siding. When the server arrived, her father muttered, "Whatever you've got on tap that tastes like another." Jessica rolled her eyes and ordered a wheat beer with lemon.

"Do you remember this place?" Gerry leaned forward. "I used to take you here when your mother was out. It was our little secret."

"Didn't she cook something and leave it for us in the fridge?"

"I used to bring the dish with us, and throw out the food in the Dumpster in the parking lot." Gerry laughed and then shook his head. "I didn't feel guilty about it either. I just wanted a burger."

Jessica smiled. "And a milkshake."

Outside, it had started to rain, a light misting rain that clung to grass or hair or pants, only soaking in thirty minutes later, after you had forgotten that you were even caught without an umbrella in the first place. Jessica touched the curls piled on the top of her head. On days like this, her head was haloed in frizz.

"It wasn't enough," Gerry said suddenly, breaking the low buzz from the restaurant around them.

"What?"

"I didn't take you here enough. I should have spent more time with you."

Jessica touched his hand with her fingers. "You were busy. It was work that had to be done."

Gerry shifted in his chair and grimaced. "Sure, sure. I saved a bog and got some tree-huggers out of prison. When God is looking at my list of sins and virtues, I'm sure those will be enough to justify the deaths of two teenaged girls."

"Dad, what are you talking about?"

"Obviously, your mother needed help. I couldn't see that because I was too busy thinking I could save the entire world from destruction. I could have been there for her—stayed home more, helped out with the kids. Even just taken you out more often. Anything. But I didn't. And look what happened." He shifted his eyes from Jessica's face to the ceiling, blinking at the fans, immobile and dusty.

Jessica looked at her father, quiet and still, his face lined and sharp, as if the last few months had slowly been shaving away skin and fat until all that was left was his essential sadness. During Donna's illness, he had held her while she shivered, cleaned her armpits with a warm cloth, trimmed her toenails as she slept. And now, his thoughts circled in on themselves until all he could understand was that he hadn't done enough. He had made those dead bodies his fault. Jessica wished she could tell him that he was wrong, that the outcome would have been the same no matter how often he got home in time for dinner, but she knew this wasn't true. If he had been home more and listened to his wife, maybe Casey and Jamie would still be alive. Maybe they would have walked out of the house, whole and intact, carrying their bags and scowling at their social worker.

She gripped her father's hand tighter across the table. "You did what you could. None of us knew any better, Dad."

Gerry looked at Jessica's face and exhaled. "That's sweet of you."

"It's the truth."

"I know." He picked up his pint glass and took a long sip. "I just wish your mother was sitting here so I could tell her I was sorry."

"And you know what she'd say. She'd tell you to stop apologizing and help her rake the flower beds."

Gerry laughed. "Even when I first met her, she didn't take any shit." He paused and looked out the window. "She was so beautiful then, with all that curly hair and that big smile. We started out thinking we could change the world. She told me once that she used to nurse injured birds and squirrels and things. One time, it was a stray cat. She kept them in the attic, where her mother couldn't find out."

"I didn't know."

"Well, I think most of her patients died. She probably didn't want to tell you that." Gerry winced at his words and, with a slight shake in his hands, picked up a menu. "Burger or pulled pork? Or both?"

Jessica watched him read, his eyes just barely rimmed in red. She almost stood up and put her arms around his neck, but then changed her mind. "Both, of course. With a side of sausage." They laughed and clinked their glasses together, feeling, for the first time in months, that laughter wasn't cruel and wrong.

—

That night, Jessica roasted a chicken in her parents' kitchen, then washed her clothes. She drank a glass of wine on the back deck after her father went to sleep, huddled in Donna's green parka against the wind that whistled down the side of the mountain. She could hear movements in the bush—crunches and snaps—and imagined raccoons and moles feeling their way through the dense vegetation, some of it dead. She had always loved this house, which sat squat and brown like a mushroom in the moss. Even though downtown Vancouver was only a twenty-minute drive away, the city seemed like just a good story you told to your family at dinnertime.

It was easy to say *My childhood was normal.* It was the sort of thing people say when they want to deflect attention, or when it was the most polite way to explain that you grew up with privilege, that your past wasn't dotted with evictions and coupons and beatings from a father who could never keep a job. It was what Jessica always said, even though she knew this statement couldn't possibly be true for anyone.

Staring at the mountain in the night, barely lit by the flood lamps on the ski hill, she remembered that her childhood, the public one, was ever-shifting, as if one more news story about a child gone missing or a predator on the loose or a mass cult wedding could twist the continuum of time or reorder the universe so that every house on the walk to school in the morning seemed ever so slightly different. A volcano erupted, and the sidewalk looked cracked and bumpy. A nuclear power plant exploded and Jessica knew that the flakes of skin on her legs were dying, peeling off one by one as the radioactivity seeped into her body. But nothing weighed down the air like the men who abducted, raped and killed children.

It was Clifford Olsen. It was Ted Bundy. It was the Paper Bag Rapist. Later, it was Paul Bernardo. If Jessica saw a windowless van parked on the street, she ran past it, head down, afraid even to blink because, in the half-second her eyes were closed, a man with a fake beard or a real beard could grab her by the waist and throw her through the rear doors, into a space padded with mattresses and old quilts. Even if she screamed, no one would hear her over the van's engine starting up. He could stuff a sock in her mouth. He could drug her. He could threaten to kill her parents if she said one word. So she ran, eyes aching with the dry air that pushed at her face.

If she thought hard enough, she knew that these things— sex, violence, death, fear—would be forever entangled in her head. Jessica knew the very first time she looked at a boy and wanted him to make her come. She was scared, but she wanted him. She knew she might die if he beat her or didn't wear a condom, but she couldn't stop staring at his face. Even now, while drinking twelve-dollar wine in a folding deck chair behind her parents' house, she could remember everything about that boy's face. The wide smile. Eyes just a touch too close together. The dimples, always a surprise. And how she wanted to watch that face as he watched her.

It never happened. That time, the fear won.

She knew, also, that the fear kept her with Trevor. He bought books for her and wrote messages on the inside covers. Brought her croissants whenever she had her period. He would cry when she died, those deep, coughing sobs, the ones that tear through a chest and hurtle through walls. There might be no one else who would love her this much. If they broke up, the next man she slept with could kill her, could wait until she was naked and lying on his couch, half-drunk, and strangle her with an electrical cord. Or simply beat her with his fists, the weight of his body hitting her head until the sounds she made were wet and involuntary, until even those stopped too. All of that could happen.

Because it wasn't just girls she didn't know who had gone missing and died. It was two girls whom she had lived with and tried to like. It was Jamie and Casey, who had breathed fear but pushed through life anyway, who had run away for one weekend and returned, brittle and angry and violent. Jessica knew that something terrible had happened during those two days. If she had to guess, she would say that men had hurt them then, as they had before and as she had always feared for herself. The difference was that she was still alive and they were not.

Jessica had always been scared—of disappointing her mother, of another job, of living without Trevor. But now, drunk but alone in the night wearing a parka that Donna had used only when she shovelled snow, she understood that fear was a doubling down on hurt. The men might hurt her anyway, or they might not, but fearing them wouldn't prevent that. It only made her tentative and sad and stuck. Being afraid of death made no difference. She was going to die anyway. She licked a dripping line of red wine on the curve of her glass.

Once inside, she saw a car parked in the front driveway, a big American sedan. She walked closer to the window. In the light of the street lamp, a man emerged from the driver's side. Chris Gallo. She put a hand to the messy bun on the top of her head and looked down at the pink long johns she had pulled out of her mother's dresser just after dinner. At least the hooded sweatshirt was hers. She wondered how much of the makeup she had applied earlier that morning was still on her face.

She opened the door and he didn't smile. There was a wrinkle in his forehead that pushed his eyebrows downward, that made him look like an over-sugared child who had just been told it was bedtime. Without saying anything, Jessica reached out and touched the wrinkle with her finger, pressing to smooth it out. When he smiled, she let her arm drop to her side again.

"What are you doing here?"

"I came to see if you were all right." He whispered, as if afraid that Gerry would come rushing out.

"I'm over it. A few glasses of wine can cure anything." She paused and looked at his eyes, set far apart and warm even when he was trying to act detached. "You didn't really come all this way, at ten o'clock at night, just to see if I was all right."

Chris let out a breath and his shoulders fell, just a quarter of an inch, but it changed everything. He was no longer the police detective who asked questions and expected them answered; he was a man who was unsure of what was going to happen next, who had a different kind of question he wanted to ask, and who didn't know which words he was going to use or what the answer was going to be.

"Do you want come for a drive?"

Jessica looked at the looming bulk of the car behind him. She had a decision to make. One that was hard not because the choices were equally appealing, but because one choice was so glaringly wrong and scary that it made her stomach flip. Yet it was precisely that choice that pulled at every muscle in her body, that made her want to dance out the door—light and happy—even though she knew with every cell in her brain that the final outcome would almost certainly have nothing to do with happiness, but rather guilt or disappointment or disgust.

She had never met a man who had said so little to her that was sweet or kind or romantic, but who nevertheless owned her fraction by fraction every time his eyes settled on hers. So as the drumbeat in her head pounded out *wrong, wrong, wrong,* the blood speeding through her veins pulsed a homologous but opposite rhythm: *this is what I want, this is what I want.*

It was thin, the space between decisions.

She said, with her head half-turned because she couldn't bear to look at his face for a minute longer, "Let me grab my keys."

⚓

If she thought ahead to what she might feel after this moment, the whole illusion that she and Chris existed in a bubble that was unbreakable, even untouchable, would rupture. She would be left with the peculiar sensation that she was simultaneously enjoying the warmth of his lips against her cheek while looking backward at it in wistfulness or with a sad, future clarity. Jessica knew this was how she could destroy the minutes she had with him. She wasn't going to do that. She kept her eyes open, turned on his broad face, her fingers caught in the curls of his hair.

They were parked in the lot at Grouse Mountain. The surrounding lights glowed orange and dim, illuminating a few garbage cans and one other car. Not that Jessica cared if the lot were full of hikers swallowing sports drinks out of non-toxic plastic bottles. She sat on Chris' lap, facing him, in the backseat. There was no talking, just their breath knocking against the windows and echoing back so slightly it was as if every sound they made was simply vibrating as it tumbled out of their mouths and into the sealed, silent air. He didn't ask her what she wanted and she didn't tell him. They were beyond that.

Death and grief and the lack of words simulated a past and a relationship they had never had. Maybe it wasn't real, but, right now, in this car, with his hands on her ass, it was real and sticky and present. It was enough. Fuck it. It was way better than enough. It was fucking genius.

At midnight, she padded into the hallway on her way to the bathroom. Chris had dropped her off, making jokes about the retro nineties radio station he exclusively listened to. "I can't think beyond Stone Temple Pilots," he said. "If the band isn't skinny and dirty with a lead singer who shouldn't be singing, I don't

131

want to hear it." Jessica had laughed, purposely pushing out all those other thoughts that meant she knew better, or that wanted to scream that this was the worst possible betrayal of her entire life, and kept her gaze on his wide smile that was bright and sharp and verging on feline. Not once did they mention Trevor or her mother or the girls. Not once did Chris' face flicker with the knowledge that he had chosen this night over his job. And not once did either of them say they would see each other again. He had driven down the hill and she had watched through the window until his car turned the corner and she knew by the minutes that had passed that he was merging on to the highway.

She knew there might be consequences. She knew no one would understand. She could think about Trevor, about how he might rage or cry or insist that she leave. She could remind herself that she didn't know Chris' middle name or where he grew up or what his favourite food was. But none of that mattered—not really, not now. The after-touch, that ghost of their skin on each other, burned all of that away. She could choose to be oblivious, just for tonight.

Tucked into the small dormer window was her mother's desk—still clean—with the pile of photo albums she had placed on its surface the night before. There was no possibility of sleep, at least not now, so, glancing at Gerry's closed bedroom door, she walked over and sat in Donna's cushioned chair. Every month, her mother had sat here, putting her bills in order, gluing photo corners until her fingers were covered in a transparent, tacky film. Jessica leaned back and felt her body settle into the grooves and divots Donna had left behind. Everything fit. Jessica's arm. Her spine. The backs of her thighs. It was as if her mother had been breaking in this chair just for her.

She reached forward and grazed the albums with her hand. She squinted and sat up, bringing her face closer to the spines lined up to the left. Each album was labelled by year. Jessica counted. They began in 1978, the year Jessica was born, and ended with 2015, the year her mother was diagnosed with cancer. She stared at one album near the bottom. 1988.

She was breathing quickly as she pulled it out, almost knocking the others to the floor. She turned the pages as fast she could, barely even noticing her mother's handwritten captions underneath each picture. *The family snowshoeing on Grouse Mountain, January 17. Matthew and his new adoptive family on his last day with us, April 2. Jessica learning how to dive, Whytecliff Park, Canada Day.* When she got to the middle, she stopped. There they were: Casey and Jamie in their backyard, digging with spades. *Casey and Jamie helping us harvest the squash, September 25.* And again: *Casey and Jamie pressing leaves into their new scrapbooks, September 29.* There were three blank spots, all of them pictures of the girls that the police had taken with them.

Donna had never left any family moment alone. In the middle of cookie-baking or weeding, she would point a camera in Jessica's face and demand, "Smile." And Jessica thought she could see the discomfort in the pictures later, even as they hung on the wall or were stuffed into envelopes to be sent to Granny Beth. Still, it was something she was used to and learned to mostly ignore. But Casey and Jamie, they swore under their breaths and deliberately turned their backs, grinning as soon as they heard Donna sigh and replace the cap on the lens. It had been a game, and they were winning.

The next set of photos was Jessica in her Halloween costume (Pee-Wee Herman) and then nothing until Christmas. She stared at the last page, decorated with holiday stickers and her mother's wobbly illustrations of holly branches and sleigh bells. Jessica's hands were in fists, her thumbs tightly squeezed in her fingers.

This was the version of her family Donna wanted to remember: happy, craftsy, nature-loving. Her whole life Jessica had thought her mother wanted to remember everything, that her urge to can and preserve meant that anything could be used and reused, even memories that weren't beautiful. But these pictures of red-cheeked contentment proved otherwise.

Jessica, her lips pursed, yanked the very last photo, a picture of her parents at a New Year's Eve party, from its tabs. She looked at her mother's smiling, slightly tipsy face. Her face was full and open. How could she hide two dead girls in her freezers for so long?

As she tried to push the corners of the photo back into place, it caught on the edge of a tab and flew up, landing face down on the album's black page. Jessica stared at the back. Another photograph was taped right behind, its edges lined up so precisely that no one would ever suspect it was there. Jessica picked it up and examined the three faces. Granny Beth, Donna as a child, and a little boy of about the same size whom Jessica didn't recognize.

He had curly blond hair and stood stoutly, feet planted firmly in the front lawn of her mother's childhood home. Carefully, Jessica peeled it away from the other photograph and looked at the back. No date, no writing, just four yellow stains where the tape had been. She squinted at the piles of albums. There had to be another photo somewhere.

Jessica started from the beginning, 1978, and pulled every print from its corners from every page. Nothing. She kept going until the pads of her fingers began to ache, as if the skin were threatening to split, dry and spent. She looked at the clock hung above the desk. One o'clock in the morning. And twenty-seven more albums to go.

At three, she was done. She stared at the first and only hidden photograph she had found. Granny Beth stood slightly apart, her hands on her hips. The two children weren't touching, but the slice of air between them was so narrow, you could miss it entirely and think their arms and shoulders were glued together. Jessica shook her head. A neighbour? A cousin? She looked at Granny Beth's face again, smiling yet unamused. Granny would know. Granny could tell her.

She wanted to cry, not just at the idea of her mother seeking solace in her childhood self, but at the idea that she was right. There had been things that Donna had wanted to remember. Donna couldn't help herself. Jessica put her head down on the desk and closed her eyes. She needed a minute. For once, she had been right.

TWELVE

IT WAS A LONG DRIVE TO LION'S BAY, ONE THAT JESSICA had not made very often. As she negotiated the turns of the Sea to Sky Highway, she tried to count up the number of times she and Donna had gone to visit Granny Beth. Ten? Twelve? Maybe not even.

The sun was out, spilling thin light that pooled over the ocean on her left. She had tiptoed out of her parents' house at seven, while Gerry was still asleep and after three hours of lying in bed, eyes open in the darkness. She had spent the night turning that old photograph over and over in her mind, half-whispering to herself, "But what does it mean?" Somehow, Jessica had convinced herself that finding out that little boy's identity would lead to other clues she hadn't foreseen, which in turn would lead her to how Casey and Jamie had ended up dead and curled into her mother's freezers. By the time she padded to the shower at six, she knew the jumble of thoughts in her head made no real sense. But still, she thought—in that way that means sleeplessness has created a peculiar logic out of the illogical—she could see the eventual answers buried underneath the mess, shimmering like shiny-gilled fish at the bottom of a murky pond. As Jessica shampooed her hair, she considered that there might be no answers at all and that she was really just rushing head-first into madness. Then she remembered one unalterable truth. Granny Beth knew something about Donna that Jessica didn't.

She glanced at her open purse, the photograph wedged between her wallet and her phone. She rolled down the driver's side window and air blew in cold and tinged with the salty, seaweedy smell of the ocean. No music, just the hum of the car climbing through the mountains.

After Donna had died, Jessica was the one who had called Granny Beth. There was no one else to do it, and Gerry— exhausted and grieving—had already spent three days in his pyjamas, alternately crying and sleeping. So Jessica had sat in their kitchen, dialling one friend after another, repeating the same sentences over and over.

"She passed peacefully in her sleep."

"Thank you. No, we don't need anything."

"The memorial will be next week. We'll send an email."

"She really loved you too."

She had left Granny Beth to the end, flipping past her name as she turned the pages in her mother's address book. Eventually, there was no one left to call, just the receiver in her hand and the silent, waiting space between her parents' house and Granny's. She dialled.

"Hello?" Her voice was wavery, uncertain, vulnerable. In her surprise, Jessica was quiet. "Hello? Is anyone there?" This time, she sounded irritated. Jessica exhaled.

"Granny, it's Jessica."

"Good evening, Jessica. How are you?"

Jessica rolled her eyes. If she didn't answer properly, Granny Beth might just hang up. "I'm fine. And you?"

"I'm doing well. I'm managing quite reasonably with the walking stick these days. Although it's not much help on uneven ground. I suppose my hiking days are over."

As Jessica listened to her grandmother's crisp summary of her general wellness, anger simmered through her body. Granny Beth knew that Donna had cancer. She knew that Donna was going to die. These were things Donna herself had phoned to tell her over the last few months. As soon as she had heard Jessica's voice—her only granddaughter who had never called before—she must have understood what she was calling to tell her. And yet, she continued with this pretense of manners, as if how polite you were made any fucking difference at all to the people you loved and lost, or the way you cried at night holding your childhood stuffed dog to your open, screaming mouth. *Fuck her*, Jessica thought.

"If you went for a hike now, you'd probably break a hip anyway," Jessica said, staring at the fruit bowl on the counter, full of apples that were wrinkled and dry.

Granny sucked in her breath. "What did you just say?"

"Granny, I'm not calling to talk about hiking or your goddamned cane. Mom died on Sunday. That's all." Jessica heard the hard words, how they cut the air with their clarity and mercilessness. But she didn't care. If Granny Beth cried now, good. She was supposed to. It was what mothers did.

"Was she sleeping?"

"Yes."

"Oh." For a minute, Granny Beth said nothing and Jessica could hear only her breathing, so measured and deliberate that she thought that Granny Beth must be trying not to weep.

But then, she spoke, her voice no different. "It's what she said she wanted."

Jessica couldn't imagine her mother telling Granny Beth anything as intimate as that. "Mom told you that?"

"In a letter. She wrote me many letters over the years. The last one arrived three weeks ago. She wrote about her death and what she wanted." Granny Beth cleared her throat before continuing. "Her letters were always addressed to me, but I often got the feeling that she was writing them for herself, to express things she never did otherwise. They were usually full of news she would have never told me over the phone. They were," she paused and Jessica thought she could hear her tapping a long, pointed fingernail on a table, "curious."

At the time, Jessica was still so angry that she felt as if her chest might heave outward and spill its hot and hard contents all over the counter in front of her, so she told Granny Beth that the memorial would be held next week and hung up. She didn't wait for an invitation to visit. She didn't wait for Granny Beth to say she would come and help clean out Donna's clothes and books. It was no use. Granny Beth would never offer those things and, even if she did, Jessica would never accept.

Now, as Jessica drove onto the exit for Lion's Bay, she wondered if she should have comforted her grandmother, told her that Donna loved her and kept a photograph of the two together by her bedside until the very last breath. But these would have been lies—big, fat, transparent lies. And Granny Beth would have known it.

The driveway to the house curved to the left, the paving stones outlined in bright green moss. Everything was as Jessica remembered it. The stubby rhododendrons. The stone St. Francis of Assisi standing by the front door. The covered windows that always made Jessica think of eyes that had been blinded by knives or shrapnel. The house was grey and short, neat and ageless. Jessica knocked.

A thin Filipina woman opened the door. She blinked at Jessica and said quietly, "Yes?"

"My name is Jessica. I'm Beth's granddaughter."

"Oh?" The woman tucked a long strand of black hair behind her ear.

"We're not close. In fact, I'm sure she's probably never even talked about me." Jessica shifted on her feet. "But I really am her granddaughter. Maybe she's mentioned my mother, Donna. She died not too long ago."

"Yes. Donna. Mrs. Worth told me she had cancer. I'm so sorry."

Jessica waved her hand. "That's all right. Can I come in?"

The woman stepped aside and held the door open, silently watching as Jessica removed her shoes and hung her coat up on the hook in the hall. When Jessica turned around, the woman smiled.

"I was making breakfast. Come into the kitchen. Mrs. Worth is still in the bathroom."

As Jessica followed her through the living room, she said, "I'm sorry. I didn't ask your name."

"Dolores."

"How long have you worked here? The last caregiver I met was Maria."

Dolores lifted the lid off a small pot and stirred the oatmeal inside. "Four months. Maria retired."

"I hope my grandmother is being nice to you," said Jessica. She laughed but it sounded too loud and empty.

Dolores tilted her head to the side and squinted at Jessica's face. "Mrs. Worth is very fair."

140

She almost replied, *My mother fucking hated her*, but instead she rubbed the back of her neck with her hand. Her eyes felt like they were being pricked with needles. A migraine, like the ones she had as child, was coming.

It had been early October and Jessica stood in the middle of the playground, the yells and pounding of recess beating around her as she stuffed her hands as far into her pockets as she could. In the corner by the chain-link fence, Mrs. Wakabayashi was staring at the looming rain cloud blowing in from the west. Jessica needed to walk over to her and tell her she was sick and that she wanted to go home, but it was an extra fifty steps. She looked behind her. The gate to her house was the opposite way. *Home*, she thought. *I need to go home. Now.* She turned around and, weaving through the groups of children huddled around the play equipment, walked through the gate and down the street.

The front step. Jessica wanted lie down right there, but she knew if she did that, she would be there for hours, or until her mother walked out at two thirty to pick up Casey and Jamie, as she had been doing lately to make sure they actually attended classes. Breathing through her mouth, she unlocked the door and pulled herself up the stairs, shoes and coat still on.

"Mom?" she called. "Mom, I need you."

She heard nothing, just the soft hum of the bathroom fan. As she walked down the hall, she saw a trail of wet footprints from the bathtub all the way to her parents' room. Jessica bent down and touched the carpet with her finger. Water pooled as she pressed. Maybe the tub had overflowed. Maybe her mother had hurt herself in the bath and had dragged herself into her room. Jessica walked faster and pushed open the bedroom door without knocking.

Donna sat on the floor with the quilt from her bed draped over her shoulders. She was dripping with water—from her hair, her nose, her ears. There were dark stains where the quilt was already soaked through. Jessica blinked. Her mother's legs were bare, sticking out like a marionette's from under the quilt. Donna was naked.

"You just missed them," Donna said.

"Who?"

Donna snorted. "Casey and Jamie. Who else?"

Jessica pulled off her coat and placed it carefully over her mother's legs. She knelt in front of her and tucked Donna's hair behind her ears.

"Oh, sweetie. Thank you."

She didn't want to know what happened. She really, really didn't.

"I was alone. I just wanted to take a bath."

Jessica chanted to herself, *Stop, stop, stop*.

"It was lovely. I had the radio on. I felt so loose and warm."

Jessica turned away and tugged at her running-shoe laces. Maybe if she didn't look at the way her mother's face was sagging and twisting around her words, this whole thing would be easier to hear.

"I didn't hear them come in."

Jessica felt Donna's hand on her shoulder. Her mother wanted her to turn around, but she didn't. She tensed her neck and leaned forward. She would not look. Would not.

"They ran in with my camera. They took pictures of me. I tried to grab them, but I slipped and fell back into the tub. They called me names—Fatso, Cunt."

Jessica flinched. She had never heard her mother say anything so hard and mean and wrong before. She put a hand on her head. It still hurt. She wanted to lie down.

"They took all the towels and all of my clothes and ran out, laughing. Do you know what that feels like, to be laughed at and naked and called names? No, why would you? " Donna paused her breathing, irregular and raw. "I'm afraid, Jess. I hear them at night, moving around the house, whispering, flushing the toilet, opening the closets. I haven't slept in five days. I haven't been this tired since I was a little girl and all those nightmares about animals and the ocean and cliffs. These girls are planning something. I know it."

Jessica jumped and turned around. She stared at her mother.

"They need counselling. I call the social worker every other day, but there are so many other children, she says. She said she knew I could get them through another week, just until the therapist's schedule opens up. She relies on me, Jess. But look at me now."

Jessica was already looking. Her head, suddenly, was clear. She reached out and wiped her mother's chin with her sleeve. In her head, she ran the same words in a circle, over and over again. *I hope they run away again. I hope they run away again. I hope they run away.*

"I just have to keep them safe," Donna said. "Just for a little while longer. No more mistakes."

In Granny's house, Jessica rummaged in her purse for a bottle of Advil. Just as she swallowed two pills, dry, she heard the door to the bathroom open behind her and the swish of leather-soled slippers on the parquet floor. Granny Beth, one hand on her walking stick, stepped into the kitchen. When she saw Jessica, she paused, her blue eyes lingering on Jessica's amber ones. She had always thought of Granny Beth's eyes as cold and honed, as if she spent her leisure hours sharpening them, a glass of brandy on the table beside her. Now, they seemed liquid and malleable. For a moment, Jessica thought she should hug her.

143

Granny Beth straightened up and smoothed down the buttons on her cardigan with her free hand. She turned her head away for only a second, but by the time she looked at Jessica again, the severe solidity of her eyes had returned.

"Jessica. What are you doing here? And so early in the morning too." Dolores guided Granny Beth to a kitchen chair before placing a steaming mug of tea in front of her.

"You didn't come to the memorial, Granny. So we never got a chance to visit."

Granny Beth nodded slightly, then tapped the table with her middle finger. "Dolores, please make my granddaughter a cup of tea. I'm afraid she's looking quite wilted."

Jessica thought that Granny Beth looked nervous, as if her entire body itched and all she could think of was scratching her skin away. She had never known her grandmother to fidget and yet she was folding and unfolding a cloth napkin in her thickly veined hands. She hadn't asked Jessica about the weather or her job or the drive. She sat, perched on her chair, waiting. Jessica wondered what Granny Beth expected her to say.

Dolores returned with a second mug of tea and a bowl of oatmeal for Granny Beth. She turned to Jessica and asked, "Toast?"

"No, thank you. I'm not hungry."

"I'm not either. But at my age, if you don't eat, you quickly disappear." Granny Beth lifted a spoon of grey mush to her mouth and frowned before swallowing. "I just wish I was eating a bowl of lobster bisque instead."

Jessica didn't respond, but instead reached into her purse and pulled out the photograph. She placed it on the table in front of Granny Beth. She could swear the air around them chilled.

Granny Beth gazed at the photograph before picking it up and bringing it closer to her eyes. As she stared at the image of this very same house, her hand, the one holding the print, shook. It was just a tremble, a slight and fast wobble, but it worked its way down from her fingers to her wrist to her elbow, until her arm collapsed on the table, knocking over her tea and launching the photograph into the air. It floated side to side until it landed, softly, on Jessica's placemat. Dolores appeared with a kitchen towel and began wiping up the spilled tea. Granny Beth, blinking her eyes hard, pushed Dolores out of the way.

"Get out," she whispered. "We need to be alone."

When Dolores had left, taking the wet placemats with her, Granny Beth narrowed her eyes and pointed a lilac fingernail at Jessica's nose.

"You have no idea what you just started."

━

The sun had shifted and was now shining directly through the skylight above the kitchen table. When Jessica was younger, she had hated coming with her mother to Granny Beth's, and as soon as she stepped through the front hall and into the common rooms at the back of the house, she sucked in her breath and held it, as if the lack of air could unfog her eyes and make what she was seeing that much sharper and greener and finer. The windows here, unlike the covered ones that faced the street, were tall and wide and the vertical blinds always open. If Jessica stood with her toes touching the baseboards, her nose inches from the glass, it was as if she were standing on a cliff, the ocean just a running leap away. If she shouted, she was sure she would see the trees on Gambier Island sway with the sound.

She sat, waiting for her grandmother to speak, looking at the view that her mother grew up with, that she had almost never spoken about. Jessica didn't think it was strange before, but now, as Granny Beth opened and closed her fists, waiting, it seemed, for the right words to form themselves into the right sentences, she thought it was a gaping hole in the story of Donna's life. Donna, who had loved the outside and the rush of fresh air as she stepped from steamy kitchen to disordered yard. Donna, whose own body had seemed to change with the landscapes she marched through. Hair like curls of young ferns. Voice like the crunch and scratch of hiking boots on gravel. If a child grew up like this, with the ocean underneath her, in front of her, pushing at her ears, that child would live forever with the scent of sea water soaked into her scalp. Or the always rippling shadow of waves moving through her face. She would be marked, like the bent and scarred arbutus clinging to the rocky overhang at the very edge of Granny Beth's property.

Granny Beth put a hand on Jessica's arm. "You'll have to understand something."

"What's that?"

"We promised each other, many years ago, that we would never speak of this, of him again." Granny Beth shook her head. "I never thought it would be me breaking that promise."

Jessica gently lifted Granny Beth's hand off her arm and held it. The skin was thin, like living, warm paper. "You don't have to tell me anything."

"Oh, I do. You've brought me that," and she pointed at the photograph lying on the table. "You didn't come all this way just to visit with me. I'm not so old and daft that I think you actually like me." Granny Beth smiled, her lips closed.

Jessica said nothing. If she laughed, the moment might pass, broken into pieces that wouldn't fit back together again. So she only looked at Granny Beth's face, at the fear and hesitation wrestling through her jaw, the muscles around her temples.

"His name was Devin," she said quietly. "He was my son. He was Donna's brother. They were twins."

There were three—men or beasts, the girls never really knew. They might have been hurting them with fists or hooves or horns. This is the way with hurt: the weapons mean very little if the asshole wielding them is angry enough or strong enough. The girls screamed, of course, but who would hear them? In this half-alley, where the closest humans were in the same pain, or a different pain that manifested in the same deafness, their cries could have been feral cats in a fight or babies from the open windows in the grimy hotel above.

When the man-beasts left, the sisters crawled to a doorstep and hunched there, pulling their clothes over themselves. There was no wind in this dead-end alley. They didn't speak, didn't cry. To the left, they could see the lights of passing cars, a plastic bag circling in the storm. That way, they thought. When they stood up, they fell, so they held on to each other and stood again.

NINETEEN FORTY-SEVEN
to
NINETEEN FIFTY-NINE

THIRTEEN

ELIZABETH ROSE PARKER HAD ALWAYS BEEN A PRAC-
tical woman. As a child in Comox, she lived with an unmarried
aunt after her parents died of pneumonia, and she learned
soon enough that her pale and silent aunt would never love
her. She left for Vancouver at seventeen with four hundred
and sixty-three dollars tucked into her stockings in her lone
suitcase. She was a waitress, then found a job as a clerk at a
stationary store. Three years later, when she was engaged to
be married to Charles Worth, she considered all her options
carefully, comparing the security of being an actuary's wife to
the shifting, dangerous possibilities of being a single woman.
Charles had been a pilot during the war, flying over Japan and
Burma and almost dying twice. Once, when they were on a
date to see *The Ghost and Mrs. Muir*, he had told her he never
wanted to take another chance, that staying firmly rooted to
the earth and coming home to a pretty wife and a nice meal
were all that he needed to stay alive and sane. He had patted
her hand. She had felt gratified.

But even as they stood in the small church off Burrard Street, Charles' face seemed to be disappearing in the yellow and red light from the stained glass windows, fading so quickly that Beth blinked and blinked, hoping that it was just her nerves playing with her mind and not a bad omen for their brand new marriage. Her hands were sweating in their gloves. The church was so hot that it was all she could do to stand there and not rip off her veil and run, panting and half-blind, into the street where the September breeze blew eastward. Once she was outside, maybe she could make it to a streetcar line and then to the train station, where she could go anywhere, do anything, as long as she could do it alone. She stared at his face, transparent in the sunshine, and tried to remember the angle of his nose, the colour of the flecks in his eyes. She couldn't. He may as well have been a fake man with a wooden skeleton and unyielding, painted skin.

The ceremony ended. She held Charles' hand. She became Mrs. Worth.

At first, they lived in an apartment on Pendrell Street in the West End, in one of those new stucco buildings with wrought iron balcony railings and Spanish-style roof tiles. It was nice and respectable, and another young couple, Walt and Laura, lived just down the hall. Walt was a veteran too and, on long summer evenings, as Laura and Beth sunned their feet on the balcony, Walt and Charles stayed in the dining room, curtains drawn against the light, smoking and whispering. Once, when Beth walked by to fill a glass of water, Charles' head was resting on Walt's shoulder and she could swear she heard him crying. She had never heard a man weep before and stood, half-hidden in the hall, rooted to her spot by the wrenching, churning noise. That night, in bed, she turned to him and was about to ask how he was feeling when he took her hand in one of his and said, "It's getting late. A good night's sleep will do wonders for both of us." Before she could respond, he rolled away from her and was silent, his back as still as the night outside.

During the day, she and Laura walked the downtown streets, stopping for tea at the Hotel Georgia when they were feeling spiffy, stopping for doughnuts and coffee at their favourite diner on Granville Street when they weren't. When the weather was good, they walked on the beach at English Bay in their bare feet until the sand was crusted halfway up their shins and they had to rinse off, holding their shoes in one hand, at the open shower by the changing rooms.

On a windy fall day, Laura sat down on a bench facing the water and pointed at the ocean, glittering with sunlight, blue and grey and white. "Where would you be if you weren't right here?" she asked, her dark brown hair blowing against her cheek.

"What do you mean?"

"What would you be doing right now if you weren't married to Charles? Where would you go? Who would you be with?"

Beth sat down beside her and buttoned her jacket up to her chin. "I don't know. I used to know how to type. Maybe I would be doing that in an office downtown."

Laura laughed and the sound circled on the wind. "Don't say anything too crazy, Beth. Don't you ever think about going to Hollywood and being in the movies? Or getting on a steamer to Europe?"

"No. I mean, maybe when I was younger, but not now. What would be the point?"

"There is none. But so what? I have to think of something, or my brain might just fall out of my head." Laura turned and smiled, her blue eyes and dark lashes like electric lights even here, in the middle of the day. "I would go to Paris and live in a romantic attic apartment and have brilliant men come to entertain me every evening."

Beth patted her friend on the shoulder. "I don't know that anyone who lives in Paris right now thinks it's very romantic."

"Oh, the war." Laura waved her hand and shook her head. "The war has been over for two years and I'm tired of it. Let's talk about where we should have lunch instead."

Later, as Beth stood in her kitchen, staring at the open refrigerator just before suppertime, she finally understood what Laura was trying to tell her. They were restless, girls pretending to be women in marriages that didn't seem quite real yet, that may have frightened them at first with their certainty, their solid beginnings and middles and endings, but that now bored them. They were waiting: for children, for bigger houses, for newer cars, for something to weigh down their desire to walk the city until their feet ached and cracked. She remembered, suddenly, how she had wanted to run away from her wedding, how her white dress had felt like a harness and leash. But it was futile to think about escape now. Her life was easy. She should appreciate that.

And yet, the next time she and Laura walked through the building's front doors, she thought about grabbing her friend's hand and hailing the first taxi they saw so that they could drive as far as their money would take them. Even if it was just to the edge of the city, where the trees and ocean choked out everything else and there were spots—muffled and brown— they would never be found.

When Beth became pregnant, Charles insisted that they needed to buy a house. For a few weeks, Beth managed to convince him that this was an unnecessary expense. After all, one baby couldn't possibly take up that much room, even if their apartment was a little small. But then, after one particularly long doctor's appointment where the nurse and doctor spent forty minutes listening to Beth's belly with stethoscopes, she had to return home and tell Charles that they were having twins. They had to move now. There was no question.

It didn't take long. Charles found a new house in Lion's Bay, an hour's drive from the city. At first, Beth thought it was too far and didn't even want to go see the house at all. But when she finally stood at the tall windows in the living room, facing the ocean, she felt like she was standing at the edge of the world, as if she could float through the windows and land, feather-soft, in Hawaii or Japan or the Philippines. She and Laura could plot their fantasies here, with the babies cooing at their feet. It would be like they weren't in a house at all.

Charles rented an office in West Vancouver, closer to home. They painted. They bought furniture—all of it white and blue. Beth told the sales clerks that she wanted their house to be light, to feel like it was perched among the clouds. Laura drove up every Tuesday for lunch and every Friday evening with Walt for supper. Soon, Beth grew too big to leave the house and Laura came every day, bringing doughnuts and Danishes and chocolates. When Beth ate, she could feel the babies turning inside her, both in the same direction as if they were in a chase, with one just a single beat ahead of the other.

One afternoon, Beth asked Laura when she and Walt might start their family. Laura shrugged and tucked a stray hair back into her impeccably waved bob. "Maybe next year.

Walt has a lot on his plate right now. Every bridge around here needs an engineer, it seems."

Beth nodded and didn't think about what Laura's words might really mean if she picked at them and tried to peel them back. Beth didn't think about much. If she began to imagine what it would be like to take care of two newborn babies by herself, in a sparsely settled town where she had to drive to buy just a pint of milk, she might curl into a ball and never get up. She had never met her neighbours. She didn't even know where the pharmacy was. It was easier to just eat her lemon curd Danish and let her mind empty as the waves flung themselves against the rocks just outside the glass doors. It was smarter to act like a fool, even if she wasn't.

—

When the babies came, four weeks early, Beth had been in labour for so long that she didn't even know she was pushing until the first one, the girl, was held up for her to see. She was crying, covered in thick, white paste. She seemed far too big for an infant who had had to share a womb. The second, the boy, was breach. She could hear the howls of her daughter at the far end of the room and yet she was still strapped into a hard, surgical bed, pushing until she felt sure the blood in her head had begun to explode, vein after vein after vein.

When the doctor pulled him out, he didn't cry, only stared at the bright lights with his mouth closed, as if he were silently appraising his surroundings. The nurses wiped him, weighed him and set him down on Beth's right side before he made a noise. Not like a baby. Like a seagull. Or a goose bleating for food. He was pale. The girl was pink.

In her head, she had already named them Devin and Donna. When she told Charles, he nodded and smiled, seeming to not even hear her. Instead, he kissed her cheek and said, "You did a good job, my dear." He gazed at the children sleeping in their bassinets. "You should sleep too." And he left, leaving behind a bouquet of carnations and fern fronds that Beth was sure he had bought ten minutes earlier in the hospital gift shop.

A kernel of worry bounced from one side of her head to the other. *Charles doesn't want them. Charles doesn't care.* But then she knew this was wrong, or at least not entirely accurate, for he had never complained, not once, when she had to sleep alone in their bed because the heat from his body made her pregnant body feel like it was wrapped in tin foil and placed in a slow-burning oven. He didn't complain when she asked him to repaint the nursery twice because the shade of blue she wanted was not quite sky, not quite cornflower. And he didn't complain when Beth was too big to stand and cook and he had to make do with Laura's boiled peas and potatoes. It wasn't that he didn't want them. That was just his way, and that was all Beth was ever going to think about it.

The babies grew. She fed them. She sang to them. She tried to knit. But every time she took out her bag of needles and wool, Donna would begin to cry, or Devin would begin to cough and she would have to hold one or the other or both, even as they swatted at each other as she balanced them on her lap. She had read once that twins liked to sleep together in the same crib, but the one time she had tried, Donna kicked away from Devin until she had scooted to the far end of the mattress, her swaddled blanket a tangle around her tummy. Devin just screamed.

After supper, Beth followed Charles around the house, asking him questions, telling him about the colour of Devin's poop or the half-roll Donna managed while lying on the rug in the hall.

"Devin needs more cuddling, it seems, doesn't it, Charles? His little hands get so cold."

"How do you think I could weigh them?"

"Tell me about your day. Tell me about it all."

Charles rarely answered and instead continued moving, from the sofa in the living room to the armchair closest to the glass patio doors and then, finally, to the Muskoka chairs set on the flat rocks outside their windows. It was February, but still he sat there, a snifter of brandy in his gloved hand, his scarf pulled up over his chin. When he passed by the babies on his way, he smiled at them, lips closed, moustache unmoving. Donna and Devin stared, silent.

The only person she talked to was Laura, who came less often, once a week, sometimes twice a month. Beth wondered to herself if Laura didn't like babies, but didn't allow the thought to grow bigger or unfurl roots in her head. If she hated babies, she wouldn't visit at all, right? Although, when she did come, she sat on a chair in the living room and barely watched Beth walk Devin back and forth until he fell asleep, or she kicked a ball to Donna with her eyes fixed on the view, while Devin sat on the floor, solidly eating his fist. She never touched the babies or talked to them or offered to hold them, not like the ladies on the street who couldn't seem to resist tickling the twins with their gloved hands as they sat, fat and unsmiling, in their double pram. Beth decided that it didn't matter. When Laura walked into the house, she brought with her a cloud of perfume and car exhaust, the smell of city side-walks soaked with rain. She came from somewhere else, the city Beth once thought of as hers, and this, she thought, as she folded diapers on the kitchen counter at night by herself, was what she valued.

———

One night, when the babies were two, Charles didn't return home from work. He had called her at five to say he needed to meet a client downtown for supper and wouldn't be home until late. Beth put the twins down and then went to sleep her-self. At three in the morning, Devin woke up whining, so she brought him into her bed and saw, groggily, that Charles wasn't there. As Devin snored through the rest of the early morning, Beth worried. Charles could have been hit by a streetcar, or he could have stumbled into the wrong club, drunk. She imagined him lying on a dirty mattress in a back room, his pockets empty and a dribble of blood inching down his face from his open, unmoving mouth. If she got up to make a telephone call to one of his colleagues, Devin would wake. So she lay there instead, face turned toward the open bedroom door.

At six o'clock, she heard the lock turn in the front door. She heard a man pissing in the toilet. Then she heard the shuffle of socked feet walking to the living room and the final, soft sound of the springs in the sofa. He was fine. He was sleeping in the other room. But Beth's eyes were dry and hot. She blinked against the dawn and looked at Devin, curled on his side, his thumb in his mouth. Even if she wanted to, she couldn't march into the hall and begin throwing shoes and words at her husband. She might wake the babies. It was the babies she had to think of. It was the babies she could never get away from.

At seven thirty, after Donna and Devin had their diapers changed and were sitting in their high chairs, bowls of oatmeal in front of them, Charles walked into the kitchen, straight-backed, eyes brighter than Beth had seen in months. He put the kettle on for tea and patted Donna on the head.

"Aren't you tired?" She was trying, but the knife edge cut into her voice, that sharpness that hones words into ticking, tiny bombs.

He pulled a teabag from the cupboard. "I'm fine. I'll just have some tea and that'll perk me right up."

Beth couldn't remember the last time he had said so much to her in the morning. Or, really, at any time. "What kept you out so late?"

"My client wanted to go to an after-hours club. You know, the one across from the steakhouse. And then he wanted coffee and doughnuts, so we went to one of those all-night diners. I can't remember the last time I ate doughnuts at four in the morning."

"So it was fun?"

Charles took a sip of tea and frowned. "I wouldn't call it fun. But it was nice to be out. We spend so much time at home."

Before she could stop herself, Beth said, "Actually, it's me who spends so much time at home."

"What's that?"

"I spend all my time at home, Charles. Not you."

"Well, someone has to go to work and pay the bills, my dear. Speaking of which," Charles glanced at the clock above the sink, "I have to have a quick shower. I'm afraid I'm running a bit late."

When he had finally gone, Beth opened the patio doors

and let in the wild, salt-tinged wind that was ripping through the arbutus trees growing on the rocks. The house still smelled of booze and man sweat, that specific odour of people jammed in tightly where there was no air and no light, only the non-trustworthy flames of candles in glass holders and cigarettes burning low. The children ran toward the door, but she held them back with her foot and they squealed in protest. *Let me smell something else, something that came from far away*, she thought. *Just for this one minute.* There it was: the faint drift of seaweed and fish both living and dead floating up from the ocean. Her chest grew and she straightened up, her spine tall and pulled tight. Maybe the twins were still crying. Maybe it was a shore bird. She didn't know and didn't care to find out.

———

Charles left. He didn't speak to her about it beforehand or tell her where he was going. He just left.

For months, he had been telling her his client wanted to be taken out again, and since he was the head of a big insurance company, Charles felt compelled to go. Beth wondered why it had to be him and not some other actuary, or even the man's secretary, but as soon as she said this out loud, Charles would shrug and say it was all so they could afford the house and the car and the new clothes she bought. There was no counter-argument.

He left on a Friday evening in March, after the children had gone to bed. Beth was reading in the living room when she looked up and saw him, overcoat buttoned, fedora pulled low over his forehead. He had one suitcase. Everything he wanted to take with him fit in one small suitcase. This, more than anything, made Beth sad.

He said, "I'm leaving. I'll send money for you, for the kids. Don't try to find me. When I'm ready, I'll write to you."

At that moment, she knew she had been too soft. She had wanted to believe that this marriage was prudent and the right decision, even though her body had screamed in protest as they stood in that church on that sunny day five years ago. She had let the idea of Charles lead her to this house on a cliff where she knew almost no one, where she chased the twins down the hall because she needed to break up a fight, where she held Devin's hand while he lay, feverish and cranky, in a bed damp with his sweat. She had let things happen to her while she wore her floral apron over her blue or yellow dress, propped up like a dumbfounded rag doll against the kitchen counter. Not again. Never again.

Charles was waiting for her to say something. Did he think she would cry? Had she been the man, it would be her leaving, not him. Sadness and tears played no part in this. She was envious, angry, full to the eyes with bitterness.

He picked up his suitcase. Beth nodded and said, "If you're going to leave, then just leave." She turned to look out the dark windows, where shapes in shadow sat hunched and still on this windless night. She heard the door close and the sound of his keys being pushed through the letter slot and falling on the tiled floor.

—

At first, it seemed as if nothing had changed. Donna and Devin kept fighting. Beth kept pulling Donna off her brother, yelling, "You're bigger than him," and Donna would sob and say, "But he started it. It was him!" Beth knew this was true. She had watched Donna cook a pretend meal for him: mud pies, fallen leaves for salad, gravel the size of peas. She had seen Devin laugh at the table set for two on the tree stump outside and, later, turned from the stove to catch him stealing Donna's dolls and pulling off their heads. He dropped them haphazardly around the house as if his sister's heartbreak meant as little to him as a trail of broken, discarded toys. But it was Donna who could hurt him with her strong arms and tight grip, even if all she was trying to do was hug him before they went to sleep. Devin wasn't small, but he caught cold after cold after cold, and couldn't run fast enough when his head ached or his throat was raw from coughing. At the very least, Beth thought, she could prevent Donna from drawing blood.

After two weeks, she called Laura, who hadn't come by like she usually did, something Beth had been grateful for since she had no desire to explain Charles' absence. But she missed Laura's fine, high laugh, the way she looked around the house from her chair in the living room, her gaze never falling on the children, floating instead at a line just above their heads. So adult. So clean and easy.

Walt answered. Beth looked at the clock. Two in the afternoon. What was Walt doing at home?

"Hello, Walt. It's Beth."

"Beth," he whispered. Even in that one syllable, she knew he was drunk.

"How are you?"

"Wonderful. Right as rain." He laughed and Beth could hear the thickness of whiskey in his throat.

"Is Laura there?"

"Why would she be here?"

Beth paused. He really was very drunk. "What do you mean?"

"Charles, that bastard. He's not home, is he?"

"Actually, no. He's likely at work."

Walt began laughing again, but the laugh ebbed out and soon she thought she heard him sob. "Holy hell. You don't know, do you?"

"Walt, I think I'd better get off the line now. I'll call back another time."

"Laura's gone, Beth. She left me. She took off with Charles. With *your* Charles."

Beth stared at the phone on the wall, at the curled green cord that led to the receiver in her hand. It was real. This was real. "It was *Laura*?"

"Yes, you little idiot. They had been carrying on for a year. I knew she was seeing someone else, but never did I think it was Charles. The man is unhinged. The war repeats in his head, all the time, every day."

"Did she tell you it was Charles?"

"She told me she wanted to be honest. I told her she just wanted to inflict more pain. Our parting words. Lovely, don't you think?" He really was crying now.

"Do you know where they are?"

"Her mother sent me a letter, said they were in Edmonton, living near the house Laura grew up in. Her mother always liked me, you know. Charles doesn't strike her fancy, it seems."

This phone, this goddamned telephone was hot in her hands. If she didn't let go, her whole body might catch on fire, flames licking at her wrist, her arm, her shoulder.

"Walt, I'd better go. The twins will wake up from their nap soon."

"Wait. Maybe we could go for coffee. Beth, please." She knew that, if she could see him, he would be wearing wrinkled clothes that he had slept in. He would smell. He would be trying to hold her hand, his own trembling because the first whiskey of the day hadn't steadied his nerves yet.

"I don't think that's wise, Walt. Just . . ." She stopped for a moment, not knowing what she should say to the weeping man whose wife had just run off with her husband. "Take care, okay?"

Afterward, she stood outside on the rocks, one hand on the arbutus closest to the house. She could go anywhere, like she had always wanted. She could sell this house that seemed to hover over the sea and take the children with her. There, across the ocean. Or back, down the highway and to the city, where lights burned through curtains in the night, where you could find music at any time on any day, if only you listened hard enough. She didn't have to stay here, where she had to wrestle her hair against the wind every time she stepped outside, where Charles' holey socks and thin underwear still sat folded in the dresser. She stretched her arm toward the water and felt the bite of salt-heavy air on her wrist. But here, she had the illusion of freedom. Here, she could wear what she wanted and say what she wanted and be certain that no one would ever know because her windows faced *out there*, where her words flew and then dropped, disappearing into the water like unseen stones. This house may have been Charles' idea, but it had since become the only place where she knew how to exist. Her touch, her smell, the evidence of her movements were everywhere, absorbed into the walls and floors as if they were made of sponge. But the house was wild too, unwatched but witness to the sky and sailboats and islands that changed every minute in small ways, but also didn't. There was nowhere to run, but you could see farther than you'd ever want to.

They would stay. The next morning, she told the children their father was dead. When they cried, she gave them peanut butter cookies and never mentioned Charles again.

The twins grew. Every year, Beth hoped that they would stop fighting, that she would walk into the living room and see them cuddled together, reading a book with a blanket over their knees. Instead, she could hear them wherever they were in the house, their voices high and angry, the sounds of toys breaking and the concluding, inevitable crying. Beth tried to talk them through it, tried to sit down and explain to them how being cruel to each other only made everyone miserable, but they didn't listen, only kicked their feet against the table legs before jumping off their chairs and running to opposite ends of the house.

Once, when they were alone, Donna said, "I love him so much, Mother. But he's always so mean, like he hates me." Beth told her to keep her distance, and she tried. But eventually, like two pieces of the same magnet, they found each other again. And the fighting continued.

She stopped trying to talk. Instead, she demanded silence in the evenings after supper and locked them in their bedrooms if she just couldn't take it anymore. There was no father here. Beth had told the children and everyone else that Charles had died, which seemed to be the easier explanation. So she had to be hard. She had to shut her ears to the soft crying from behind their locked bedroom doors, even though in her head she could see the two of them, each curled on a bed, each with eyes closed tight against the tears that were falling out anyway. It didn't matter. If they wouldn't stop fighting, she would make them stop.

By the time Donna and Devin started school, Beth could see her methods were working. Donna began making pets of the small animals that scurried through the bushes around the house. She lay on her stomach on the rocks outside, chin resting on her hands, watching for any small movement, her breath seeming to still whenever a vole or a baby crow came looking for the line of nuts and bread crumbs she left for them every morning. Devin stayed indoors, where he built towers and cranes out of his Erector Set, and then smashed them with an old wooden spoon that Beth let him have. They made friends—separate friends—and never seemed to notice each other anymore. Beth, for the first time since Charles had left, sighed with relief.

But, still, sometimes in the night, Devin called for her and she stumbled, her dreams still hanging off her body, trailing after her, into his room, where he would be sitting up, crying into his sheets, his forehead hot with fever or bad dreams or both, and she would have to crawl into his single bed with him, half her body hanging off the edge, cold in the night air.

It was dawn one morning as Beth lay there, eyes shut even though she knew light was beginning to push through the curtains. If she looked at the clock, it would be five thirty or six, and the spell of sleep would be broken and she would be curled around her son, tense with the anticipation of his waking self, the one who asked her for cookies fifteen times in a row until she flushed all the cookies in the house down the toilet. The one who crept into her lap whenever she sat down, burying his face in her neck like a baby. So she lay there, eyes closed, her nose in Devin's hair.

She thought she was dreaming at first, that she had fallen back asleep in the hazy morning silence. She was on a boat or a train or something that moved with a discernible beat, a one-two, one-two. She felt soft, cossetted by warmth. It was a dream. Of course, it was a dream.

But it wasn't. It was Devin moving underneath her arm, making noises like a kitten trapped under a sofa. It was Devin, with his hand in his pyjama pants, masturbating.

At first, she thought, *He must be asleep*. But when she looked, his eyes were tightly shut, so tightly that his eyelids were wrinkled and the lashes pressed down over the tops of his cheeks. No, he was awake, and trying to imagine himself somewhere else.

Does he remember I'm here? I need to leave. I need to leave.

Beth began to slide out of bed, her arm behind her to feel for the carpet on the floor. She would do this quietly and he would never notice. It would be like she had never been here, and she could forget that she had witnessed anything at all. But just as her fingers grazed the carpet beside the bed, Devin reached backward with one arm and grabbed a handful of her nightgown, his grip stronger than she knew was possible. With one hand on his mother and the other in his pants, his eyes never opened, never even seemed to flicker with the acknowledgement that Beth was there with him and knew what he was doing.

She didn't move. She stayed. When he was done, he rolled over, on to his back and sighed, his body limp and weighed down with sleep. Not until his breath was even and heavy did Beth leave the room, her bare feet cold as she hurried down the hall.

In her room, she sat down on her bed and stared out the window at the bush outside. The sun was out with a vengeance now, yellow and unsubtle and thick. She wondered if she was going to cry, but no tears came to rinse away the warm spot on her hip where Devin's hand had rested, or the smell of his unwashed hair in that hot and narrow bed. He was only eight. Surely she could talk to their doctor; surely he would know what to do.

She reached over to open the drawer on her nightstand, where she kept her address book. She could phone in an hour when the receptionist arrived. But just as she pulled the drawer open, she remembered the whispers she had heard last year at the twins' school. A little girl had disappeared, though her older brother was still attending. One of the other mothers had told Beth, in a mean, sharp voice, that the girl had been setting fires around the schoolyard and at home and her parents had sent her to Woodlands, an institution where disturbed children remained tucked out of sight and never wore anything but their nightgowns and slippers.

"It was for the best, really," that other mother had said. "They couldn't have her burn them all to death in their beds."

Beth had agreed but was left with the image of children staring into space behind windows reinforced with chicken wire, floating like ghosts in hallways lit so brightly they seemed like shadows in comparison. Now, she saw Devin there. Medicated. Still. No trouble, but incapable of anything else besides a quiet acceptance. No one ever asked if the children were happy at places like that. The answer was obvious. Beth pressed hard on her stomach with the palm of her hand, feeling the loose skin that still wrinkled over her abdomen, the skin that had stretched for both of her children at the same time, the skin that would never contract and be smooth again.

It would be okay. She was the only one who knew. As long as it stayed here, in the house, she could manage it. The next time he cried out for her in the night, she would make sure to leave his bed well before morning. She heard Donna turning on the taps in the bathroom. The day was starting and this day, more than any other, she had to convince everyone that nothing was wrong.

Donna and Devin hated her. Not always and not for the same reasons, but they hated her often enough and with enough ferocity that she worried when the house grew too still. In those moments, she could feel the animosity in the air, thick. She worried about a plot, about the possibilities that the two of them might work together to run away. But then, they had never worked together for anything. They just hated her, separately.

One evening, after the children had finished their homework and Beth was putting away clean laundry, she found, in the back of Donna's closet, a small pile of droppings. There was no doubt that these were from some kind of small, furry, brown animal, no doubt that the neighbouring shoebox filled with rags had been a bed. Beth could smell it—that undeniable smell of fur hastily cleaned by a small, pink tongue, the funk of a living creature squeaking in an airless closet. The droppings were old, were ringed by a dried, dark stain on the carpet. Whatever had been living here had long since been released back into the bush or had died.

The longer she stood there, staring at the mess, the angrier she became. It had probably been a common field mouse, the kind that snuck in through holes no bigger than a thimble. The kind that proliferated in underused garages and abandoned wheelbarrows. The kind that wasn't worth saving and whose smell would be impossible to wash out.

Donna was sitting in the living room, curled into the yellow armchair, reading a library copy of *Little House in the Big Woods*. Beth walked over and placed the makeshift bed on the coffee table in front of her. Donna looked, saw the shoebox and sat up, the book sliding off her lap and onto the floor.

"What happened to it?"

Donna stared but said nothing.

"Did it die? Did you kill it?"

Beth could see the tears pooling in Donna's eyes, but she

couldn't stop. She needed to get it out. She needed someone to hear the frustration bouncing inside her body.

"You thought you were saving it, didn't you? You thought if you brought it home and loved it, you could fix its broken leg or whatever else was wrong with it."

Donna looked around her—quickly, desperately—as if there could only be one escape route and her mother was blocking the way.

"It was all right for a while, but then after a few days, it stopped eating. It stopped trying to run away. It just stopped." Beth paused and pointed at the box. "You found it, in there, not moving, eyes open. And you knew you had killed it."

Her daughter was crying, those deep, eight-year-old sobs that are both childlike and adult at the same time: rapid, deeply hoarse.

"You buried it. In a little bag outside, with a stone marking the grave. But you couldn't go back to the closet and clean up the box or the mess. You didn't want to remember its life or its death. You just wanted to forget."

Beth could sense Devin behind her, his body half-hidden by the corner of drywall that bordered the hallway. It was a trick of motherhood that she could swear she heard his ears turning toward her, like radio antennae looking for the clearest signal.

"Well, there's nothing we can do about that poor, dead animal now, is there? Except clean up the shit and piss it left behind." Beth cocked her head toward Donna's bedroom. "You are going to clean up your closet until you can't smell the stink anymore. When you think you're done, you're going to put your nose down to the carpet and sniff as hard as you can. If you can smell anything, you'll have to start all over again."

Donna sat, limp and curled over, in the chair. Her head nodded, just barely.

"Go on, then. The cleaning rags and detergent are in the basement. Go."

Donna left, her blond hair matted at the back of her head. On another day, Beth might have stopped her and brushed and braided the curls into a tight French braid, but not now. Her children needed to be afraid of her, needed to know that Beth was far more than cuddling and soft. She was the one they had to answer to.

—

It was a wild November, the kind where every windstorm threatened to blow their little house off the cliffs and into the angry, tossing sea. The twins were stuck in the house every weekend and Beth kept them apart as much as she could, but they still had to eat together, still had to share the same bathroom. They were ten now, and their arguments were no longer violent, but their voices, both strangely adult, were like knives twisting into Beth's ears every time they bickered over the last scoop of shepherd's pie or the toothpaste.

One night, after dinner, Beth stood at the oven, waiting for cookies to bake. If in doubt, she told herself, feed them. They can't say anything with their mouths full. Rain struck the house at a vicious angle, leaving slashes on the windows. If there was anything outside beyond the patio doors, she couldn't see it. For all she knew, she was in a spaceship, hovering in a starless universe, alone.

She heard Donna screaming, a wordless cry that seemed to come from everywhere and nowhere all at once. Their steps pounded, running and running until they burst into the kitchen,

Devin first, Donna second. She was chasing him, her hair wet and dripping, and wearing only a pink T-shirt and underpants. She was sobbing so much she seemed in danger of being overcome and simply collapsing on the floor. Devin only laughed as he ran. Beth stepped forward and tried to tear off her oven mitts, but somehow they seemed stuck to her hands, glued there by invisible layers of unwashable cookie dough. She bent her head to look closer at the elastics around her wrists when she heard the patio door open. They were chasing each other on the rocks out there, in the dark, in the rain.

The fence, she thought. *It won't hold them.*

When they had first moved in, Charles had put up the fence, made of thin, plastic-coated wire and skinny metal poles drilled unevenly into the rocks. Beth had said she wanted something that wouldn't obscure the view. But now, she ran to the door, a scream forming in her mouth even as no sound emerged.

When she stepped outside, she saw Devin climbing over the fence and dropping to the rain-slicked rocks on the other side. Donna was behind him, struggling to get a foothold in the small, pliable, wire-lined holes.

Beth yelled, "Come back! Come back now!"

She reached Donna in six steps and grabbed her shoulder. When Donna spun around, Beth hissed in her ear, "What is going on?"

Her daughter's face was flushed, patches of pink blooming, lit by the lights that shone through the windows behind them. Her eyes were wide open, so wide that the whites were visible all around her irises. Donna coughed as she tried to speak.

"I was having a bath, Mother, and singing in the tub. And he barged in. I told him to leave, I did, but he wouldn't. And then he pinched me, all over. Here," and Donna pointed at her chest, "and here too." She put a hand between her legs and looked down at the rocks. "I hate him so much. I hope he dies."

"Donna. You must never say that. Never."

On the other side of the fence, she heard Devin's voice. "She was pinching herself, Mother. In her privates. I saw her, in the tub, like a whore. *I saw her.*"

Before Beth could say one word, Donna had started climbing. Devin walked backward, making faces at his sister through the wire, calling her names.

"No," Beth said. "Stop!"

Maybe they couldn't hear her. The waves were crashing, crashing, an assault on the rocks and air and ears. Beth yelled louder. It made no difference. As she reached out to grab any part of Donna she could, Donna finally landed on her feet and turned to face her brother. Devin began to dart behind the arbutus, his hand reaching for the trunk. But Beth knew the tree was wet too, slick the way old wood in a storm can get. His hand slipped and he fell backward. He landed on his bum and began to slide down the rocks. He reached back and tried to steady himself with his hands on the ground, but his palms seemed to only glide over the gravel and stones as if they were coated in oil.

"Donna! Help him!" Beth was two steps away from the fence. Donna was running toward him, her legs oddly steady on the loose ground. *Please, God*, Beth thought. *Please make sure she gets there in time.*

Devin slid and slid. Donna reached down with both arms, as if she were going to grab his wrists and pull him toward her. But then she straightened up and, through the storm, Beth could swear she saw her daughter push her heel into her brother's chest. He rolled backward, over, and was gone. In the dark, the edges of the cliff, the sky, the ocean—it all looked the same. Black. Empty. Surely he was still there. Surely he was clinging to something, even though, that close to the edge, there was nothing to grasp anymore.

Donna stood with her toes pointed out toward the ocean, her blond hair waterlogged and flat. A solid girl. One who would never be so foolhardy as to fall into the sea. One who was too strong and too practical to ever allow herself to be pushed. No, just the opposite.

When, finally, Beth had climbed the fence and looked, she could see nothing. She heard nothing but the waves and the rain and the foghorn farther down the shore. Beth was his mother. If he was screaming, she knew she would hear it. The storm continued even as she stood there, waiting for a human voice to float up toward her.

When they walked back to Hastings Street, a taxi driver saw them in his side mirror and recognized the stagger of girls who had been raped. He stopped, tucked them into the back seat and drove them to the hospital. They stayed until the next afternoon, but they would not say what their names were, where they lived or what had happened. The nurses told them a social worker was on her way, so they pulled the intravenous needles from their wrists, put on their old, filthy clothes and walked out into a city washed clean by a windstorm.

They went back to the foster home. When asked, they said they had spent the night in Stanley Park, sleeping in a gazebo by the Rose Garden, the faded petals in a cyclone around them. Their foster mother believed them because she wanted to. In her gut, she probably knew better.

Later, as the days went by, the girls knew they had changed, but the change was huge and still growing and impossible to contain. They were pissed off. They were sad. They ate everything they could find in the middle of the night. And they woke up in the morning pissed off again. It was an ever-expanding mass and they didn't know how to stop it, or if they should. Anger, the older one reasoned, was better than sadness. They could think. They could laugh. They could push the hurt outward. And so they held onto the rage, and it was sharp and dangerous.

TWO THOUSAND
AND SIXTEEN

FOURTEEN

JESSICA DIDN'T KNOW IF SHE SHOULD CRY OR STORM out of the house or wrap her arms around her grandmother's thin shoulders. The migraine, muted with painkillers, throbbed gently behind her eyes, and she pressed the heels of her hands to her forehead. She looked at the photograph again. Devin looked hard in the eyes, like Granny Beth, but she thought she could see the uncertainty in his smile, as if he knew that his future was wavering and unformed, as if thinking about his grown-up future might be useless. She had seen that look before, with children who had been ill, or who had been home-less and were used to travelling from one thirty-day shelter to another. Donna looked as she did in every photograph ever taken: beatific, sunny, smiling as if this were the most important moment in the history of the world.

"I blamed her," Granny Beth said, her eyes red and damp. "Even though I was never certain that she had kicked him over the edge. I was crying and the rain was so fast and heavy. Who knows what I saw? I blamed her until the end, even though she was only a child then. I couldn't stop. I didn't stop. She begged me to move to Vancouver, to sell this house, but I wouldn't because it was something *she* wanted. I put her in an all-girls' school down the highway, made her take choir, and she hated every second of it. When we agreed never to speak of Devin again, I still blamed her in my thoughts and, whenever she saw me, she knew it. I told her I didn't want to see her unless I had to, and she honoured that. Later, she began sending me letters— she would try to explain the accident or write about how her life was about making sense of the tragedy and creating something good from it. After a while, I simply sent them back unopened. It was only recently, after she phoned to tell me she was dying, that I began reading them again. Death, when you're as old as I am, makes everything else seem small and blameless."

"But was she blameless?" As soon as she said it, Jessica wondered if the answer even mattered.

Granny shook her head. "They were only ten years old. Even if she had pushed him, would she have really known that he would fall all that way? Did she think ahead to what life without him meant? I've spent fifty-seven years trying to explain it to myself. I don't think Donna herself knew if she had meant to hurt him or not. Not then, not later."

Jessica knew Granny was right. What difference did it make? Except that there were two girls, twenty-eight years later, whose deaths should have made a difference and didn't. And her mother's past, this storm-scarred childhood, was where she had started, where she had watched her brother die, where she might have wished for his death and then kicked it into existence. She had loved him. She had tried to love Casey and Jamie too.

"The hardest thing I ever had to do was write to Charles to tell him Devin had died. He never did write me back, but he kept sending his cheques until Donna turned eighteen. He may very well be dead now too. I never tried to find out."

"Mom told me he died when she was little."

"Yes. I never told her differently."

Jessica reached out and turned the picture over. "Do you want me to leave that here?"

Granny Beth looked up and stared. She wiped her eyes with her sleeve and laughed, short and loud. "No. I have plenty of those. They're in a box at the back of my closet. I used to look at them sometimes, but not in many years."

For a moment, Jessica considered telling Granny Beth about Casey and Jamie, about the police investigation and the toll it was taking on Gerry, on her. But as the sunlight shone on her grandmother's sleek white hair, she knew it would be too much. Granny Beth had just told her a story she had never told anyone. A story Donna herself had never allowed to be launched into life. Granny Beth would only wonder if what she had done or not done had started a chain of regrets and mistakes that led to the deaths of two girls who had teetered on the brink of being forgotten. Until now.

After Casey and Jamie had returned home after running away, Donna allowed Jessica to go to her friend Danielle's house by herself. Jessica had been asking for days, but Donna kept saying, "We have to be together, to make the girls feel secure." Jessica had wanted to shout, *What about me? What if I hate this house and those stupid girls?* But she didn't. Finally, Danielle's mother had called Donna, saying that Danielle really needed Jessica to help her through the death of their first kitten.

On the way there, Jessica sang the theme song to *The Littlest Hobo*. When she breathed in, she straightened up as tall as she could.

Just as they had settled on the right clothes for their Barbie dolls, Danielle's older brother came and stood in the doorway to the bedroom. Danielle looked up and rolled her eyes.

"Go away, Jason. We're busy."

"Obviously. Mom just wanted me to tell you that she made some brownies."

Danielle didn't answer, just blew the hair out of her eyes and continued dressing her favourite Barbie in an iridescent teal ball gown. Jessica looked at Jason sideways but was careful to keep her head down so he wouldn't catch her.

"Hey, Jessica, can I ask you a question?"

Jessica almost gasped but managed to swallow her surprise. "Sure."

He leaned forward slightly and dropped his voice. "That Casey girl. Does she have a boyfriend?"

She felt as if she had magically, suddenly shrunk to the size and significance of a field mouse. "I don't know. Why?"

Jason stuffed his hands into his jean pockets and shrugged. "No reason. I just heard she was sort of going out with Scott and maybe that new kid from the Island." He turned around and took a step down the hall. "I hear a lot of things about her. When you talk to her, tell her to watch her reputation. Bad things happen to pretty girls like that."

Danielle threw a Barbie shoe at her brother, hitting him in the shoulder. "Get out of here. You're disgusting."

Jessica felt stupid and young, and pushed the doll she was holding under the bed until she could no longer see it. Danielle sighed and stood up.

"We can go into my mom's room, if you want. She lets me play with her makeup as long as I wash my hands first." When Jessica didn't say anything, Danielle touched her on the shoulder. "Don't mind him. He's just gross. Brothers are like that."

It took an hour and a plate of brownies for her to forget the heavy wave of disappointment that Jason, with his blue eyes and floppy hair, had found Casey pretty and worth thinking about. She was new and dangerous with her black hair and long eyes. Jessica was Jessica. Solid around the middle. Skin and hair and eyes the colour of two-hour-old dishwater. When she walked home again in the fading sunlight, she tried to imagine how she might look with pink cheeks and lilac lipstick. Like a little girl who might one day grow up to be pretty. Who could do whatever she wanted, as long as it impressed her mother.

She looked out the window past her grandmother's head. For now, Jessica could keep her own secrets.

"You want to leave, don't you? Stay. Stay and come for a walk with me. It's a shame to waste a lovely morning." Granny Beth tucked her hair behind her ears and pressed her lips into a smile.

"Sure, Granny. We'll go for a walk." Jessica stood up and offered her grandmother her arm.

Granny Beth stared at Jessica's body, her eyes travelling down, then up. "Are you wearing your mother's clothes?"

"Yes," she said. She didn't want to explain the fight with Trevor and the sleepless night she had spent in her parents' house, so she just laughed, one hand pulling on the red knit tassels hanging from the hem of Donna's sweater.

"Well, you must really miss her, then. I'll never understand why Donna insisted on looking like she was woven out of bran." Granny Beth stood up and put her hand on Jessica's arm. Steady.

Before they turned into the hall, Jessica looked one more time out the patio doors. The wire fence was no longer there, replaced years ago by a wrought iron barricade. In the morning sunlight, the rocks were benign and simple, just shades of grey dotted with moss and lichen. She wondered how Granny Beth could live here so long, watching the same landscape change in small, incremental ways that added up to almost nothing. That cliff was where Devin had slipped and fell, where he had skidded, grasping and afraid, onto the hard-edged rocks below before rolling into the cold black ocean, his sister standing above him. This was where Granny Beth had grieved and where she was grieving again, now. But then, Jessica understood that people became tangled in their sadness, that the constant reminder of loss could also be a reminder of love, even if it was love that had long since passed. Gerry was no different. And neither was she.

She and Granny Beth stepped out the front door and took the path through the woods, where they could hear but not see the ocean throwing itself against the rocks.

Jessica lay in her childhood bed and stared at her childhood ceiling. She had no idea what time it was, only that it had been daylight for hours already. She could smell herself in the room, as if she were under the covers with a sweatier, heavier Jessica, who had eaten cheese at midnight and wiped her mouth on the sleeve of her pyjamas. Slowly, she peeled back the quilt and sat up, running her hands through her long, tangled hair.

It had been three days since she had left her apartment, two since she had driven with Chris to Grouse Mountain. She hadn't told Gerry about her visit with Granny Beth or the photograph with Devin. While they were eating dinner last night, she thought about asking if he knew any of this, if Donna had ever told him about the brother she lost. But

Jessica and Gerry talked about the first season of *True Detective* over their microwaved chicken pot pie as Brahms played on the radio. She told herself that if he did know, if there was any way he could explain her mother further, he would. The lack of answers consumed him too.

Jessica hadn't called Trevor either or answered any of his calls. Instead, she had let her mind circle and circle over every conversation she could remember, as if she were looking for a crack, a tiny hole he had left unfilled that would mean he had somehow let the cheating in, and therefore she had done nothing wrong when she had fucked the detective who was investigating her family. She thought of the time Trevor had told her about his childhood friend who had died of the flu. That time he had sung the entire soundtrack of *The Sound of Music*, just to prove he could. His early morning whispers in her ear, describing the previous night's dream.

They had talked about having children only once. After they had been living together for a month, Jessica had turned to him as they lay in bed and asked, "Should we have a baby?"

She didn't know why she asked him like this. She could have said, *Do you want to have a baby,* or *Sometimes I think about having babies,* but instead she asked him if they should, as if she knew he would have the right answer just waiting, curled underneath his tongue.

"Do you think the world needs more children?"

Of course, she thought. *Of course that's what he would say.* She drew an invisible circle on the middle of his chest. "Not necessarily. But it wouldn't be just any child. It would be our child."

Trevor sighed and ran his hand through his unruly hair. "I hear you. But think about how many kids you see every day who are unwanted. If we really wanted to do some good, we'd adopt one of them."

Jessica was quiet. Those children whose faces she looked at Monday to Friday were broken or scarred and glued back together haphazardly. Their pasts were tangible, erupting whenever a little girl touched herself the way her stepfather had done, or whenever a little boy punched a classmate in the genitals. These were the children she and Trevor could adopt. She pulled the covers up to her chin.

"I don't really want babies. I just wanted to know what you thought." As the words tumbled out, she wasn't sure if this was what she meant. It wasn't so much that she wanted children, but she wanted to know the possibility was there, that a man who cared so much for the rest of the world could care for a skinny, mewling infant with his chin and her nose. She wanted to know that he loved her so deeply that he would have babies with her, despite himself. Despite what was good for the planet or society or his own ideologies. Instead, he had told her no, even before she had had a chance.

Trevor smiled. "You're too smart to join the mommy brigade anyway." And he kissed her, pulling her body to him as the sun thickened behind the blinds. She thought, *He's right. Of course, he's right.*

Remembering Trevor was easier than phoning him. It was easier than thinking about Chris, even though all she wanted was to close her eyes and remember the way his chest felt under her palms and the looseness of his face when he came. But thinking about all of that was tangled up with present-day Trevor and how Chris wasn't him and how maybe that was what made her want him in the first place.

She didn't want to think about Granny either, or about the child who had died but whose presence had hovered beside Donna no matter what. They had been born together, touched each other without meaning to, looked at each other and seen their own features—re-ordered and re-angled but still the same—looking back at them. Twinship was something magical, something that compelled myth and witchery and the mutterings of old women. What was it like to be joined by flesh, to never know a moment without the breath of someone else just like you but different? How long did they believe they were the same person? Jessica pulled on the ends of her pony-tail until she felt sharp prickles in her scalp. After her mother had chased Devin to the edge of the rocks, put her foot on his chest and watched him sliding through the dark and down toward the sea, did she feel as if she were falling too? Did she know what it felt like to plummet through salty air, to slice through wind knowing you were going to die? She knew. Of course, she knew. She had relived that moment throughout her life, walked up hiking trails with Devin dragging behind her, still attached.

Jessica let go of her hair and moaned. It was easier not to think, but she couldn't even manage that.

Sitting on the bed, she held her phone to her ear and called her boss. "Karen? It's Jess. I hate to call you on a Sunday, but I don't think I can make it into the office tomorrow." She flipped through one of her father's old copies of *National Geographic* as Karen murmured vague reassurances about grieving and accumulated vacation days. This had happened last Thursday and Friday and now today. After she hung up, she knew she would cook breakfast, lunch and dinner for her father, drink wine and sit on the deck, watching the sun disappear west-ward behind the mountain, the house hunched in shadow. She was glumly satisfied with this.

Every two minutes, despite herself, she thought the same thing: *My mother lost her twin. She might have killed him.* When Granny Beth had said that Donna was trying to create good,

Jessica had known it was true. Everything her mother had cooked or said or grew was for the specific purpose of atonement. She had been the reason Devin was running outside on the wet rocks. She had been the one who could have saved him but might have pushed him instead. So she had to be the one to make up for his missing life. She brought strange children into her home. She saved them. She gave back the years she had watched fall from a cliff into the ocean. She had meant to do good, and it had been working.

Until Casey and Jamie arrived.

They had picked and scratched, peeling back the shell Donna had grown over her younger, guilt-ridden self. Underneath, they had found the girl who had let her rage chase her brother to his death. They had reminded her of Granny Beth, who was cruel, intentionally and unintentionally, who had created a home where anger simmered low until it boiled over, catastrophically. They had reminded her of Devin, of the love and hate that had knotted her and her brother together, even now. They had picked a cavity big enough that all of this came bubbling out. And whatever happened, happened tragically. Jessica stared at the quilt and remembered one night. A night she had forgotten about on purpose.

Ten-year-old Jessica woke and sat up, eyes open wide in the dark. She pressed her hand against her chest, feeling the skitter of her heart underneath the skin. There were noises. She could hear them seeping through the walls.

She stood up and tiptoed to the door. She turned the knob, holding her breath, hoping the slow separation of the door from its frame would be silent or at least not so loud that whomever was moving up and down the hall would hear it. An inch of space now. Jessica exhaled. Six. She cocked her head and looked out.

None of the lights were on, not even the one on her mother's desk on the landing, which Donna sometimes left on if Gerry was working late. The air gently blowing in from the open bathroom window was cool and tinged with damp, the sort of night air that foretold a rainstorm in the morning. Jessica could just make out the pictures hanging in the hall and the potted rubber plant at the end, next to her parents' bedroom door.

Maybe she had been dreaming. Maybe there was nothing to worry about.

But then she felt a sharp breeze, a stinging gust that closed her eyes. When she opened them again, her arms, tense and unmoving, were covered in goosebumps. She heard their voices and the rustle of plastic. They were at the other end of the hall, standing by the stairs.

"How is this going to work?"

"Look. I found some bologna in the fridge. And pickles. Let's take it to the bedroom, before anyone wakes up."

"Case? I didn't mean the food."

"Do I have to go over this again? We'll just have to be careful. We can take my stuff over next weekend, or sooner if we skip school."

"Does it have to be his place? Can't we take the stuff to Mom's?" Jamie sounded scared. Little. "Don't you remember what happened last time?"

"This time will be different. We'll be safe, I promise."

"But *I'm* going back to Mom's later. Right?"

Casey let out a breath. "Yes, of course. Once they stop looking for us, we'll take you to Mom's, like you just got tired of living on the street. You'd be going back there anyway, once this foster shit is all sorted out. But no one will allow to me to live with *him*, unless they don't know and just think we've run away." She stopped for a minute and Jessica could hear her finger tapping the wall. "I promised him, James. He just got his own apartment and everything. You have to help me."

"Yes," Jamie said. "I know."

Jessica stared at the dark bulk of her bed and dresser. They were planning another escape, a permanent one—Jamie to their mother's house, Casey somewhere else. Her head pounded. But she stood up straight, so quickly she stumbled into the door jamb. Her mother was coming, she could feel it.

"What are you plotting, girls?"

For a moment, no one spoke. No one had turned on any lights. All Jessica could hear was the breathing of three people, the dampness of air being cycled in and out and in again.

"I asked you a question."

It was Jamie who answered. "We were just hungry. So we were going to get a snack, that's all."

"I could smell it from my bedroom. You like my husband's junk food, do you?" Jessica had never heard her mother's voice like this, sharp and mean, the way Granny Beth some-times sounded on the phone. "I don't suppose you're going to tell me what else you were talking about."

"We don't have to tell you anything." Casey's words were tough enough, but she spoke quietly, as if she were tired, or scared.

"No, you don't. I might have cared once, but I really don't give a shit now." Jessica pushed down on her chest with her hand so she wouldn't gasp. "Since you don't like talking to me and would rather eat, why don't we go down to the kitchen and see what else you might like?"

"No, we're fine. We'll just go back to bed."

"Come on now, girls. I insist. As a matter of fact, there is quite a lot of food in the fridge that is on the verge of going bad, and it would really help me out if you two would eat it. Since you've been so hungry lately."

"We're full."

"Did you not hear me? I insist. I will sit in the kitchen and watch you eat all the leftover and dried-up food you can handle. And then, you can throw up and eat some more. Come with me."

Jessica heard the girls start to cry, the deep breaths that meant they were still trying to prevent the sobs from coming, even though they knew they never could.

"Why are you crying? It will be fine. It will only take a couple of hours. As long as you apply yourselves."

Through the crack in the door, Jessica saw her mother push Casey and Jamie toward the stairs. At first, the girls dug their heels in and tried to push back, but Donna bent her head and said, "If you don't, I will tell the police that you have been communicating with the disgusting man who got you pregnant, and then we'll see how well your plan works out. Don't fight me, girls. I've had lots of experience dealing with brats like you."

Jessica stepped back and closed her bedroom door. For the rest of the night, she didn't sleep. She huddled in her bed, covers over her ears so she wouldn't hear any of the noises coming from downstairs. She knew, with all the certainty her brain could gather, that her mother was doing something terrible, but it was the middle of the night, so maybe she hadn't heard or seen anything and she was dreaming, lying sleeplessly in a dream house just like the real one. Maybe in the morning it would be forgotten and, if glimmers of this appeared during the day, she could dismiss them as nonsensical and absurd. Jessica felt tears at the corners of her eyes but she didn't know why she was crying. She wasn't sad. She was just scared shitless. She ran those two words over in her head, the grown-up coarseness of them heavy and deliberate. Scared shitless. That's what it was.

Jessica walked down the hall to the bathroom, a towel balled under her arm, shaking off the sticky coarseness of the memory. In this hallway, she thought her footsteps sounded like her mother's, like that heavy tread she had always thought of as clumsy and loving, all at once. *I come from a family of psychopaths.* She thought of how little she cared about Trevor's feelings anymore, about how she never seemed to do any good at work, about how she felt no regret about the night in the car. *That's the problem, right there. Maybe I'm a psychopath too.*

Naked, Jessica pulled back the shower curtain and looked down at the blue tub. On the bottom were dark green rubber flowers, stuck down so that the young Jessica and all those foster kids wouldn't slip as they washed their hair. They were now peeling at the edges and outlined in black mildew. Jessica bent down and tried to pry one up with her fingernail, but it wouldn't budge. She sniffed. It smelled like feet.

Turning, Jessica sat down on the bath mat, back against the wall of the tub. Why hadn't her mother gotten rid of those rubber flowers twenty years ago, when everybody else's mothers were renovating their bathrooms? Instead, she had left them to collect mould and moisture until they could no longer be separated from the tub at all and had grown sticky little strings of muck like glue. She bent her head and rested it on her bare knees.

There was one summer when there had been no foster children and Gerry had been busy with a criminal trial for one of his clients. Every day Jessica and Donna ate breakfast together on the back deck, silently watching the ants hatching in the lawn and flying in clouds over the fence and down the alley. The breeze smelled like drying grass, like things had stopped growing just so they could rest in the sun. Afterward, Donna would turn to Jessica and ask, "What should we do today?" Jessica didn't suggest anything outrageous, so Donna granted her wishes, driving them to the beach or Granville Island or just letting Jessica lie on a blanket in the grass, watching the clouds blow and morph as the wind sped up and slowed down. If she fell asleep, she would wake up in her room, tucked into her bed, with a glass of water on the nightstand beside her.

Jessica wiped her nose on the back of her hand. In her head, Devin's death was knotted together with the deaths of Casey and Jamie. Her mother's guilt and desperation to assuage that guilt had led to how hard she tried with the girls. She wanted to save them, like every other child who had lived in their house, but she wanted to save them *more*. They were more damaged, more resistant, more angry. Donna had tried harder, had grown just as angry, and then released her rage into the house. She had been trying to build a life that would put Devin's death to rest, but it had accomplished exactly the opposite.

Casey and Jamie, tangled up in their cruelties, both small and big, had reminded her mother of Devin. Of the way she had loved him and he had loved and hurt her. It was Devin, clinging to her, who had made her hate those girls, made her fear them, made her wish they were dead.

The only sound in the room was the whirring of the bathroom fan. In here, with the tiles and tight walls, she couldn't hear her father, or the occasional car outside, or even the starlings shrieking as they pecked at the moss in the lawn. In the silence, she heard Granny Beth's voice. *I didn't stop. I blamed her until the end.* She didn't need to blame Donna. She would have blamed herself anyway. Like all mothers, good or bad.

Poor Ginny, Jessica thought as she stood up, knees creaking. She stepped into the blue tub and turned on the hot water.

Ginny must still wonder. Jessica stared at the spray of water hitting her in the chest. *Ginny would still be alive.*

In a flash, she wanted to shout, *The truth matters.* All this time, Jessica had wanted the truth, even though she knew it would turn out ugly and frightening and almost impossible to comprehend. Ginny must have spent years spinning the possibilities in her mind—from homelessness to prostitution to death to new identities. The truth would end that. She would no longer be a mother stuck in a dizzying game of *maybe this* or *maybe that.* Together, she and Jessica might be able to cobble together the truth, or, at the very least, a kind of truth that fit the missing spaces just well enough.

Jessica soaped and scrubbed as quickly as she could, banging her elbow on the tiles as she rushed. She hadn't done any laundry and her dirty clothes were hanging limply over the towel rack, but it didn't matter. Ginny wouldn't care what she looked like.

She was easy to find. One online search yielded her home address, a basement suite in a beige stucco house in the southeast, just around the corner from a strip of Vietnamese noodle houses, bubble tea cafés and liquidation outlets. Another search turned up a short obituary for Bill on a longshoreman's reunion website, dated 1989, the year after the girls had disappeared. An hour later, Jessica sat in her car across the street, staring at a white iron fence. There was no lawn, only a thin layer of gravel with a stained water fountain stuck in the middle. A squat Chow paced the upstairs front porch, his black tongue dangling out of the side of his mouth. Jessica didn't like dogs. She thought she could smell his mange through the open driver's side window.

She didn't know what she was waiting for. All the way over, she had been practising what she was going to say. *I have news. I'm so sorry. I knew them. I lived with them.* But as she had pulled her car over, all those words withered on her tongue. They were insubstantial. They didn't begin to explain what she knew, how she knew it and why she was here. Ginny had lost her children. Maybe she thought they might still be alive. Maybe she sat at home every night with the door unlocked, waiting for Casey and Jamie to burst in, mouths spilling over with tales of adventure and danger and triumph. Or maybe she knew, with a mother's certainty, that the girls were dead, and spent her days imagining all the different ways they could have jumped off a bridge or been murdered by a pervert who preyed on teenaged runaways.

How could Jessica, the daughter of the woman who had, at the very least, failed to protect the girls, walk in and expect communal crying or gratitude or catharsis? No, better to wait until she knew, really knew, what she needed to say.

I think my mother really tried. She meant well, until she didn't. I'm so sorry.

In the rear-view mirror, she saw a small Chinese woman with short hair. She carried two cloth shopping bags in one hand and wore a light blue jacket. She walked with her head down, looking only at the progress of her feet and the pavement below. She was like many women Jessica had seen shopping at the Chinese malls in Vancouver. Efficient, sensibly dressed, free of makeup. But even as they walked with set faces and purposeful steps, there was always a hunch in the shoulders and neck, as if their bodies were folding into the air, intent on making themselves as invisible as possible. Jessica could guess what had happened to each of these women hurrying from alley to alley in Chinatown or waiting for the bus stop at Main and Hastings to make them walk like this. She felt as though cold rain were dripping down her back.

Jessica straightened in her seat and put a hand on the door. It had to be now. Or she would never do it.

As the woman turned into the front path, Jessica jumped out of the car and hurried to the gate. She caught up and the woman's bobbed head turned back and looked Jessica in the face. She had the same long eyes as Casey, but hers were turned down at the edges. She might have been pretty once, but Jessica doubted she had ever believed it.

"Ginny?" she whispered.

"Yes?" She tried to pull her jacket closed, as if she needed the protection.

"My name is Jessica Campbell."

Ginny frowned and began to back away.

"Maybe you remember my mother. Her name was Donna."

"Donna," Ginny said quietly. "The foster mother." She paused and looked up at the overcast sky. "The police were here last week."

Of course. Jessica felt stupid. Of course, the police had come to tell Ginny that they had found her daughters. Of course, she already knew they were dead. She half-turned her body, ready to walk away at this very moment without one extra word, just a broken conversation hanging in the spring air, dissipating as both women began to forget. But then, Ginny placed a hand on her wrist.

"Is there more?" she asked. "Do you know what happened?"

Jessica stopped moving. Ginny's eyes were wide open, like she couldn't look away.

"Is it all right if I come inside?"

Ginny nodded and opened the gate, waving for Jessica to follow her. They took a side path around the house and came to a narrow white door lit by a 60-watt bulb in a cheap aluminum shade. Ginny opened the door and switched on a light.

"Can I get you some tea?" She slid off her sneakers and stepped into a pair of terry cloth slippers. She walked toward the tiny kitchen. Jessica stood by the door. The living room was neat, with space for one loveseat and a low coffee table. A table with two chairs had been pushed up next to the kitchen counter. Every surface was clear. Even the fluorescent lights mounted on the ceiling were dust-free.

"No, thanks. I'm fine."

"Have a seat." Ginny pointed to the dining chairs and sat down herself, sighing as she leaned back.

"Do you work close by?" Jessica had no idea what she was saying. She just needed to hear Ginny talk about herself for a while. She needed to hear that she was all right. That losing her daughters hadn't ruined her.

"No. I work at that big private girls' school on the west side. I'm a lunch lady." And she laughed as she touched the top of her head. "I wear a hairnet."

"Do you enjoy it?"

"It's okay. I like the students. I like being around young girls." A tremor moved through Ginny's face. "You're not here to talk about my job though, are you?"

Jessica thought she might throw up or, more precisely, that her stomach might leap out of her body through her skin and empty its contents on the linoleum underneath their feet. She gripped the edge of the table with both hands.

"I've been trying to find out what happened."

Ginny said nothing, only stared at Jessica's face.

"I haven't found much, only the foster care files. And those were mostly about their lives before they came to live with us. I don't need to tell you about that."

Ginny began to shake. Her face contracted, as if conflicting thoughts were blowing through the skin and muscle, pushing at the flesh in waves. She touched her cheeks, her fingertips just resting on her closed eyes. After a minute, she looked up and then sat on her hands. "Yes. I remember everything."

"I'm sorry. I'm upsetting you. Maybe I should just go." Jessica leaned forward and put her hand on Ginny's shoulder. After a moment, Ginny shook it off.

"Don't go. Tell me what you know."

Jessica told Ginny about Casey and Jamie's arrival at their home, how they ended up hating Donna and had acted out. She told her that Donna had been trying to save the girls because she had lost a twin brother when she was a child. As she listened to herself, Jessica realized that she had found nothing conclusive, nothing that pointed directly to how the girls had died or why or with whom. When she was done, she looked at the kitchen table, listening to the emptiness her words had left behind.

"I used to see the girls every week at my mother's apartment in Chinatown. They told me many things about your mother, things they hated. I told them over and over again to behave and just get through it, one day at a time, and soon we could live together again. The last time," she smiled, a tight, small smile, "we talked about New Kids on the Block."

"Did they say anything that was unusual, anything you remember specifically?"

Ginny started to cry, not even bothering to cover her face or wipe her nose. "No. There was nothing strange at all. When the police asked me, all those years ago, if I thought they had run away, I said no. But the officers kept saying that's what probably happened until I started to believe it. I started to think of Casey and Jamie as runaways, even though, in the beginning, I knew it couldn't be true." Her eyes were open and fixed on Jessica's face, but even Jessica knew that Ginny wasn't looking at her. The grief was an opaque veil and Ginny sat in her own particular dark.

Quickly, Ginny reached out and held one of Jessica's hands. "Did she kill them? Do you think your mother did it?"

Jessica could swear she felt her mother's curls brushing her cheek then, but when she reached up to brush them away, she felt tears instead. *Fuck you, Mom*, she thought. *Fuck you for making me do this*.

"I don't know. I hope she didn't but every time I think about it, I think she must have."

After a few minutes, Ginny blinked hard and released Jessica's hands. "Why them? Why not you instead?" She looked away. "I'm sorry. I shouldn't have said that."

"It's okay."

"My daughters weren't monsters, you know. They used to be happy. We used to make them happy." Ginny folded her arms over her chest. "There were nights when I imagined them being beaten or starving to death in a dirty basement somewhere. When the police came last week and told me they were dead, I was relieved. It was like I could walk by myself again, instead of walking with both of them on my back."

Ginny stared at the wall behind Jessica's head. She said nothing for several minutes and Jessica wondered if she should just leave. But then Ginny said, "I used to think it was all his fault."

Jessica thought she might have heard wrongly, so she leaned forward and asked, "What did you say?"

"Wayne," Ginny said louder. "The man who got Casey pregnant. I used to blame him."

"Of course."

"But as I got older, he seemed less important. I had more time to think backward and backward again. It never ended, how far back I could think to get to the one thing, the one day that started all of this." Ginny turned and looked at Jessica, her eyelids heavy and red. "First, it was Bill moving out, then it was him losing his job, then it was our marriage. Not too long ago, I decided that trying to find the one person or the one minute that could have changed our lives was pointless. So I stopped. And then they told me the girls were dead. I haven't done much thinking since then."

"I'm sorry." Jessica tried to remember how many times she had said those words and not meant them. If she could, she would take all those moments back just so this one conversation would have the density that signified real sorrow, the weight of true, kindred grief.

Ginny didn't respond, but nodded her head with her eyes on the table, as if she were agreeing with a voice Jessica couldn't hear. Wayne. Jessica hadn't thought of him much and had only considered him as the man who had victimized Casey. But as she sat in Ginny's apartment, her bare feet on the cold linoleum floor, she wondered if that was really what it felt like. Casey had loved him. He might have been a sexual predator or a manipulator or just a man who had made a series of bad, bad decisions.

"Do you know what happened to Wayne?"

"He moved up north to see if he could get into logging, but he didn't last long. He was a city boy, after all. The last time I heard anything about him, he was still living with his parents and was working at the mall downtown in maintenance. But that was ten years ago. Sometimes," Ginny paused and picked a hair off the table, "I think I want to talk to him."

"Why?"

"He's probably the only one left who remembers. My mother is dead. Bill too."

"How did Bill die?" Jessica asked quietly.

"Accident. They said he was hit by a bus crossing the street." Ginny stood and steadied herself on the lip of the kitchen counter. "But if you ask me, he stepped into the road on purpose. He felt a lot of guilt. It was just as well, I suppose. His trial was supposed to start the next day."

Before Jessica could say anything else, Ginny slid past her and opened the door. "I need to be alone now."

"Wait. Let me give you my card." Jessica reached into her purse and pulled out her nondescript Ministry business card. "If you ever want to talk, or need anything, my cell number is on the bottom."

Ginny shrugged and stared at the strip of gravel and footpath outside. Jessica backed out, clutching the hem of Donna's sweater. "Goodbye," she said. Ginny was silent as she shut the door.

FIFTEEN

JESSICA SAT DRESSED FOR WORK IN HER COMPACT, efficient car, her practical, roomy bag on the passenger seat beside her. Chris was in her head—his face, his one hand undoing the hooks of her bra, the painful slowness of his movements when she thought she wanted him to be fast but he somehow knew she really didn't. Here, in a hot car, staring at the front door to her mouse-brown, low-rise office building, she wanted to hold him in her cupped palms. She wanted him to be small enough to fit, or maybe she just wanted to be big enough to contain him, for her life to have a space he could slip into.

But it wasn't possible. And it wasn't what she actually wanted anyway. He had filled a role for one night. He was the other man, the opposite of Trevor, the man who had appeared on her parents' front step unbidden and self-exposed, and she had been unable to refuse what had seemed like an outland-ishly generous gift. She didn't love him. But she couldn't stop thinking that she could if circumstances were different. And this was the thought that hurt.

Her mother was dead. Casey and Jamie were dead. Chris was trying to find out why and so was she. They had fucked and it was good. The rest of it—the dark, swirling mass of the work they had to do, how she was pulling back layers of her family's bad decisions and subsequent traumas—created no room for her and Chris to be together again. If this were a romance novel, Jessica would have stopped reading and tossed the book into her closet.

She had said yes because she thought she didn't need to care. But she did. And her feelings were like ravens with one clipped wing, flying in concentric circles, calling to each other in a conversation that was really just a series of echoes saying the same fucking thing. *You can't. You can't. You can't.*

Finally, Jessica let go of the steering wheel, grabbed her purse from the passenger seat and climbed out of the car, making sure to press the lock button on her key fob. She took an elevator to the fifth floor and walked down a short hallway to her cubicle, where she sat and turned on her computer. Waiting for her email to load, she took in the piles of unfinished work that had accumulated in her absence. Photos of children waiting to be adopted. Binders from other offices, with children from Dease Lake or Trail or Nanaimo. Old files that needed to be archived. Jessica slumped in her chair and wiped her nose on the sleeve of her peach sweater. Another one of Donna's, embroidered with nubby red poppies. She couldn't remember if she'd combed her hair this morning.

She picked up a stack of photos. Each child wore a different expression. Some grinned widely, others looked away from the camera, corners of their mouths tucked in tightly.

One little boy stared straight at the camera, a defiant tilt to his chin. *Go ahead,* he seemed to be saying, *adopt me. See if you can handle it.* The corresponding files were on her desk, but she knew without looking what they said.

History of abuse. Fetal alcohol syndrome. Oppositional defiant disorder. Attachment issues.

It wasn't hard to write each child's story in a way that obscured the truth. She couldn't lie, of course, but she could make every biography seem just needy or normal or adorable enough. Potential parents read her words and gazed at the pictures and felt the child's arms around their necks, the magic warmth of child's breath on their ears. Once they said yes, then it was over. She could move the file to someone else's desk and start all over again, with a new set of hurt and aggressive and emotionally cold children. Whether the parents could handle the challenge was something she didn't need to consider. Before today, this relieved her.

She tapped on her keyboard.

"Justin is a four-year-old boy who fears and hates men. He was physically abused in his birth home and has lived with three foster families. He has tortured small animals and cannot be trusted with cutlery. He needs a home that can contain his rage and minimize the possibility that he will one day become an abuser himself. He enjoys water sports."

No surprises. But probably no parents either. Jessica laid her face down on her desk and shut her eyes. She thought she heard Donna's voice. *If I hadn't chased him, things might have been different. If he were alive, things might have been different. I tried to save everyone. But I couldn't.*

When Jessica sat up, brushing the hair out of her eyes, Parminder was leaning on the edge of her desk, arms crossed.

"I thought you were asleep," she said, patting Jessica on the top of her head.

"I wish."

"Come on. You know you can't live without all this glamour." Parminder waved her arm at the rows of cubicles and laminate desks.

Jessica laughed. "I told Karen I would be back tomorrow, but I woke up at six thirty, so here I am. Lucky you, getting me one day early."

Parminder leaned in. "Did you find anything useful about those girls?"

"Not really. I mean, I'm still looking, you know?" Jessica shrugged and began to flip through a green binder to her right.

"I've been thinking about this a lot lately and I just keep coming back to the same thing." Parminder leaned in even further so the fabric on her blouse was brushing Jessica's cheek. "Donna couldn't have killed those girls. It's just impossible. She was a foster mother. She was basically a *professional mother*. I mean, I know she wasn't perfect, but she was as close to a saint as we get around here."

Jessica nodded and reached for a pen.

"Your whole family is made up of people who just want to help. How proud was your mother of you? You're a social worker, your job is to help kids. The police are lunatics if they think anyone in your family had anything to do with this. Maybe I should call them myself, volunteer my services as an investigator on the case." Parminder laughed and straightened up. "You're following in your mother's footsteps, you know. Good for you."

Jessica stared at Parminder's brown eyes, so wide open, so full of earnest goodwill. "Yes, that's exactly what I've been doing. Following in my mother's footsteps." *How stupid*, she thought. *How utterly, completely stupid.*

All her working life, she had been trying to help people but ended up failing. She had been trying to be her mother, to be the woman who always knew the right thing to say, or the right casserole to bake, or the right time to start weeding someone else's garden because they had been too sick all spring. But instead Jessica had taken children into foster care who should have stayed home, or left children with parents when they should have been removed. Now, she sold damaged kids to desperate families and together the confusion only grew, leaving children who ran away or parents who began to drink their fears into oblivion. In all this time, she had assumed it was the system's fault, that her failures had to do with the rules they had to follow or the lack of resources, but now she knew it had been her all along. She wanted to be her mother but there was always a part of her that knew it wasn't possible. There was a part of her that didn't want to help anyone at all, that just wanted to stand somewhere empty—an unused path in an unnamed green belt, a mall at dawn—and feel the uninhabited air lick at the skin on her arms and neck. No certainty, no feeling that she was only following the smell—thick and musky, warm and yeasty—her mother had always left behind.

And now, she knew. Her mother had failed too. Spectacularly.

If Jessica kept her job, how much damage would she leave behind? Who else would she sleep with, just to feel that she was teetering on the edge, living out the danger that she spent her whole career trying to subvert? Looking at Parminder's face, she straightened her shoulders, then reached for her purse.

"Where are you going?" Parminder asked as Jessica pushed past her into the hall.

"I'm going to see Karen. I'm quitting right now."

"What? Why?"

Jessica turned and took Parminder's hand in hers. "It's the right time, Parm. If I stay any longer, I might just go insane."

At the end of the hall, Karen's office door was open. It was going to be easy. For the first time in years, Jessica felt like she could dance her way across the industrial-grade carpet. She didn't even take one last look around.

———

It was easy for Jessica to say to herself, *I'm going home.* It was even easy to say, *I'm going home to pack my stuff and leave my boyfriend,* because those words, said in a steadfast voice in her car with the windows up, meant very little. They were a plan, an outline, but didn't describe the messiness of trying to sneak in when Trevor wasn't home, or of calculating more boxes than she thought she would need because she didn't want to go back twice. In the car, she didn't allow herself to question her use of *home,* when, in truth, the apartment Jessica had been living in had ceased to be a home the very moment seven weeks ago when she had looked at Trevor and felt an unsettling in her stomach. The sight of him didn't make her sick exactly, but the image of him standing in the small kitchen in a pair of stretched-out underpants seemed to pass right through her, leaving a visual trail on her insides that made her slightly dizzy and forced her eyes closed.

Jessica dragged a pile of empty boxes up the stairs and into the hall outside her apartment. She stared at her key ring for a half-second, trying to remember which key opened the door. Slowly, she turned the lock and peered in. No one home. Thank fuck.

Quickly, she began emptying out her half of the closet and the two shelves she used in the medicine cabinet. She was grateful she had never accumulated much, that most of the art (photos taken by journalists in war zones, usually of empty-eyed civilians with dirt or flies dotting their faces) and furniture were Trevor's. Once upon a time, she had meant to decorate with throw cushions and maybe some wallpaper, but never got around to it. After a while, she didn't notice the dun-coloured beanbag chairs and second-hand television bench. They were just *there*. As she had been.

Jessica pulled books off the shelf in the living room and dropped them into a box, enjoying the thud they made as they landed. She began to sing to herself, an off-key version of "Moondance" by Van Morrison. This was the last time she was going to look out this window at the alley and the Dumpsters, smell the rotting bananas from the produce market around the corner. She laughed and tossed a copy of *The Wealth of Nations* over her shoulder.

"Jess? What are you doing?"

Jessica turned around and saw Trevor standing in the open doorway, bicycle helmet still on his head. She took a step back but there was nowhere to go. She had planned to leave a note. It was more humane than a text, but not as messy as a face-to-face explanation. *Fuck.*

"Hi."

Trevor pulled off his helmet and placed it on the kitchen counter. Slowly, he turned to look at her. "Are you packing?"

"Yes," she said quietly. Then, she stepped forward, trying to smile. "I think it's time for us to be apart. I've been at my dad's so much anyway, and all that time alone made me think about what I want from life. I need to just be by myself, to figure things out. And you deserve someone who is really ready for a long-term relationship, you know?" Jessica knew that she was uttering every break-up cliché she had ever read in a fashion magazine, but it was all she could think of. She hoped Trevor wouldn't notice.

"I'm not stupid, Jess. What's the real reason?"

It was only yesterday that she had said to herself, *The truth matters*. It did, she knew that, but standing here with a paperback edition of *Sense and Sensibility* in her hand, she knew that speaking the truth would bring it into existence, give it a size and form that Trevor would recognize and never forget.

"It's not just about you, or us. I quit my job this morning. I just—" she paused and looked up at Trevor, so tall and lean, an unwavering manifestation of what it meant to be right and good. "I just can't be part of your world anymore." Before he could breathe in or respond, she said, quickly, "And I slept with someone else."

For a moment, she wanted to take the words back. Then maybe they could be the way they were, when Trevor was just enough certainty to make her feel like she was unafraid and her place was permanent and purposeful. They fit together then. But she remembered, when the moment passed, that Chris was the push she had been looking for.

He hadn't moved. "Who?"

"You've never met him. It doesn't matter."

"How many times?"

"Only once." Strange, how the number of times was important, how having sex only once made a difference in the calculation of betrayal. Jessica almost smiled.

Trevor walked toward her. "I'm not a traditionalist. You know that. If you say it was a one-time thing, then we can work it out."

She stared at his thin face, the ears that stuck out farther than she thought a grown man's should. "Why are you not angry?"

"I love you. My world has always included you. We work so

well together. We know what's really important. Only you, Jess. Only you understand this."

Jessica wanted to laugh. This was the very thing she needed to leave behind: this earnestness, the idea that one person could be greater than all the rest and change everything. She wondered if Trevor would ever know how ridiculous he was. She didn't want him anymore. Her mind was clear.

"That's what I can't be a part of anymore. I've lived my whole life trying to be my mother and save every last child on this earth. But even she couldn't do it. She *failed*."

"What are you talking about?"

She hadn't planned on explaining anything about Donna or the girls to him, but what difference would it make? Jessica looked down at the floor. "I don't know if she murdered those girls. But it was because of her they died. She didn't protect them like she was supposed to. She didn't act like the grown-up. She let them down. She let their mother down."

On the last day Jessica had seen Casey and Jamie, they ate breakfast together, silently. She had walked to school with Danielle. As she trudged down the front walk, she looked back and could see her mother standing in the living room window, handing the girls their coats and school bags.

At three thirty, when she returned home, Donna wasn't there. An hour later she came back, dumping the car keys on the table by the door. "They must have gone out after school," she said. "I waited for forty-five minutes in that parking lot. Well, this isn't the first time they've taken off." At bedtime that night, the girls still hadn't come home and Donna called the social worker.

By mid-afternoon the next day, everyone assumed that they had run away again. Their coats and school bags were gone, along with the money that Donna kept in a jar in the kitchen for emergencies. The social worker came by for a meeting and to gather up the few pieces of clothing Jamie and Casey had left behind. "You did your best, Donna. Don't worry. We'll find them."

Jessica saw a quick darkness on her mother's face that disappeared as soon as she squinted to look closer. Quietly, Donna said, "I just hope they haven't been abducted."

The social worker nodded as she shifted the plastic bag of clothes from one hand to the other. "The police know about the possibilities. Trust me."

Donna turned and ran a finger across a layer of dust on the hall table. "Of course."

Jessica watched it all. No one asked her any questions. She lay down on the sofa in the living room and felt the air touching her skin—light and empty, free of the girls' hot and sharp breath. She smiled to herself. It was over.

Trevor pulled her hands away from her lap and held them with his long fingers. "I get it, Jess. I'm so sorry." Most of the time, Trevor was cold, a quaking skeleton. But right now, he was warm and steady and if this had happened three months ago she would have laid down on the rug and pulled him over her so that they could sleep, just like that. He cleared his throat and said, "She meant so much to you."

"But do you see? I tried to be just like her, and she failed. All I do is fail. I mean, I even failed you. I can't do it anymore. I won't."

"We can work on it together. We'll go to counselling. This doesn't have to destroy us. You don't have to be a social worker. We can find something else that makes you happier, that fulfills you so none of this happens again." Trevor inched closer. His nose almost touched hers.

Jessica felt herself believing him. Maybe there was another way. Maybe she could still help someone and be good at it.

Maybe she could make up for what her mother did. Maybe one night with another man was simply a small blip in the continuum of their relationship. Trevor wiped his cheeks with the back of his hand and grinned.

"Come on, baby. We could be like superheroes together. Defending the ninety-nine percent. We could be legends."

Jessica balled her hands into fists. She wasn't her mother. She was never going to be. "Sometimes I think you don't even hear yourself," she said. "I don't want to be in this relationship anymore, Trev. I don't want to save the world. Maybe it's petty and small-minded, but I just want to eat chips and watch reality television right now. I'm not a hero. I don't want to be."

Trevor kicked away one of her boxes with his foot. "Well, I'm not a dick but I'm going to sound like one for a minute." He pointed at her. "You need to get your head out of your ass, Jess. All you've been doing is staring at yourself in the mirror thinking about how bad you have it. Get over it. You're not homeless. You've not been gang-raped by child soldiers. You're an upper-class white girl who just thinks about herself and fucks another man at the worst possible time. Go ahead. Leave. I have better things to do than convince you to stay." He stood up and walked to the bedroom, where he closed the door so quietly, Jessica wondered if he had simply disappeared.

In fifteen minutes, she had loaded all the boxes into her car. She pushed her key under the front door and stared at the sliver of light coming from the apartment. He was going to be fine. Tomorrow, he would start writing songs about how she had betrayed him. Two weeks from now, he would pack all of their photos and ticket stubs and gifts in a box and shove it into the back of the closet. In a month, he would join an online dating community. And, maybe, in a year, he wouldn't be angry at her anymore.

It was dark as she drove down the alley and into traffic. She could hear the car tires turning on the road, each revolution propelling her forward—fast. She looked up through the windshield and wondered if she would see transparent, tissue-thin versions of herself floating off into the night air. She was shedding. First work, then the apartment, now Trevor. Soon, she would be down to her very core, even if she didn't know what that looked like yet. She had spent the last nine days trying to unearth who her mother really was because she thought that would lead to how Casey and Jamie had died. But now, as the street lamps lit the smear of grey clouds above her, she finally understood that she would never know. She was driving headlong into a vast, howling future, so empty that it blistered her skin with its cold aridity. She knew enough. Any less and she would have never realized that her life, crafted to be just like her mother's, was foolish and ineffectual. Any more and this feeling of rushing air and bottomless stomach would evaporate, replaced with the weight of knowing, of unalterable truth. Jessica turned on the radio. Taylor Swift. Of course. She sang along. She had never felt so light.

That night, Jessica lay on a thin sofa mattress, an open book beside her on the mismatched sheets. Parminder had made up the bed while Jessica unpacked her overnight bag.

"You can stay as long as you want," she had said, tugging the elastic over a corner. "I know it's small, but it's free." Parminder had laughed loudly. Jessica wasn't sure if she should have joined in.

She pulled the duvet up to her chin and stretched, her foot kicking the leg of a laminate desk. A green light on a folded laptop blinked slowly. Green. Green. Green. The room had no window, only a mirror hanging on the wall, meant, Jessica supposed, to simulate a feeling of space. The light in the ceiling was round and frosted, like a cold fake nipple.

This den, with its thin drywall and oatmeal-coloured carpet, was miraculous to her. The architect who had designed it could never have imagined that this was where Jessica Campbell would strip away her old life and begin, slowly, to construct a new one. This entire building had been developed to maximize square footage and budget and to satisfy the predictably consistent desires of condo buyers. Every unit had granite counters, one and a half bathrooms, a balcony bordered with glass. No one had thought about the first breaths of transformation or the possibilities within windowless dens for chrysalis and birth and progress. Jessica clasped her hands over her stomach and held them tightly. If she let go, she might break into a mad, happy dance.

Her phone rang. She peered at the screen, waiting for it to display the caller's number. It wouldn't be Trevor. He would be at home still, sitting on the floor, wound up tightly in his rage.

Chris Gallo, it said.

"Really?" Jessica whispered. She answered. "Hello?"

"Hi, it's Chris." He spoke slowly, carefully.

"It's eleven o'clock."

Chris stifled a laugh. "I know. It just occurred to me that I haven't talked to you in a while. You know, since the other night. So, how are you?"

"I'm fine."

"Of course, of course. Why wouldn't you be fine?" In the background, Jessica could hear male voices, sloppy and loud.

"Are you drunk?"

Chris snorted. "What? No. Well, maybe a little."

"You're drunk-dialling me. That's hilarious. What are you, fifteen years old?"

"It's not like that. Or maybe it is. I don't know. I was just out with my friends and I started thinking of you." His voice was growing quieter with each word, as if he couldn't quite understand what his brain was making him say. "So I called. Although I probably should have called two days ago. Fuck, I sound ridiculous."

Jessica laughed. "Yes, you sound ridiculous. And drunk. Don't forget drunk."

"I mean, I should call you again tomorrow or something. You know, catch up."

It was the banter of courtship, the careful choosing of words so that they meant nothing and everything at once, so that the surface was easy and funny, but the subtext carried with it the weight of sex and the tumbling of feelings inside the gut. Jessica knew that he was asking her, without saying so, to take his hand if they should ever walk down the street together. He was asking to crawl into her bed at midnight and not leave until daylight shone through the window so they could see, finally, their unguarded faces lined with sleep and barely awake. He was asking her to take him on, this man who was Trevor's opposite but also not, who could swallow her up as Trevor had until she was the police detective's girlfriend, the one who nodded at his stories and kissed his cheeks when he came home, distraught over someone he wasn't able to save.

He wasn't Trevor. But he was. She blinked and was surprised at the tear that spilled out.

She imagined Chris lit by a dim bulb in a crowded bar, each crisp angle made blurry by shadows. His eyes gleamed brown and pulsing and generous and if she were with him right now, she could hold his face with both hands and kiss him, tasting the beer and beef and hot sauce on his tongue. She could bring him here and they could quietly, beautifully touch and fuck and giggle. She could run out and meet him. She could do it. She could.

But as much as she had been trying to forget it, he was still the police officer who was trying to prove that her mother or father had murdered two foster girls and whose relationship with her could very well cost him his career. And she was an unemployed social worker who had just left her boyfriend because she no longer wanted the job or him or anything but the great emptiness that now, finally, surrounded her. As she sat on Parminder's mattress and listened to the hiss of her phone in her hand, she knew that being with Chris would fill up her life again. No, she wanted to run through the space she had created. Alone.

And what she couldn't forget was that she had used him. Without him, she may have never left Trevor. Without him, she may have continued on as she was, hunched over with the weight of her job and her mother and an apartment she hated. She had used him and she knew she didn't need him anymore. She shuddered with the coldness of it all, the dialogic feeling that she could love him, if she tried, but that it wasn't necessary. It was him now, or someone else later, or no one at all.

"I don't think you should call, Chris. Unless we have police business to deal with, maybe we shouldn't talk again. I'm sorry."

He didn't say anything for a minute and all Jessica heard were the rhythmic sounds of a vigorous drinking game. They counted, then they cheered. She smiled.

"You're right," he said finally. "The post-mortem report is supposed to arrive on my desk next Monday. Not that I'm allowed to tell you that."

"Thanks for letting me know."

"You know, if things were different, I would take you out for dinner. Hell, I might even cook for you. It's not all sex in cars, Jess. I can be a gentleman. Really."

"I know."

"Well, goodbye then, Jessica Campbell. Next time, I'll drunk-dial your father instead." They hung up, both laughing.

She felt the weightlessness of the dark. It just barely ruffled the fine hairs on her arm and swept like whispers across her face. Jessica had spent the entire day cultivating this sense of possibility, of runways and hallways waiting to be hurtled through. Finding the truth about her mother didn't matter anymore. Because this—this silent, soulless room—was what she had been waiting for.

But as her thoughts blurred together and she started to fall asleep, Casey's face, as she had seen it in her mother's kitchen twenty-eight years ago, flashed through her head. The girls. What about them? They had disappeared, leaving only a ripple in the space they had once occupied in Jessica's life. No one had understood that the truth might be stranger and more gruesome than just a simple escape from foster care and the birth family that had appeared to be hurting them. The truth—before, during and after—would have meant something to them.

Jessica stared into the dimness. Casey had gambled everything for Wayne. He knew what that felt like. Somewhere in his head, no matter what he was doing or where he was living, he remembered. Jessica sat up and flipped the light switch. The laptop sat on the desk in front of her and she pulled it close, balancing it on her crossed legs. She would have to wait at least one more day for her new beginning.

SIXTEEN

WAYNE WAS A GHOST. ONLINE, JESSICA COULD FIND no trace of him. Not a post on a discussion board, not a mention at a class reunion, not even a blurry face in a group photo tagged with his name. She stood up to stretch her legs and glanced at the clock hanging on the wall. Three fifty-three and still nothing.

She closed the browser on Parminder's laptop and, as she was about to turn it off, she saw, in the corner of the screen, the small, grey icon that all social workers used to log into the province's databases. When they were out assessing a family or at a meeting with psychologists and teachers, they could find the files they needed with just a name or a social insurance number or whatever they had. She stared. That morning, before she had left the office for the last time, she had watched her boss delete her email address and password from the system. "Security," Karen had said, frowning. "You know how it is."

Maybe Parminder had saved her own login and password. She tapped on the icon and a window appeared. The fields were already filled. Jessica smiled. Technology. Magic.

Quickly, she typed in Wayne's first and last names and waited. One file. Two. Three men that shared his name who had accessed services through the province of British Columbia. She scanned the details. The first man, born in 1991 and currently out on bail, was too young. The second was a three-year-old that had been taken into care. The third, born in 1951, had last received income assistance two years ago when he had been living at an address on Kingsway in East Vancouver. No phone number, no email. Just an address. And a note that he no longer qualified for financial aid.

Jessica typed the address into her phone and lay down on her side, her head deep in the pillows. Wayne existed. Two years ago, he was living here, in this city, seeing a financial aid worker, trying to pay rent and eat on $610 per month. Maybe he had found this demeaning and near-impossible. Or maybe he hadn't cared and had spent his days in his bedroom, slowly blowing cigarette smoke out his open window and into the damp, fumy air.

She could find out today. In six hours, she would get up, shower and find him. She closed her eyes and didn't sleep. In Parminder's windowless home office, she wasn't even sure when it was dawn.

◢

She stood in the doorway, under a stained, once-white awning, and shivered as the rain dripped around her and onto the sidewalk. The apartments were on the second floor, above a bakery that looked like it hadn't been open since 2007. Across the street, a car wash and a series of produce markets and convenience stores, all with windows fogged over with condensation. Jessica had pressed the buzzer once already and was trying to decide whether she should press it again when a female voice crackled through the air.

"Hello?"

"Yes, hello. My name is Jessica. I'm a social worker. I'm looking for Wayne." She winced as she said this, knowing that she wasn't lying but was instead fuzzing the truth just enough.

"Wayne doesn't live here anymore."

"Do you know where he's gone?"

Ten seconds of silence. Then, "Why?"

"I need to ask him some questions about a case I'm working on. Please." Jessica's voice rose. "It involves children."

"Hang on. I'll come down."

A woman in her fifties emerged from the stairwell wearing a chocolate brown track suit and pink flip-flops. Her yellowish, greying hair was twisted into a collapsing bun on the top of her head, and she held a black, skinny dog in her arms. She stared at Jessica through the glass doors for a moment before twisting the lock open. She stood, half-in and half-out, her hip resting on the edge of the door.

"What did you say your name was?" The dog sniffed in Jessica's direction and bared its teeth.

"Jessica."

"A kid, huh? Wayne never had any kids."

Jessica pulled her jacket tighter against the wind whipping toward them. "It's not about a child that he was ever taking care of. It's an old case." She could see that the woman was waiting for her to continue and was not going to answer any questions until she was satisfied it was worth her time. "He was friends with the family until the children went into foster care."

The woman narrowed her eyes. With her face drawn in, she and the dog looked so alike that Jessica wanted to laugh. The dog growled. "Did he do something to them?"

"No. Well, not anything illegal."

"That sounds about right. Wayne never actually did anything illegal. Maybe they were wrong or stupid, but never *illegal*." She shifted the dog to her right arm and reached into the pocket of her hoodie. "I haven't talked to him in two years, not since his mom died. She left him the house, you know, and a bunch of insurance money, so he didn't need me anymore." She laughed but then started coughing. "Sorry."

"Don't apologize."

She scrolled through a phone. "There. His parents' address. I don't know why I even still have this in here. It's not like I ever go over for tea." She read off a number and a street in Strathcona, just east of Chinatown.

"Thanks so much. I'm sorry, I didn't even ask for your name."

The woman smiled and swept a strand of hair off her face. "It's Heather. You can tell that shit stain that I still hate his ass. But Pluto here says hello." At the sound of his name, the little dog barked before Heather stepped backward and let the door fall shut again.

—

It was just before noon by the time Jessica had stopped to buy coffee and a muffin and pulled up in front of Wayne's house. She sat in her car, windows rolled up, and ate, barely tasting the blueberries and cinnamon and sugar. All she could think about was what Casey would want her to say to the man she had loved but never said goodbye to. If Casey had grown up and lived through the past twenty-eight years, Jessica was certain she would no longer be with Wayne, that their relationship would have been one of those moments in a woman's life that defies explanation, that requires a suspension of sense to even remember. But she didn't grow up and she didn't live, so all Jessica could consider were the wishes of a fourteen-year-old Casey, the girl who had made decisions with resources both meagre and remote.

She would want him to know that she'd loved him. She had always intended to be with him. She had never, not once, changed her mind.

Jessica ran through the rain to the front door, faded grey but with streaks of red still clinging to the wood. No door-bell, only an old brass knocker that she could barely fit her fingers in. Her knock was louder than she expected and she half-turned to look behind her, in case the neighbours had heard and were streaming out of their houses to watch the ruckus. But the street, with warehouses at one end and small, wood-sided houses on the other, stayed empty. She knocked a second time, more quietly, and a third. No answer.

She stepped on the path that led around the side and to the backyard. Jessica could hear Chris Gallo scolding her in her head. *This is unsafe*, he said. *You're alone, walking into the backyard of a man you've never met but whom you know has done his share of harm. What are you doing?* Of course, she knew this could be unsafe. Of course, it was possible Wayne was angry and violent. But it was also possible he was sad and forgotten, that he had been waiting, all this time, for the girl he loved to come back to him. Jessica turned the corner and found herself standing on a concrete pad just outside the basement door. There, hunched underneath the sagging porch, was Wayne.

He was facing her, and she supposed he had heard her foot-steps on the path. He looked confused by her, but nodded when she put up her hand in greeting. He was tanned, with deep lines on his forehead and around his mouth. His eyes, narrow and set close together, were ringed in red. Slowly, he pulled a pack of cigarettes from the front pocket of his denim jacket.

"Mind if I smoke?"

"Not at all."

The lighter flared and Wayne closed his eyes as he inhaled. "Are you with the city?"

"I'm sorry?"

"The neighbours. They told me if I didn't clear out the weeds, they'd call the city." He waved his hand toward the back fence, where blackberry brambles grew over the pickets, tangled and sharp. Burdock pushed up through cracks in the empty driveway.

"I'm actually a social worker, not a bylaw officer."

"Social worker? Why are you here?"

She stepped forward until she was close enough to smell the beer and smoke soaked into Wayne's clothes. "I used to live with Casey and Jamie. In their last foster home."

Wayne reached out and gripped one of the mossy posts holding up the porch. Ash from his cigarette fell onto his canvas sneakers, but he didn't even seem to notice.

"I don't know if anyone told you, but the girls didn't run away. Someone found their bodies a week ago. Actually, it was my dad and me. We found them."

She couldn't see the expression on his face as he stood, bent over. Finally, he dropped the cigarette. "I knew it."

"Knew what?"

"I knew they didn't run away. That's what the cops kept saying, after they figured out I had nothing to do with it. I told them that we had plans, Casey and me, and that we talked about them over and over again. She wanted things. She didn't want to be a street kid. But they didn't listen. Why would they? I was just a pervert to them and, besides, girls went missing all the time back then, the kind of girls cops don't give two shits about." He paused and raised his head. "How did they die?"

"I don't know."

"You said you found them. What do you mean you don't know?"

Jessica looked to her left, at the mountains half-obscured by grey clouds. On days like this, she often felt that the city shrank, that nothing else beyond the rain even existed. "After my mother died, we were cleaning out her things and we found them in her freezers. I don't know how they got there. The police say they're working on it."

"Did your parents kill them?"

"My father didn't, I'm sure of it. As for my mother, I used to think that she wasn't capable, but now I don't know what to think."

Wayne nodded, as if this relinquishment of certainty made the kind of sense he understood. "The police never tell anyone anything. They don't care if not knowing makes us want to kill ourselves. They just don't give a fuck."

"Do you think about her still?"

"All the time. Awake. Asleep. Whenever."

"Would you mind telling me about her? Anything you remember?"

He looked up at Jessica's face for the first time since she had stepped into his yard. She could see the man he used to be—the blurred lines around his jaw and cheeks that were once sharp, the wrinkles around his mouth that meant he used to smile and smile hard. He blinked once.

"What for?"

"They were forgotten by a lot of people twenty-eight years ago. I want to remember them."

Wayne released a new cigarette from its box and stuck it, unlit, between his lips. He had wanted to love once. He had wanted to be understood. Maybe he still did.

"Fine. Let's talk. But first, I'm going to need another smoke."

They would say to each other that they didn't want to take it out on their foster mother, that they didn't mean to scare her or make her cry, but they both knew that they really did. Why else would watching a grown woman collapse into a heap on her bed feel so satisfying, so fucking right? In those moments, they weren't happy, but they could forget that they had been hurt. And what did it matter if she hated them? They had tried to leave peacefully, to run toward the life they wanted without inflicting harm, and it had backfired. Goodness seemed like a futile endeavour. No one would ever know, or believe, how good they had tried to be.

Goodness didn't pay. Cruelty didn't either, but at least they hadn't failed at it. Not yet anyway.

NINETEEN
EIGHTY-EIGHT

SEVENTEEN

WAYNE WOKE UP IN HIS PARENTS' HOUSE AND PULLED on his dirty Lee jeans from the night before. He ate breakfast by himself in front of the television as his father silently packed his toolbox for work. There was nothing to say, really, because all of their conversations began or ended with his father yelling in Cantonese, "You need to get a job and move out." So Wayne just watched Norm Perry read the news and said nothing while his father slammed and locked the front door.

His mother was scrubbing the congee pot in the kitchen. He brought his cereal bowl to the sink and kissed her on the cheek. She grunted but leaned her body into him, the best hug she could manage with her hands covered in rubber gloves. Wayne put on his cracked leather jacket and shoes and went into the backyard, where he smoked two cigarettes while staring at the drying leaves on the cherry tree next door.

That afternoon, Bill came by in his rusty, second-hand Buick. "You want to go for a ride?" he yelled from the open window. Wayne jumped in and they careened around the corner as Wayne's mother watched from the front step, hands on her hips.

They drove and drove, through downtown and across the bridge, past the fancy shopping mall and along the water. The houses had enormous windows, like blind, unblinking eyes pointed toward the inlet. The sun was thick but cold, as it often is in the fall, but both men had their windows rolled down, the wind circling through the car, whistling through the fabric of their sleeves.

"Did you ever notice that the ocean out here doesn't smell like anything?" Wayne shouted.

"No," Bill said, smirking.

"When you go to New Brighton or down by the train tracks, you can smell fish and wood and salt. Out here, it's just fucking *clean.*"

"You notice the weirdest shit."

And it was true. Wayne did notice the weirdest shit. Everywhere he looked, there was something to see, something to tuck into his brain for the future moment when he would notice something else that would turn that one old, remembered detail into an epiphany. As he sat in Bill's car, he thought about how here, in West Vancouver, the waterfront was pristine and lined with tidy houses with gardens cleaner than his jacket. Not six blocks from his parents' house east of Chinatown, the waterfront was dirty, littered with the garbage of work: split and gnarled two-by-fours, Styrofoam coffee cups, puddles of spilled motor oil. What was the difference? It was the same water, but long ago, someone decided which portion would be worth looking at and which would be used to power and clean the plants and refineries and shipping containers. It seemed unfair to him, but he couldn't figure out why.

Bill turned left onto a small road that was poorly paved. Wayne could reach out and touch the cliffs on the side if he wanted, but he kept his hands in the car. He didn't trust nature. Plants could make you itch. Animals and bugs hid in every crevice.

"Where are we going?" he asked quietly, in a voice that could have been a child's.

Bill threw a cigarette out the window. "Lighthouse Park. Ever been?"

No, Wayne had never been. He had kept to the familiar confines of downtown, East Vancouver and, sometimes, Chinatown, if his mother wanted him to help with the groceries. He thought of Stanley Park and its well-ordered seawall and rose garden and bowling lawn, but he knew just by staring at this park's gate (painted and green and looped with rusted chains that may very well have been chewed on by bears) that this was something wilder. As they walked on the uneven paths, kicking aside pine cones and fallen branches, Wayne briefly thought about running back through the trees and into the car. He would feel less buried there, less held against his will by the darkness of the tall firs and spruces. But he kept up, not wanting to disappoint Bill, who strode along without hesitation, as if he weren't an immigrant East Van boy with a Chinese accent he had uselessly tried to erase. As if he had grown up in a forest with squirrels and whatever bird that was calling like the three-note chime of the shiny white SkyTrain.

Finally, they burst through the woods and stood on a flat, wide rock. Ocean and more ocean. A sailboat. The lighthouse on a point farther west. Wayne swallowed, trying not to throw up.

"You see," said Bill, "sometimes you need to get out of the city to get some perspective."

Wayne's perspective had never included parks that clung to the edges of cliffs, where nothing stood between you and the raging water below. He wasn't sure he wanted it to.

"It's beautiful, right?"

Wayne cleared his throat. "Sure."

A spider floated down on a thread and landed, delicately, on Wayne's nose. At home, if a spider touched him, he would swat it away immediately, not caring if its carcass lay on the floor of his bedroom for one day or three weeks. But here, he let it crawl over his nostril, his right cheek and down to his jaw. He thought he could feel its little feet pricking his skin, feeling with its legs the strange, soft human underneath. When Wayne finally breathed, the spider lifted off on his exhale and away. He tried to find it among the cracks in the rock he was standing on, but he saw nothing, only bits of moss and pebbles that could have been spiders but weren't.

He had lost it. But he still felt the trail of its movement on his face. It was unbearable, feeling the smallest touch like this as if his skin had been stripped off and he was nothing but nerves in the sunshine. He didn't feel like throwing up anymore, but he wasn't sure this was better. Rubbing his hands over his eyes, he tried to remember the cockroaches and geckoes that had crawled over the floors of his family's old, grubby apartment in Hong Kong, but he couldn't conjure them up. He was five when they had left and the memories often shifted and faded until he was no longer sure if they were real or made up.

Bill turned. "Had enough? You look ready to get the fuck out of here."

Wayne nodded. "What should we do now?"

"Let's go back downtown and get some lunch. And I should go see my girls tonight. Ginny leaves for the night shift at nine. We'll bring some beer."

"Beer? For the girls?"

Bill let out a roaring laugh, sharp and explosive. "No, dumb-ass. It's for us. The girls will fall asleep by ten. And then we can have a little party. You in?"

Wayne nodded again. He had nothing else to do. Might as well tag along, watch his friend play with his daughters and drink. If he played this right, he wouldn't see his parents again until tomorrow.

That evening, Bill parked his car in front of his old home and turned off the ignition. Wayne reached for the door release, but then he saw that Bill wasn't moving. Quickly, he leaned back in his seat and stared through the windshield at the car parked in front.

"You see that?" Bill nodded toward the house.

Wayne had seen that yard and front step and chipped siding many times before, so he wasn't sure what kind of answer Bill was looking for. He nodded slowly. He hoped he looked wise.

"That was my house. I used to pay the rent."

"I know."

"And now my wife hates me so much that I have to sneak in when she's not home just to see my kids. It's fucking crazy, is what it is." He slapped the steering wheel with his hand.

Wayne nodded more enthusiastically. "No doubt."

"I sleep in a shitty room in a shitty hotel. No one cleans. Let me tell you something, Wayne." Bill turned and pointed a finger at Wayne's nose. "Never get married. Women will mess you up."

Secretly, Wayne had always wanted to get married. Sometimes, just before he fell asleep at night, he imagined the kind of woman he might marry. She was pretty, of course, and small (because Wayne himself was on the short side), and knew how to make soup with dried bok choy just like his mother. When he came home from work, she would wrap her arms around his waist and whisper how glad she was to see him, her breath honeyed and warm on his chin. And then she would step out of her dress, right there in the living room, before pulling off his work pants and pushing him to the floor.

"Women," Wayne said quietly. "Nothing but trouble."

As they walked up the path, the front door swung open and light spilled onto the porch. Casey stood on the threshold, holding a mug and wearing grey wool socks pulled high over the legs of her pyjamas. She smiled at her father. She stepped forward and then noticed Wayne, his hands stuffed into the pockets of his jeans. Her face rearranged itself and stared blankly. But even then, Wayne could see the swirling in her eyes, deep pools that never quite stopped moving, even as the rest of her was still.

"Bear, you remember Wayne," said Bill as he took the mug she handed him.

"Sure."

Bill stepped inside and nodded. "Bring him some tea too, will you?"

Wayne had to slide past Casey to get into the house as she stood holding the door open. Her long black hair smelled musky and sweet, tinged with berries or apples or some kind of fruit that Wayne was too muddled to remember. How old was she the last time he had seen her? Eleven? Even without looking, he knew there was an adult body underneath those layers of flannel. She was warm, radiating in a way only a grown woman could. When she walked into the kitchen, he looked sideways at her ass. Bill coughed.

"She's a pretty girl," he said and Wayne felt his ears turn hot. "Stubborn, though. Marches to her own beat, if you know what I mean."

Jamie ran into the room and Wayne was relieved to see she still looked like a proper little girl—bony elbows, hair fine and tangled, a smear of food on the front of her shirt. She pulled a binder off the shelf beside the couch and sat down on Bill's lap.

"It's my social studies report, Dad. Look—I got a B."

Jamie walked her father through the parliamentary practices of Japan. Wayne stared at the ceiling. Circles of plaster ebbed and curled. He thought of his mother, the dead slug he found in the yard this morning, the spent cigarette butts in the ashtray in his room. Anything but Casey, whom he could hear as she moved around the kitchen behind him.

"My girl's a genius, Wayne."

"Yeah. I can see that."

Her voice came from behind. "Your tea."

Wayne turned in his chair. Casey, a half-smile on her lips, holding out a steaming mug. He wondered what it would feel like to take her narrow, pointed face in his hands, his thumbs along the lines of her jaw. Quickly, he looked down.

"Do you want the tea or not?" she asked.

Wayne took the mug and turned back to Bill, who was tickling Jamie as she screamed with laughter on the couch. Casey sat down on the floor, facing the old, unusable fireplace.

"Are you working?"

Wayne jumped in his seat. "What?"

"I said: Are you working?" She smiled and shook her head.

"No. I'm between jobs."

"Oh, like Dad."

Wayne couldn't tell if she was being sarcastic or if she was just stating a simple fact. He felt on edge, as if one wrong step could send him plummeting, dizzy and confused. Strangely, he liked it. This was not how he felt sitting with his parents watching *Jeopardy*.

"How do you like school?" he ventured.

Casey snorted. "It's all right. I mean, grade eight was boring and grade nine won't be any better. I can't wait to leave. Mom wants me to graduate, though. So I have *options*."

He could hear the sarcasm now. He smiled. "I didn't finish high school."

"Exactly. You're still a decent human being, right?"

Wayne wasn't sure this was true. He had meant to tell her that he was jobless and lived with his parents and couldn't finish reading a newspaper, but he didn't. She looked up at him with those long eyes and all he could do was nod.

"Are you happy?" Casey asked this easily, as if this was a question Wayne was asked every day. But the truth was he had never been asked about his happiness before. Not once.

"No." It was all he could say.

"Really? Why not?"

She was fourteen years old. There was no way she would understand how his life had started out with emptiness and goals and a great, winding future. But then one job lost led to another job that sucked, which led to discontent and an unlawful strike and weeks and weeks of unemployment. Here he was, thirty-seven years old, still cobbling together days of work that added up to hardly anything, only enough to keep him in cigarettes and beer while he lay in his childhood bedroom, kicking at the twin footboard with his man-sized legs. He couldn't answer Casey's question with all of that, so he sighed and swallowed. "Things just didn't turn out the way I thought they would."

"There's still time. You're still young. Ish."

Wayne laughed and leaned forward so he could speak quietly. "What about you? Are you happy?"

Casey blushed. "I don't know. Sometimes. I'm happy when Dad's here. Like right now." She smiled at him as if he weren't that loser who didn't own a car and was only five foot six. He could see that, to her, he was a fully-formed man, one who was just as strong and capable as every man she had ever met. She didn't know about his failures, but he knew she wouldn't care, because to a woman as new as she was, the past meant nothing because she hadn't been there. He stared at her lips. Pinker than he had ever thought possible.

For another hour, Wayne and Casey chatted quietly, about how she had asked her mother for a cat even though she knew it was pointless. About the docks, where Wayne had worked when he left high school and where the men moved stuff and grunted until all they could do was sit still for fifteen minutes, just long enough to finish a smoke and a cup of coffee. She asked questions, because she was interested and didn't know, but made no pretense of knowing more than she did, as children do when faced with the strange and new. Instead, she listened and looked up at Wayne with her bottomless eyes until he squirmed in his chair and had to get up to use the bathroom. Looking in the mirror, he thought that he should go home and never come back, but she liked him, honestly liked him even though the only woman who ever looked at him these days were the hookers who shivered in the night air on Powell Street. So he stayed.

At ten fifteen, the girls went to bed. Casey patted Wayne on the shoulder on her way and said, "Good night. It was nice talking to you." The spot burned. He watched her walk into the hall, each step like electricity travelling through the floor and straight into his body.

Bill and Wayne sat in the backyard, smoking and not saying much. After an hour, Bill turned to Wayne and said, "Thanks for coming. I appreciate it. It's not easy, this thing with me and Ginny."

"No problem."

"I'm a stranger here. It sucks. And after everything I tried to do." Bill pulled on the cuff of his jacket. "Are you coming by with me next week? I mean, if you have the time."

Wayne hesitated. Bill heard the pause and spoke quickly to fill the silence.

"I know you could be out having fun, being a single guy and everything. I was going to fix up this house, put up new curtains and paint the walls and shit. At least, if you come with me, I can forget all of that. Damn Ginny."

What could he say? His buddy needed him. It would be mean and irresponsible not to come. Wayne set down his bottle and punched Bill lightly on the arm.

"I'll come whenever I can."

The night shimmered with house lights and car lights and the lights on Grouse Mountain. Wayne's heart beat like a swinging hammer. It hurt. But he suddenly knew that he had been a sleepwalker his entire life, a man who had barely breathed to pass the time. Until now. He was awake. Startlingly, painfully, joyously awake.

The next morning, Wayne woke up from a long, complicated dream, soaked with sweat that was starting to turn cold and clammy on his skin. He sat up and shook his head, but it didn't matter what he did, the smell of last night's beer still blanketed his body. He needed a shower. He needed to eat.

Standing under a dribble of hot water, he tried to remember his dream. He knew he had been humiliated, that this feeling of unease puddling in his gut was there for a reason. He soaped his arms, then his chest. As he reached down to wash his groin, it came back to him so quickly, he had to reach out and steady himself on the tiled wall. Casey. She had touched him, run her small hands down his belly and kissed him, putting her mouth everywhere he wanted her to, even as he remained silent. But then, just as he lifted her into his arms and she wound her smooth legs around his waist, Bill appeared, except it wasn't Bill, but a giant spider who, strangely, was still unmistakeably Bill.

His hairy pincers pulled Wayne up and out and soon he was spinning, his eyes covered with white, woolly threads as thick as the rope he used to see in coils on the docks. Bill's voice, tinged with a largeness Wayne had never heard before, whistled into his ears. "You want to fuck my daughter. I'll destroy you."

It was then that Wayne had woken up. Now, he stood, weeping in the shower, his face in his hands. He was a sick fuck. She was a child. He was her father's best friend. He deserved no better than what he had. No, he deserved even less. He was a disgusting, short pervert. He knew it now.

He avoided Bill for a whole week, not answering the phone, telling his parents to take messages as he sat in the living room with the curtains drawn. Whenever he heard a car door slam outside, he ran out the back and down the alley, sometimes without a jacket, often without any money. When he returned, he crept from tree to lamp post to Dumpster and slipped in through the basement, where he could listen for the sounds of anyone other than his mother or father. He slept when he wasn't smoking.

One day, Wayne walked through the alley to the corner store, just enough money in his pocket to buy a bag of dill pickle chips. It was risky, he knew, to be out in daylight like this, but he had managed to not see Bill for eight days, and he thought his luck would hold. After all, Bill could take a hint. He understood things. As he rounded the corner on to Dunlevy, he heard a sharp bark behind him.

"Wayne! That you?"

He looked to the right and left but there was nowhere to hide, not a rhododendron or a garbage can or anything. He stopped, fingering the coins in his front pocket. Then he turned around.

"I thought that was you. Where've you been?" Bill was leaning against his car, half-hidden behind a courier truck.

"I've been around. Just busy."

. "Yeah?" Bill squinted and pushed himself to a standing position. "Busy with what?"

Wayne paused, but then stood up straighter. "I've been looking for a job."

"Any luck?"

"No, not really."

Bill stepped forward and put his arm around Wayne's shoulder. "I know, buddy. It's not easy out there, is it?"

Together, they walked to a café a few doors down and ordered coffee and Danishes. "I'll pay," said Bill. Wayne sat as still as possible, worried that any movement might break the goodwill or betray what he had been thinking for the last week. For several minutes, Bill didn't seem to notice. But then, after he had stirred another spoonful of sugar into his cup, he looked at Wayne's eyes and sighed.

"What's bugging you? You look like shit."

Wayne didn't know what to say. He stared at his hands

on the table top, smoothing and smoothing his paper napkin until it was flat and limp. Could he say, *I can't stop thinking about your teenaged daughter because I'm a dirty old man?* He glanced up at Bill's hard face and the thickness of his neck. No, he couldn't. It had to be a secret.

Bill leaned forward. "I've been meaning to talk to you for a while."

Wayne jumped in his seat. He wondered if he could get up and run out.

"I know how hard it is to not have a job, and to be living in a situation that pretty much just sucks. I just want you to know that I'm here for you."

Wayne thought he might cry. Instead, he blinked hard and drank some more coffee.

"We need to stick together, man. You and me." Bill reached over and knuckled the top of Wayne's head.

Finally, Wayne spoke. "You and me."

Bill grinned. "I should swing by the house tonight to see the girls. Want to come?"

Every joint and sinew in his body screamed *no*, but Wayne thought of Casey's innocent questions and the way she listened as if his answers really mattered. It couldn't do any harm just to talk to the girl. He couldn't touch her anyway, not with her father and sister there. They would be safe, spinning around each other in their own little conversation, insulated by family. He rubbed the back of his neck before saying anything.

"Sure. Why not?"

It was just like the last time. Casey greeted them at the door, they chatted quietly for an hour in the living room while Jamie and Bill played cards in the kitchen. At ten, the girls went to bed and the men sat out back, smoking, drinking and not saying much. The quiet of the night was light and perfect and neither wanted to break it with the weight of words that didn't mean much anyway.

Wayne began watching the house lights. Next door, the kitchen remained lit until eleven. Across the alley, every room was dark until someone turned on a lamp for a minute and then turned it off again. Wayne imagined a man and woman, each dreaming peacefully until the man began to scream and swat the air with open hands. The woman sat up, turned on the lamp on her bedside table and shook her man awake. And then, he rolled over with a grunt and she fell back on the pillows, slipping away again into the swaddles of sleep. No words exchanged. Just breath.

When Wayne looked over, Bill was asleep, his head resting on the back of the nylon deck chair. For a while, Wayne thought he looked like a child, his mouth slack, his cheeks rounded by his quiet snoring. But then he turned and his jaw grew tight again and Wayne was reminded that Bill was a hard man, one who had never taken his failures in stride. Years ago, when they were in high school, a white kid with a greasy ducktail had snickered when Melanie McIvor had turned down Bill's request for a dance on Valentine's Day. That night, Bill had waited behind the trash cans in the schoolyard for that blond ducktail. He beat him quickly and efficiently, uttering no words so that the only sounds that echoed off the blacktop were the boy's moans. Wayne had watched, as Bill expected him to, but felt himself shrinking inside, as if his guts were trying to make themselves invisible. Bill's rage simmered constantly, even when he was simply chewing gum, even now. It was only a matter of time before it boiled and spit and burned. Wayne hoped he would never see it again.

As silently as he could, Wayne walked back through the kitchen and into the bathroom. There was no way to mask the sound of a grown man pissing in a short toilet, but he had to go, even if the noise was nuclear at midnight in a house full of sleeping people. When he was finished, he crept out into the hall, looking for his shoes. He would just walk home by himself.

In the doorway to the kitchen, Casey stood so still that Wayne might not have seen her at all if she hadn't cleared her throat. She was wearing a white T-shirt and blue flannel pants, her hair long and falling straight over her shoulders. There were no lights on, just the weak glow of the street lamps through the uncovered window over the sink, yet Wayne knew exactly how beautiful and slight she looked. He knew the outline of her body under her clothes. He knew the way her eyes bored into his face and down into his belly that she could see everything he wanted. She wasn't afraid. She wouldn't be standing there, waiting, if she was.

"I heard you in the bathroom," she said evenly. "Is Dad asleep?"

"Yes," said Wayne, so softly that he wondered if he had even said it at all.

"He does that. Falls asleep outside or in my mom's room. He always manages to wake up before she comes home, though. That's how much they hate each other."

Wayne ached for the sadness in her voice. He knew that Ginny and Bill didn't hate each other; in fact, they loved each other with so much ferocity that Ginny could no longer watch Bill fail, and Bill could no longer stand the disappointment in her eyes. Casey needed to know that. It would make sense to

243

her. He could be the one to tell her and make everything in her heart right again. He stepped forward and took her hand.

"They love each other," he began, "they just can't live together, that's all." This was a poor rendering of the complicated truth that he held in his head, but it was what he could do. "They'll work it out, Casey. I know it."

"What they have isn't love. It's bullshit." She looked down at the floor and Wayne thought she might cry, but she didn't. Instead, she lifted up her chin to face him. "I want better than that."

She tugged at his hand and he stepped into her, his body square and thick against hers. When they kissed, he felt the warmth from her lips in every last cell of his skin. He might have burst into flame. But he didn't care.

He picked her up and carried her through the kitchen and down the basement steps. She clung to his neck, but she wasn't shivering. Her grip was deliberate and steady. She knew what was happening and she sighed, a deep release that sounded like the wind off the ocean on a hot, hot day. When he laid her down on an old yellow sofa and pulled off her clothes, he gazed at her body—lean and tan, with perfect, triangular breasts. She stared at him in the night and smiled slightly, crookedly. He held her hips in his two hands and kissed her.

He watched her open her mouth and inhale sharply before sitting up and grasping his shoulders. "Yes," she said.

Together they moved and he thought he might never be happier or more in love. He felt like melted chocolate coating the tongue of the girl he was fucking and he knew this moment might never come again but it didn't matter. Because it was here and he held this shimmering creature in his arms while she breathed like she wanted this, like this was the man she had been waiting for and this was the love that she knew she deserved. He shivered against her cool skin and she bit his ear.

When they were done, she played her fingers down his back, running the tips against his skin. They might have laid there for five minutes or an hour. Wayne didn't know. He didn't count the seconds or her breath or the beat of his own, wildly skipping heart. After a while, she pushed at his chest and he raised himself on his elbows. That face. What kind of girl had a face as perfect as that?

"You should go," she said quietly. "Before Dad wakes up."

Quickly, Wayne dressed and gathered his shoes and went upstairs, still buttoning his jeans. Casey followed and held open the front door as he leaned back in to kiss her one more time.

"You'll come again, right?"

Wayne knew the prudent answer, but the flush in her cheeks wanted another answer altogether. He pulled her in close and breathed into her ear, "As soon as I can." And as he stepped backward on to the front porch, she shut the door. He stayed until he heard the lock click into place.

———

That was how they started, and how they went on for five more weeks. It became so easy that Wayne began to visit even when Bill didn't, taking advantage of the long hours that Ginny spent away from the house. Eventually, Jamie figured it out, but kept her mouth shut and stayed in the bedroom with the door tightly closed. Wayne and Casey always chose the basement. It was neutral, a place that belonged to no one and was therefore only theirs.

They talked too. Long conversations about how they could be together. Wayne tried to convince Casey that they should wait to tell anyone until she had graduated high school, but she only laughed at this suggestion.

"That's four years," she said. "I might be dead by then."

And so, they agreed to wait until she had finished grade nine before telling her parents. Wayne hoped she would reconsider before then, but he knew, deep down, she wouldn't.

"I can still go to school and live with you. We'll get an apartment. It doesn't have to be fancy. We'll just need to find jobs first, you know?"

It all seemed so easy when she talked like that, as if it was just one step that inevitably led to another that eventually led to happiness. Sometimes, at two in the morning, he started to believe her. Of course, it could be simple. Of course.

But then he remembered that she was fourteen. And that her parents would be furious. And that none of this would ever be easy. He tried to tell her that once, but she kissed him and he thought, *I can love her right now and deal with the rest later.* And so he did.

One night, as Wayne sat in the backyard with Casey's head in his lap, she opened her eyes wide and smiled. "I have something to tell you."

"What's that?"

"I think I'm pregnant."

He jumped up, shaking her off him. "What did you say?"

Casey stood up too and grabbed one of his hands in both of hers. "My period's late. I think I'm pregnant. Are you happy?"

That question again. Wayne began to think that she didn't even know what it meant. "But you're a kid!"

"Excuse me?"

It was the wrong thing to say and Wayne knew it. But it

had never occurred to him that a fourteen-year-old girl, even one that he believed was a woman, could get pregnant. He felt thickly, indisputably stupid. He breathed out and looked up at the night sky.

"I didn't mean that. You just took me by surprise."

Casey stood with her hands folded over her chest. "Is it so bad? To have a baby?"

"No, of course not."

"Well, then we can tell my parents about it tomorrow. I mean, they'll be mad, but once they get that there's going to be a baby, it'll all be okay."

No, Wayne screamed in his head. *No, it won't be okay.* He said, "We don't have to tell them."

"What do you mean?"

"We don't have to keep the baby."

Casey stamped her feet on the hard ground. "Do you mean have an abortion?"

He winced, but there was no going back now. "Yes."

"I'm going to have your baby! This isn't a random baby with someone I just met on the street, Wayne." And she sat down on the porch steps with a thud, hands covering her eyes.

She was right: this baby was his. This whole mess was his fault. He should have known better. But it was too late now. He stared at Casey's small body hunched on the stairs. Her jacket pooled around her, baggy and red. As short and thin as she was, she was also solid, a densely packed ball of muscle and skin and unbreakable bones. She might have been an optimist who believed that Wayne was the perfect man, but she was also unwavering. Once she knew what she wanted, there was no convincing her otherwise.

He sat down beside her and put his arms around her narrow shoulders. "I'm sorry. This is our baby. I know."

She looked up at him, eyes red and swollen. "We can tell my parents tomorrow?"

Wayne sighed. "Sure. There's no point in waiting."

Casey kissed his neck before whispering, "It'll be fine. You'll see."

Wayne didn't see. But he let the warmth from her breath blow into his collar and wrap itself around his throat. If they stayed still like this, maybe nothing would ever change and it would be night in this yard forever and forever. No babies. No Bill. Wayne blinked. He couldn't cry. Not now. Not until it was all over.

———

That evening, Wayne sat on his parents' front step waiting for Bill to pick him up. The plan was to act as if everything was normal until Bill had drunk exactly two beers. Only one, and he'd still be sober. Three and he might be raging. After they talked to Bill, Wayne would wait until Ginny came home at five, and then they would tell her too, stressing that this would be her first grandchild. A baby. A beautiful, chubby baby. Wayne hoped it would work.

He also hoped they would see there was no way around it now. Casey was pregnant. He wanted to be with her. He could leave her or deny his involvement. Instead, he was going to tell them how much he loved her. Maybe they would respect that. Maybe they would see that it could be worse.

As Bill's car turned the corner and pulled into the curb, Wayne bit down hard on his lower lip. The blood was warm and thick on his tongue. *Still alive*, he thought. *Good.*

It took only two minutes to drive to Ginny's house. Bill drove with one hand on the wheel and another holding a lit cigarette. He winked at Wayne and said, "What's got into you?"

Every muscle in his body strained with the effort of smiling. "Just tired."

"Yeah? Well, we won't stay that long. Just long enough to have a couple of beers."

The night progressed as it always did, except this time, Casey and Wayne watched Bill closely, checking for mood swings or bad news or fast drinking. But there was nothing out of the ordinary, just Bill sitting on the kitchen floor while Jamie tried to braid his collar-length hair. After his second beer, Bill got up and walked to the bathroom, humming "Great Balls of Fire."

Casey said to Wayne, "We have to tell him when he comes back."

He felt like he was crumpling from the outside in, one inch of skin at a time. He nodded at Casey and then closed his eyes. He slid down the wall until he was sitting on the floor. Maybe he could just disappear.

Wayne felt a tap on his shoulder and heard Bill's voice. "Are you okay? You look sick."

When he opened his eyes, he saw Bill kneeling on the floor beside him and Casey standing behind. He thought he might throw up. "Yeah, maybe I'm not feeling so good," he muttered.

"Dad, I have something I need to tell you." Casey stood with her hands on her hips. *Battle-ready*, thought Wayne.

"Is it important? Because I think I should take Wayne home."

"He's not sick." Casey sounded irritated, which made Wayne smile a little. "You have to listen to me right now."

Bill shook his head and stood up, facing his daughter. "All right, spit it out."

"I'm pregnant."

For half a minute, Bill said nothing, only stood still, his

eyes locked on Casey's face. She didn't move either. Wayne thought he saw a tremor of fear pass over her face, but then it was gone and all that was left was her defiance, which he had once fallen in love with but was now worried about.

Finally, Bill cleared his throat. "Pregnant. With whose baby?"

Casey cocked her head slightly and looked at Wayne. It was his turn.

"Mine." He said it so quietly he was sure no one had heard. But he was wrong.

Bill turned around and stared. "Excuse me?"

Wayne still sat on the floor, his back against the wall. Even if he wanted to, he couldn't stand up. His legs had turned to rubber. "The baby is mine, Bill. Casey and I have been together for a while now." He stopped talking for a moment to look around the room, hoping that, somehow, none of this was real and he would see he was in his own bedroom in his own bed. "We're in love."

Suddenly, Bill tipped his head back and laughed. "That's funny. Are you really pregnant? What's going on here?"

Casey waved her hands in the air. "You're not listening, Dad. Wayne and I are in love. We're having a baby. We're going to get an apartment when Wayne finds a job and—."

And then Bill was on top of Wayne, punching at his head as if it were a balloon he was madly trying to pop. Wayne heard his nose break and then he could no longer see, only feel Bill's fists on his face and his foot on his ribs. He tried to speak, but the blood pouring into his mouth made him choke, and he could only spit and breathe. *Where was Casey? What was she doing?*

He heard her yell, "Daddy! Stop!" And then, mercifully, he did stop. Wayne rolled over on his side and held his nose in his hands, afraid that it had become so brittle that it would break in two and fall, with a slap, on the wood floor.

"You're a whore. Do you understand that? A little snot-faced whore."

Wayne heard a thump and Casey screaming, a wordless scream with no syllables, no pause, just a long, slicing wail. He wiped at his eyes and tried to stand up, but he could only lift his head and blink toward the sound, hoping his head would clear.

Slowly, the room came into focus. Casey lay on the floor. Bill stood over her, foot raised.

"Bill! What the fuck are you doing?" Fear. Stinking, fetid, cold, cold fear.

Casey covered her stomach with her hands. Bill kicked them away before looking at Wayne, who crawled slowly forward. Bill shook his head, raised his foot again, and stomped, as hard as he could.

"No, no, no, no," Casey whimpered.

Wayne saw Jamie sitting in the corner of the couch, a comic book open on her lap. He shouted at her, "Help her. Now!" She jumped up and kneeled down beside her sister, her eyes so wide it seemed like they had lost their lids.

"You see?" Bill asked. "You're a fucking pervert. You've ruined everything. Fucker."

Jamie began to half-drag Casey toward their bedroom. Bill stretched out his arm and pulled Jamie backward by the collar of her shirt. She let go of Casey's shoulders and her head made a dull thump as it hit the floor.

"You," he said to Jamie. "Did you know about this?"

She was still and silent. As Wayne began to pass out, the last thing he saw was Bill's fist hitting Jamie in the face and her body staggering backward toward the fireplace. The baby was dying. Casey might be dying. Bill might kill him right now. "Maybe," he whispered to the rug beneath his cheek, "it's for the best."

What they did, in the aftermath, that's what everyone remembered. After all, what's one missing weekend in the course of one life, or two? We reminisce over beginnings. We dwell on endings. We say the middles take too long. We shrug. And so, the girls who were once happy, who were wrecked, who were angry for a reason, became lost. In no time at all.

TWO THOUSAND
AND SIXTEEN

EIGHTEEN

JESSICA STOOD ON THE FRONT LAWN OF HER PARENTS'
house with her father. It was the May long weekend and the
garden was already full and bursting. Peonies, the magnolia
tree, lilac. She felt drunk in the sun.

The house was empty. The last moving truck had just
driven away. Gerry was supposed to meet the movers at his
new condo with the key, but he had stayed, feet planted in
the thick grass, hand on his daughter's elbow. He hadn't said
anything for ten minutes, so Jessica didn't move, just blinked at
the pink magnolia blossoms waving in the wind. Finally, Gerry
turned to face her. "I guess we'd better go."

"I guess."

"Your mother would have never let me sell this place." They
rarely spoke of Donna these days, each unsure of the words
they might use.

Jessica sighed. "I know."

"It feels good. Like I can go anywhere."

"I know." And she did, because this feeling that you could

stand with your arms as stretched out as possible and still touch nothing but air, this is what they both finally had. Every morning, Jessica blinked at the clean, white walls of her new apartment. One sofa. One bed. A desk in the corner. No photographs. No clutter. Just this blank of a room—quiet, unstained, smooth.

"At first," Gerry said, "I wanted to stay. But after a while, it felt like Donna was on top of me all the time, perched like an eagle on my shoulders. All I could do was think of her and those gummy stews she made us eat. The way she laughed like a man. Her hair. All that hair."

Jessica leaned to the side, her shoulder touching her father's. He was shaking, just a little.

"I didn't think I wanted to stop thinking about her, but I do. Just sometimes, you know, when I feel like it." Gerry turned to Jessica, his eyes damp in the corners. She nodded, remembering, and he nodded back.

A week before the girls died, Jessica had crept up the stairs to the landing and sat on the floor, head resting on her mother's leg as Donna sat at her desk. Casey and Jamie were watching *Dynasty* in the family room with the door shut. Gerry was reading files in his study. Jessica pulled her knees up to her chest and exhaled. Her body felt boneless. She smiled.

Donna sat here every Friday night. Usually, Jessica never tried to see what her mother was doing. If she asked, Donna smiled and shook her head. "Nothing you'd care about, munchkin." But Jessica knew. Donna was gluing or reading or collecting, trying to make sure that the foster kids never forgot her, or that she never forgot them. Jessica sometimes heard her talking to herself.

"This is the right spot."

"What a beautiful face."

"I can't find the right word."

When Jessica was younger, she would fall asleep, her body curled around the feet of her mother's chair, her cheek flat against the pile of the carpet. She would wake up in her own room in the morning, so she knew her mother had put her to bed, no matter what she had been working on. The foster kids might swirl around her during the day or even cry for her in the night, but at least—the very, very least—her mother had never left her sleeping on the floor, half-hidden by the desk.

One night, Jessica sorted the photographs her mother had thrown to the floor, the ones not clear enough to warrant a place in the albums. Two-year-old Timmy from last spring who danced whenever the radio was on and cried whenever Gerry came into the room. Anya, who spoke only Russian and pointed at pictures in the Sears catalogue to show Donna what she needed. Dishes meant food. Towels meant bathroom. Jessica by herself, turning her head as the shutter released so that the image was all hair and motes of light and movement, only flat.

"Mom, why am I an only child?"

For a moment, Donna stopped moving. Jessica saw how completely immobile her mother's legs were, the pause in sorting and cutting and smoothing. But underneath the silence and stillness she felt a vibration—the kind of buzz you hear only in the middle of the night when everything else is quiet. The kind that could be mechanical or human or animal. The kind of buzz that you can never identify.

"Well," said Donna, "after you were born, we tried for a few years to have another, but we just couldn't." Donna sighed. "Sometimes you can't control these things."

"Does that make you sad?"

"Me? Not at all. If you had a brother or sister, I would never have thought to work with foster children."

"Oh." Jessica wasn't sure what kind of answer she'd expected, but it wasn't this.

"Does it make *you* sad?" Donna was speaking quietly now and Jessica had to pull herself forward from under the desk to hear her.

"No. I just wonder what it would be like."

Donna pushed with her feet and rolled her chair back. She slid off and sat down on the floor, cross-legged, facing Jessica. "I don't know what it's like, either. It was just me and Granny Beth. And that was no fun at all."

"Was she mean?"

Donna frowned and then looked down at the carpet. "No, not mean exactly. She just wanted me to be a certain way and I wasn't. She wanted me to be like her. The kind of lady who always does the right thing and whose clothes are always perfect." She laughed, a hand on her own knee. "God knows that was never going to happen."

Jessica leaned forward and patted her mother on the arm. "But you do the right thing. Most of the time."

Donna laughed and then looked into Jessica's eyes. Jessica squirmed. Finally, her mother spoke. "Honey, thank you for saying so. But we all make mistakes. Sometimes, they're the kind of mistakes that you spend the rest of your life thinking about."

Even then, Jessica knew there was deeper, more complicated meaning behind Donna's words, one she couldn't quite hear. After several minutes of picking lint off the carpet, it came to her.

"You know what, Mom? It's okay if you're too tired to hang out with me sometimes. The foster kids need more than I do. I understand."

When Jessica looked back at her mother's face, she saw

tears running down her cheeks and falling off her jaw onto the knees of her corduroys. Jessica pulled the sleeves of her sweatshirt over her hands and tried to wipe the tears away, but Donna began to laugh and shake her head from side to side.

"You're a gem, you know that? Come on, Jess, let's see if we can dig up some ice cream from the freezer. It'll be a secret, just between us."

For five minutes, neither Jessica nor Gerry said anything, standing there in the yard. A sparrow pecked at the lawn, then hopped up the walk to the stairs. If Donna had been here, she would have scooped him up into her wide hands and stroked his smooth head. Gerry sneezed and the bird flapped his wings in a panic and flew away, circling higher and higher.

"I almost forgot," Gerry said, reaching into the back pocket of his pants. "This came for you in the mail today."

Jessica stared at the thick white envelope, at her name handwritten in black ink. The return address was for the RCMP detachment. Below the postal code, another hand-written name: Chris Gallo. She looked up at the blue sky, at the lone cloud drifting toward the city. Quickly, she dropped the letter into her open purse. She might read it later. Or tomorrow. Or never.

"Let's go," Gerry said. "I don't want to see this house ever again."

Jessica opened the driver's side door in her little red car before looking back. After they had found the bodies, she'd spent a lot of time trying to understand who the true Donna actually was. It was only now, standing on the street, staring back at the windows she used to peer out of, that she really, really got it. Her mother was earthy, haphazard, committed. She could never shake her past; she kept secrets, hid her rage and thought she knew better. She was a miraculous gardener

259

and a terrible cook. She created life once, and took it away—
by accident or neglect or worse—three times. She was all of
this and there was no point in separating any of it. From now
on, when Jessica thought of her mother, she would think of
her as mashed up, asymmetrical, stuck all over with bits of hair,
crumbs and seeds. She was everything she had ever touched
or eaten or loved or despised. Like Jessica. Like everyone.

When she had first tried to find Ginny, she thought she had
needed to tell her about the girls' deaths. After all, Ginny was
a grieving mother, a woman who had tried but didn't succeed,
who had worked harder than Jessica would ever need to just to
survive. Jessica thought she could help. But now, she knew that
what she had actually needed was just the opposite. Ginny and
Wayne had told her everything. The beat of the lazy days Casey
and Jamie spent in the summer. How Casey's hair smelled as
she walked past, the air like fingers running down your face
as you breathed in. The shrill squeal that Jamie let out when
she was happy, a girl caught in the vortex of her own joy. They
were small, those details that alone meant little but when added
up could build into the fleshy, three-dimensional figures of two
teenaged girls. Jessica had needed to know the shape of their
loss. That Casey and Jamie were more than the words she had
used to use at work: *at risk, behaviourally challenged, victims.*

What Wayne and Ginny were grieving, Jessica now knew
like she knew the weight of her mother's hand. Familiar.
Resonant. Necessary.

The girls had been more than Donna's mistake or her
attempt at making up for the loss of her own brother. And
now that Jessica understood how much more, she could finally
believe she was not her mother. Not a psychopath, not the
inevitable result of two generations of people who raged
at things they couldn't change and made mistakes trying to

change them anyway. She would find another way, eventually. When enough time had passed, she might want more. She might want to feel cozy again, cosseted by things that were hers because she had deliberately chosen them. She might want to be held by a man who came to her without purpose, who loved her with no plan, who asked her if she wanted a baby without anticipating her answer. A small yard. A job she could do well. One day: when the voiceless wind now filling her life lost its newness, and she began to reach for throw cushions, a pepper mill, a cat sunning itself on the sidewalk.

They drove down the street and onto the highway, and Gerry closed his eyes against the wind coming through the open windows. She had not told him about Devin or her meeting with Wayne. It would have made no difference anyway. Jessica still didn't know how the girls had died or if Donna had had anything to do with it. Her father had decided to let go of the house on his own, so she knew, really, that there was nothing more for him to finish. As she steered around the curve, she could almost swear that the sharp breeze was really her mother's breath as she brushed her hair at night. *You have curls just like mine. It's a lot of work to keep them under control.* Jessica smiled at the windshield. Donna's hair had never been under control, had sprung from her head like crackling wires, softening only when it rained and she was caught without an umbrella. Her mother had said a lot of things even while her physical person—so loud, so full of effort and missteps— defied her best intentions. She had tried to make her world kind and beautiful and productive, and yet she had stomped and broken and served food that was dense when it should have been light. But if it were possible, Jessica would lean up against Donna right now, arms wrapped around her waist, head buried in her stained and limp apron.

A logging truck sped past, its load trembling as it careened down the slope of the highway. Gerry spoke. "I miss her anyway, no matter what." When she looked over, his mouth was slack and he was snoring. He was talking in his sleep, but it didn't make what he said any less true. She missed her too.

ACKNOWLEDGEMENTS

To everyone at ECW Press, in particular Jack David and Crissy Calhoun, for facilitating my writing rebirth and for welcoming me so joyfully and unreservedly.

To Carolyn Swayze, for always believing in my abilities.

To June Hutton and Mary Novik, for never loving my writing too much, but always loving me just enough.

To Troy Anderson, for being the catalyst for this book through his unwavering commitment to the people who live on the margins, and for being the best father our son could wish for.

To Brad Watson, for sharing his valuable insights into the world of social services and foster care, and for being the only boss I ever had who is also a friend.

To Shawn Krause, Carrie Mac, Brendan McLeod, Andrea MacPherson and Adrian Picard, for reading drafts upon drafts of this novel, and for listening to me blubber about work, life and transitions.

To my sisters, Linda Lee, Pamela Chin, Tina Lee and Emma Berg, for being the best examples of how girls really do run the world.

To the British Columbia Arts Council and the Canada Council for the Arts, for their financial support in the development of this novel.

The writing of this book has straddled the biggest changes of my work and personal lives so far, and there are many people who have supported me while I was convinced everything was falling apart. So, to Théodora Armstrong, Carolyn Cameron, Sandra Chu, Dena Cheney, Rosa D'Amato, Amanda Growe, Marilyn Harrison, Michelle Harrison, Nicole Harrison, Amanda Leduc, Angie Lee, Vicki Leung, Amy Mazzone, Tamiko Ogura and Vicki Yan, thank you with everything I have and everything I feel.

And, finally, to Oscar and Molly, for being permanent residents in my heart, and for reminding me each day and night that this is all worth it.